If the Shoe Fits

by

Shirley McCoy

If the Shoe Fits

Cover Art by *Kristian Norris*

The Wild Rose Press, Inc.
PO Box 708
Adams Basin, NY 14410-0708
Visit us at www.thewildrosepress.com

Publishing History
First Fantasy Rose Edition, 2016
Print ISBN 978-1-5092-0804-3
Digital ISBN 978-1-5092-0805-0

Published in the United States of America

Dedication

To Derek,
for bringing so much love and laughter into my life.

Chapter One

Cringing, Juliette held out her foot to the tiny man in royal livery kneeling before her. The last thing she wanted was the humiliation which would surely come of this. Any fool could see that her foot would never fit into that little shoe.

Yet, her mother, Beatrice, perched on the edge of the settee near the bay window, believed otherwise, her anticipation clear for all to see. In contrast, Rosalind, her older sister, sat, hands folded primly in her lap, beside their mother waiting her turn.

Juliette noticed Beatrice's quivering hand and wondered why. All the familiar signs were there, signs she'd witnessed in her mother throughout her life. Her stomach churned. When Beatrice was as excited as this, then disappointed, the consequences to those who thwarted her were always severe. Juliette inwardly shrugged and allowed the servant to slide the shoe into place.

Her mouth dropped open and her knees turned to water from sheer relief. The shoe fit! But how? She knew good and well that her feet were several sizes bigger than Celina's so how on earth was she sitting here with her feet encased in a beautiful glass slipper?

Then all her relief dissipated as if it had never been. This was magic! If there was anything she couldn't stand, it was spellwork. She was her own woman and would never be subject to something so capricious as enchantment. She imagined taking off the offending slipper and smashing it. An image of the shoe in a thousand glittery bits formed in her mind's eye. The desire to destroy the thing was so strong, she nearly threw it to the floor, but then the duchess caught her gaze. Only one person in this world frightened her: Beatrice, especially when she was in a rage.

As her sister's foot eased into the glass slipper as if it belonged there, taking the shoe that was meant for her, Rosalind fled from the room.

"Mother, what have you done?" Juliette asked.

"I have got the prince for you, darling. Now be quiet," Beatrice murmured between clenched teeth.

She did as her mother told her, because simple shock kept her from doing anything else. In a daze, she heard Beatrice accept the congratulations of the royal footman and the invitation to the palace for that very next morning. Soon enough, however, the footman left and her mother rounded on her. The back-handed slap was painful, but in no way unexpected.

"You almost ruined everything! That complicated bit of spellwork was no easy task and you almost gave the game away." Beatrice sat back on the settee, breathing like a bellows, and said, "The things I go through for you girls. Children just don't know."

"You know what else children don't know?" Juliette shot back, "Why the gods would ever send me a mother like you." With that last parting shot, she escaped.

****

"Are you certain about this, sire? It is an awful lot of trouble to go to for a girl," Lord Robert asked the prince.

Few would have the privilege of speaking so freely to the future king, but, as a close personal friend since childhood, Robert Weston claimed that right. He and Prince William had grown up together in the Kingdom of Camston which was considered the strongest in the world.

The country had the great good luck to be located in a very fertile area. Farmers prospered and as his father told him, full bellies first, full minds follow. To Will's father, this was no mere platitude, it was a tenant by which he lived. Mere survival was not enough. So when the new printing press was invented, Henry was the first to invest. As a result, Camston had more presses and more printed material than any other country.

In military might, no other power could hope to match them much less threaten them. This had been the case for over seventy-five years, since Will's great-grandfather's time. As a result peace reigned and in peace, the people prospered. Goods such as fine silks, spirits, rare spices, wood, and even other luxuries such as books were produced in abundance and made available for trade. The country was, in fact, built on trade and was best known for their wine.

William Rutherford was the first of his name, latest of the royal line and heir apparent of a dynasty which had ruled unchallenged for over one hundred years. For it to remain so, he must produce an heir. To get said heir, he needed a wife. So, for the good of the kingdom which he would one day rule, Will had to marry. He accepted that. What he did not accept was that his bride would be chosen for him. He would wed who he wished. He would marry the woman he'd met at the ball. The damned ball had been designed with one purpose in mind after all, to help him find his destined betrothed and by the gods, he had.

As it was early evening, they lounged in the prince's private library, a comfortable room with brown leather chairs, a large marble fireplace and an amazing collection of rare tomes. It smelled of paper, ink and wood. Will often invited Robert for a drink there after dinner. They would exchange opinions on current events or sit in companionable silence. At times they would read or discuss books they had already finished. The chamber was one of Robert's favorite places.

Tonight Robert studied his prince, for the first time conducting an objective evaluation of the other man's looks. Prince William Rutherford was just shy of what could be considered tall, with black hair, and brown eyes which sparkled with mischief as often as not. His dignified bearing marked him as royal and he had the straight nose and well defined cheek bones which marked him as a prince of the blood. His build was lanky, but he was well-muscled. With a body honed by weapons training, hunting and other pursuits, he would be a catch for any female, whether he was royalty or not. Full lips and a mobile mouth he was sure most women would think was made for kissing completed the assessment.

"For the right woman, there is no such thing as too much trouble," Will stated. He thought of that one perfect moment when he removed her mask, that one beautiful instant when their lips met and he knew he would remember it for the rest of his life. And he knew beyond the shadow of a doubt that she was worth any sacrifice.

"And you are sure she's the right woman, that she's the one? More, are you sure you are ready to be tied to this one woman for the rest of your life? You don't have to decide now. Taking time to consider is no crime. You are the prince, after all."

"True, but I have my duty."

"As you say. But there's nothing that says your duty has to be only that. It's you who has to wed and bed whoever you marry so shouldn't you choose the right person? The right wife and the right queen is essential. It takes time to be sure."

"I know that. Trust must be earned. But that doesn't change what I feel in my heart." At his friend's skeptical look, he added, "I can't explain it, but I know that time will confirm what I already know to be true. She is my one true queen."

"By all the gods, Will, you spent, what, four hours at the ball with this woman? How can you possibly know that?" burst out Robert.

"I just do. Look, relax. I don't plan to marry the woman tomorrow you know." He clapped his friend on the shoulder. "Before I can do anything, we have to find her. C'mon."

****

Will had slept very little and thought of nothing but his mystery woman since he first saw her. Searching for days had brought them no further forward and gained him nothing. Despite an announcement sent by messenger to every village throughout the land begging the woman to make herself known, the lady had not appeared. With no other options, Will and his men scoured the countryside. Every village within a twenty-mile radius had been searched and every female that fitted the description of his mystery woman was presented to him. No trace of her had been found.

Being awake for an eighteen-hour stretch had taken its toll, leaving him no choice but to return to the palace to rest. Grateful for the brief respite, he headed without pausing to his private apartments, sank down on his comfortable feather mattress and was asleep all but instantly. He had closed his eyes for no more than a moment when a hand on his shoulder shook him awake. Eyes tired and vision blurred from lack of sleep, it took him a moment to recognize Robert.

"Majesty, those you sent out have returned. Forgive me for waking you, but they say they found her."

Wide awake at the first sound of the words, Will assured his friend, "I'll be right there."

****

Juliette could not stay still. All she could do was pace and desperately try to remain calm. What could she do? Beatrice had to be stopped, but how to accomplish that was beyond her. If only she could think. But how could she when panic threatened at every second to overwhelm her? She was expected to go to the palace, to convince the prince she was the one he danced with at the ball and then fell for. Not just that, she was also to wed and bed him, all the while living a lie and committing the basest kind of treason. Unless she got caught and summarily executed. At the thought of that, her knees, still weak, would no longer support her so it seemed a pretty good idea to sit down on her bed for a moment.

One fact stood out. Beatrice would never stop with

making her daughter queen; her ambitions ran deeper than that. Making that bloody shoe fit was the first step on a long twisted road that would, if Beatrice had her way, culminate in Beatrice's rule. She would be queen in fact if not in name. Juliette's very blood chilled at the thought. No, she vowed, that would not happen, not while she lived. What was more, if she gave it a bit of time, she could come up with something. Some scheme would occur to her. Of course it would. It had to.

More composed now, she began to pack. For the time being, she would behave as if she intended to go along with the entire charade. No sense in alerting the opposition, not at any rate, until she had a viable plan and was quite ready.

****

After her undignified exit from the parlor, Rosalind retired to her own chambers to recover as best she could from her shame in private, but now that Beatrice had returned to her rooms, she joined her. At the curt command to enter, she did then studied her mother. Piercing green eyes, which Rosalind herself had inherited, set just a bit too far apart were quite arresting and were arguably her best feature. Men still fell at Beatrice's feet when she turned that sparkling gaze on them. Or they withered when that same gaze grew cold and ruthless. Her lips were thin and stiff, testifying to the fact that she did not often smile, not genuine heart-felt smiles anyway. A chin that was firm and uncompromising and a large jaw dominated the rest of her face. Though she was nearer fifty than forty, with her clear porcelain complexion, she could pass for thirty-five and often had.

Today she was dressed in her finest red satin

polonaise gown with the low square-necked bodice embellished with embroidered leaves of gold and gold lace edging the pagoda sleeves. Her ebony colored hair was powdered, as was all the rage at present, and twisted into a chignon so tight Rosalind wondered it didn't give her a blinding headache. A ruby on a thick gold chain rested between her breasts. Rosalind knew it to be one of the few items of value her mother had not sold when Lord Dubois died and she wanted to rip the stone from around her mother's neck. Or perhaps tear the elegant dress to shreds. Anything to ruffle her mother's unshakeable composure as she sat in front of her dressing table removing pins from her hair as if nothing out of the ordinary had happened. Instead Rosalind asked the one question dominating her very being. "How could you?" she all but shrieked.

In answer, Beatrice shrugged. "Only one of you can wear the shoe."

"But why her?"

"You know as well as I there are certain elements of magic that are unpredictable. I could spell the shoe. I could choose who it wouldn't fit, not who it would."

Rosalind's mind whirled then went quite blank with astonishment. "But that would mean you know who the shoe belonged to. You know who danced with the prince."

"Of course I do."

"But how? No one had any idea who she was." Again her mind ground to a halt. She recalled her utter conviction that she knew the woman in the prince's arms even though she couldn't quite place her, a conviction she'd subsequently dismissed. Then the dreamy way her stepsister had sailed through her morning flashed through her head. In a rush accompanied by an almost physical pain, it all coalesced. "Celina is the one, isn't she?"

"So she is. What does it matter?"

For the life of her, Rosalind could find no answer to that. What did she care who the prince danced with since it wasn't and never would be her?

Beatrice cleared her throat. "Now if you've calmed yourself, I have a task for you."

"You have a task for me? After this? You take Juliette to the palace and the prince while I'm to stay here. To add to that insult, you have a task for me? What pray tell? Let me guess, I will have charge of everything here. I will keep this place running, do all of the work with the help of our steward, whatever his name is."

"You would have done all that in any case. No, you must make sure, very sure, that Celina stays exactly where she is."

"What? Why? You can't be worried she'll tell. Who would believe her?"

"Still, no one must know who she is or where she is. Above all, the prince must not know he danced with your stepsister. Is that clear?"

"Very. I'm to play nurse."

"Yes. If you do your part and we succeed, all of this will be yours." Her mother gestured vaguely at the nearby window where the grounds of the Dubois estate could be seen.

Rosalind made an indelicate sound of derision. "While Juliette gets the prince and you get the throne."

Beatrice grabbed Rosalind's chin, jerking her so they were nose to nose. "The Dubois lands are more than I ever had at your age. Be grateful." Then the duchess turned on her heel and stalked away.

Grateful? Ha! Not bloody likely!

****

The longer Rosalind thought of it the more furious she became at being left behind, all the more so because there was nothing she could do about it. Fate, the one force more powerful than magic, had decreed the slipper would fit Juliette, not her. Still, she had not survived all of these years without knowing how to pick her battles. Perhaps she should view this as an opportunity. The estate would be hers to run, for weeks, perhaps months. For once she could do things her own way with no interference. At last her life would be her own.

Looking at things from that perspective, why then involve herself in treason? Once Beatrice was caught— and she would be, Rosalind had no doubt—the Dubois estate would be hers for the taking. Until that time there was always Celina, a card to play if ever there was one. If she did not like the outcome of her mother's scheme, she could threaten to expose the entire plan, with Celina as living proof. That would put her mother in a bit of a pickle, now wouldn't it? Just thinking about that made Rosalind smile.

****

Summoned by one of the daughters of the house, Jonathan mused. He was called by the one that haunted his dreams and intruded upon his daily consciousness with increasing regularity. What could she possibly want with him he wondered? Well, he'd soon find out.

When he knocked, a deep yet feminine voice within bade him enter. He stepped inside to find her seated at an elegant ladies' writing desk, but at his approach, Rosalind Alexandra Dubois rose to greet him. The sapphire gown she wore made her look like a mermaid just come from the ocean. Sunshine glinted darkly on hair black as ebony and made her porcelain skin glow. Her statuesque but petite figure fascinated, but nothing captured him so much as her eyes. Eyes he had long since realized were green as mythical serpents from out of the depths of the sea. Looking into them now, he knew he could lose himself in them so very easily.

To distract himself from his fascination with her, he studied the chamber he found himself in. Without question, it belonged to her. No typical ladies parlor done in soft pastels, the settee was covered in cream and piled high with pillows in shades from pale, grass-green to the rich emerald that matched her captivating eyes. Rather than the light pine that most ladies favored, her desk and chairs were made of dark oak. A thick burgundy rug covered the flagstone floor. Along one inner wall, massive bookshelves held numerous books. Two winged back chairs upholstered in forest green faced a large bay window. Instead of embroidery, a novel with a page marked with a ribbon lay on a small table placed between the chairs.

"You sent for me, my lady?"

"I did. We will be working closely together for a time. That being the case, I desired to meet with you." In a few sentences she informed Jonathan of her mother and Juliette's departure to the palace. "So to all intents and purposes, I'll be in charge for the duration. I'll need someone to help carry out any orders, that's where you come in. I want things to continue to run smoothly without my having to worry overmuch about it."

Jonathan nodded. "I see. You want me to do my job and yours."

"Essentially, yes." She beamed.

Dazed, he blinked, distracted by her smile for a moment. It was like the sun and even reached her eyes, his befuddled mind informed him. Refocusing, he managed to force his brain to re-engage. "No."

"No?"

"No," he repeated in a firmer tone.

Her eyebrows winged up, but all she said was, "Why?" When he didn't answer, she added, "Given the fact that I, the de-facto lady of the house, am giving you a direct order it would behoove you to obey or at the very least offer some explanation for your refusal."

"One: my authority as steward has limits. I doubt your mother would be pleased were you to extend it. Two: I will be too busy with my usual duties. Three: I don't want to." He enumerated the points one by one on his fingers. The scandalized scoffing sound which escaped her lips almost made him grin.

Rosalind held up a hand to tick off her own points. "First: it is I who will be making decisions for the foreseeable future, not my mother. You would do well to remember that. Second: as your mistress, your duties are what I say they are. Third: explain why your wishes should matter in the least."

He flushed and every muscle of his body tensed. Heated words were out of his mouth before he could check them. "I am as human as you so my wishes ought to be taken into account. I say you are a spoiled child who's never done a hard day's work in her life. The change will do you good."

Speechless with fury as she was, he decided it might be wise to leave well enough alone and beat a hasty retreat before he could ruin his life any further by saying something that would get him killed. Recovering her accustomed self-possession after such an exchange was surely difficult, but, in his opinion, Rosalind managed it. She did not throw anything at him, at any rate, as he knew she was wont to do during an argument. Halfway to the door, her voice made him halt. "Wait. I'm not finished with you yet."

It took all of his considerable self-control not to reply with a very natural 'Oh, yes, you are.' With a superhuman effort, he turned back to face her.

"You should know Celina will be unable to perform her usual duties until my mother returns."

"Is she traveling to the palace as well? Fine time for her to be gone. Very well, I'll see to it her duties are attended to."

"You misunderstand. She will remain here, but unavailable."

"Is she ill? I didn't realize. What is the matter with her?" Much as he was loath to reveal any weakness before this woman, he could not keep the sharp, tight edge of fear from his voice.

"Oh no, she isn't ill. Merely...indisposed," Rosalind assured him with a small smile which this time got nowhere near her eyes.

Instinct roared to life. Whatever was happening to Celina, she most definitely was not 'merely indisposed' but in danger. Every bit of his intuition confirmed it. Intuition that was, in truth, also backed up by his experiences of Rosalind and Beatrice. He knew that both of them could be ruthless and was quite certain they were being so now. Without conscious thought, he took the infernal woman by the shoulders. "What have you and that beast you call your mother done with her?"

When he touched her, her skin remained as cool as her voice. "Nothing. My dear stepsister is quite safe I assure you. Safer than you will be if you don't remove your hands from my person."

He hadn't the least intention of releasing her until he got some answers. Besides, it was high time to start thinking with his brain and not his cock. "Just how did Lady Dubois manage a personal invitation for an extended stay at the palace?"

Rosalind said nothing, just gazed at the strong hands still grasping her upper arms with bruising force. Resisting the urge to give her a vicious shake took great effort, but he released her, showing her his hands, open and unthreatening. "If I'm to work so very closely with you, I need to know everything that's going on. How else can I protect you?"

After a long pause, with as little embellishment as possible, she explained the situation as it stood thus far to him.

"So, you need Celina out of the way, at least until the prince is made to marry Juliette. I won't even ask what Juliette might have to say about her future being determined in this manner. Nor will I mention that the whole business is treason of the worst sort. I ought to go straight to the prince with all of this."

For a moment he saw the shadow of her mother in her face, merciless, lethal, lacking conscience and without compunction and he trembled just a little. "You could try. But consider this; it's your word against mine and my mother's."

"In spite of the fact that I am a servant, I am well respected. I may not be nobility, but my word is good. What about Lady Beatrice's? Even with her less than pristine reputation, perhaps she would be believed initially, but Celina has a very different story to tell which the king might find most interesting."

"He might, but your head could just as easily end up in a noose. If, say, Celina were not available to tell that story of hers what then? To make such a serious charge without definitive proof is a bit of a gamble. I suppose the question then becomes do you want to risk it?"

He assessed her for a long moment. "I don't think I will, at least not yet, on one condition."

A small laugh escaped her. "You're not in a position to make conditions."

"Nevertheless, Celina is not to be harmed. If she suffers so much as a scratch at your hands, I will bury you. Are we clear?"

"Crystal. I've no wish to harm the little mouse. She's of zero interest to me. So, we're agreed?"

"For the moment." Bowing, he left before he could do the vixen a serious injury.

****

As the carriage rolled along a drive toward the castle, Juliette leaned out of the window to catch her first glimpse of the place which would become her home. It was worth the trouble, she decided when a massive stone structure came into view. It was like something out of a dream, made of gray stone with turrets at each corner, battlements connecting them and grand towers in the center. It was larger than any other structure in the land. Never had she seen the like.

"It's quite something, isn't it?" Beatrice remarked, when she noted Juliette's interest.

"Most impressive," agreed Juliette, but said nothing more.

"All of this could be yours. If you follow my lead and stick with the plan, you will be queen in no time."

Unwilling to encourage such talk from her mother, Juliette kept her eyes forward, surveying the landscape beyond. The castle, with its wide stone walkways, and high wall protecting the entire keep, was magnificent but deep down she knew it would never belong to her.

Set at the highest point of a hill in the middle of a meadow, all approaches could be seen for miles. Not only decorative, she judged, but in a strong defensive position. A deep, dark moat surrounded it as well, acting as a last barrier. As they approached, the drawbridge was lowered and the portcullis raised to allow them entry.

Undoubtedly, it was a romantic prospect, one she might have appreciated under different circumstances. Yet as it was, all she could envision was being thrown into the deep dark dungeons she could not see but knew the castle possessed. Taking a deep breath, she gathered her things and disembarked.

****

Will could scarcely contain his excitement as he awaited his future bride in the main audience chamber later that morning. With little expectation of finding her so soon or even perhaps at all, once told she had been located, he was over the moon. He wore his finest clothes, black knee breeches with white silk shirt beneath a dove gray waist coat. His cloak was white with the royal seal dyed in black on it. Boots of dark gray polished to a gleam encased his feet. As crown prince, he of course also wore the silver circlet passed down from father to son which marked him as heir.

His father entered, then sat on his throne. Made of oak and a lighter cedar, the royal seal was carved into the back with the edges etched in gold, it was a masterpiece of craftsmanship. The seat cushion was filled with swan feathers and covered in purple velvet. According to legend it was one of the most comfortable, yet regal thrones in the world. As befitted his exulted station, the king was dressed for the occasion in his most formal attire: powdered wig, royal robe of red with white fur at the collar, white silk shirt, scarlet waist coat and black knee breeches. Golden, bejeweled crown and scepter were also, of course, in evidence.

The early morning sun poured in through the stained glass windows which ran down the entire length of the place, but Will could not appreciate the beauty of the day while he waited at the far end of the bright and airy room. Standing on the dais beside his father, he had to remind himself not to pace, something he often did when impatient or over-eager. He longed to know whether she was as lovely as he recalled or if the evening had been no more than a fantastic dream.

"Are you ready, son?" King Henry asked.

"More than, Father."

"The Lady Beatrice Dubois and her daughter, Lady Juliette Forbes," the herald announced.

The massive oak door opened to reveal a woman of perhaps twenty-five or twenty-six, with a mass of red-gold curls and hazel eyes as changeable as a stormy sea. His heart, which had leaped into his throat, fell. She wore white with a stomacher embellished with sky blue flowers and a simple blue ribbon of the same shade at her throat. Not her, he realized. She's beautiful, he decided, but this is not the one I danced with. He had no time to say as much to his father. In seconds the two ladies stepped forward and curtseyed.

King Henry acknowledged the women with a nod. "You are most welcome, Lady Dubois. Lady Forbes, my son looks forward to renewing your acquaintance."

With another deep curtsey, Beatrice replied, "We are honored, sire."

Two expectant faces turned toward their prince. He blinked, gazed down at the women below. He had to pull himself together if he was to deal with this fiasco. Jaw firming, he did just that. "We are…most pleased at your arrival. In fact, we wonder at it. Even our greatest hopes are exceeded at seeing your face again so very soon." His tone, cool and brooking no nonsense, had both his father and the girl flushing, but for very different reasons.

King Henry shot his son a quelling look, then took the two steps down to catch Juliette's hand. "Please forgive my son. He is overwhelmed by your beauty. You must be tired from your journey. Allow my servant to show you to your quarters."

****

"Do you mind telling me what that was about?" Henry demanded once they were alone in the king's withdrawing room. His father's voice, rough at the best of times, was almost a growl.

Henry did not use the area often. It had been built during his grandfather's time when it was often necessary to conduct audience after audience with diplomats from various countries. After hours of such interaction, the former king needed a place to refresh himself or ask advice of his privy council. So the nearby room was furnished with a comfortable chair, with a seat cushion covered in red velvet, and a table of highly polished oak with other less ostentatious chairs about it for the council. These days, Henry had little need to withdraw, as there were fewer diplomats to deal with and if he needed advice, he would be sure to get it ahead of time. Still, today the chamber was convenient, and they made use of it.

"She is not the woman I danced with."

That stopped his father in mid-tirade. "What?"

In a reasonable tone, Will repeated, "She is not the woman I danced with at the ball."

"The shoe fits her and from what I understand it would fit very few. The entire company was masked for the whole evening. How can you possibly know that for sure?"

Will shrugged. "The curve of her face, her coloring, the shape of her hands, her bearing, the shade of her eyes. I could go on."

"But she is as you described: blonde, well, auburn, hair, delicate, blue eyes."

Will just shook his head. "No, I can't explain it except to tell you there's magic at play here. The woman we just met, whoever she might be, is tall, and has hazel eyes."

"It's easy to mistake eye color, even height in the dark. She—"

Before his father could finish contradicting him, Will interrupted, "Only I saw her up close. I alone saw her unmasked. I am the only one who spoke with her for any length of time. She is not the same woman and I will not marry her."

His father's entire face went a bright red, always a clear warning of an impending explosion. "I don't care if she's the bloody queen of Siam! You swore an oath to marry the woman who fit the shoe. Any woman. So you will wed her. Whether there is magic afoot or not makes no difference to me. I don't even believe in such things as you well know. She seems a nice enough girl, spells or no, and her birth is beyond reproach. Resign yourself, my boy. You will be a husband to her."

"The woman I enjoyed the ball with is the only woman I'll ever love. Do you not understand? I was hers from the moment I laid eyes on her and no one else's."

"Don't be ridiculous, Will," Henry scoffed. "There is no such thing as love at first sight. What you are feeling is not love, it is lust."

"I'll not deny a desire to bed her, but there's more to it. She is my fate as surely as I am hers. I won't stop searching for her." Seeing little point in further discussion, Will turned to leave.

Progressing from red to a deep shade of puce, his father spluttered, "I forbid it!"

Will raised his eyebrows. "Really? How will you stop me then? Will you disown me or execute me? Foolish, as I'm your sole heir. My death is what it would take to stop me, you know. I will find her."

"I'll restrict your movements. Place you under house arrest if I must," Henry threatened. "Be sensible."

Will said nothing more, just turned on his heel and walked away.

Chapter Two

"Oh, gods, he knows!" When this got no reaction from her mother, Juliette continued, "You saw his face! Prince Will knows. He is writing the orders for our execution as we speak!"

"Get a hold of yourself, Juliette," Beatrice commanded. "He won't be executing us because he has no proof and he never will. The worst is over. We are in."

Juliette placed a hand to her forehead, wishing that simple action could stop the blinding ache building behind her eyes. "Mother, we can still stop this. It isn't too late. We can tell the king that it was all a mistake, an honest, regrettable mistake. Surely if we are truthful, he'll—"

Beatrice cut her daughter off with a sharp gesture. "Whatever you are thinking, whatever you are planning, stop. If you don't, I promise you will wish you had. I won't sit by while that common strumpet is put on the throne."

"What strumpet? You mean the girl the prince actually danced with? You don't know she's a strumpet or even a commoner for that matter..." Juliette's voice died away as certain bothersome, curious facts fell into place. "He danced with Celina didn't he?" The look on her mother's face was all the confirmation she needed. "What did you do to her when you found out? Spelled the shoe of course, but where is she, Mother?" For the first time in her life she dared to lay hands on her mother, grasping her upper arm none too gently. "Where is she?"

With a look of pure fury, Beatrice jerked her arm away. "She's quite safe I assure you."

"Where?" The word was a shout, which did not faze the older woman in the least.

"Home, of course. Where Rosalind will make sure she stays. I mean to rule through you. You had better get used to it," Beatrice stated in a matter-of-fact manner Juliette found maddening.

Shaking as temper coursed through her, Juliette could not string two coherent thoughts together, much less give them lucid expression. Yet one thing was clear, the last of her fear had dissipated, leaving rage in its place.

****

The poorly restrained violence emanating from the prince surprised Robert so much that it took a moment before he could manage to ask what the trouble was. His shock increased when Will didn't answer, but grabbed the nearest goblet and smashed it in the hearth. When he looked ready to destroy the decanter as well, Robert found his voice again. "What is wrong, majesty?"

When the prince said nothing and instead took hold of another glass, clearly intending it to go the way of the first, Robert lost his own patience. "That is very expensive crystal and, with all due respect, you've broken enough of it. What happened? You were supposed to meet your bride; I assume something went wrong since you are furious."

"Furious would be an understatement. I'm livid because she's not. Not my bride, not the woman I danced with, and most definitely not my future queen."

"What? How is that possible?"

"I don't know exactly. I do know two things, however. This fiasco was no accident and I am not marrying Lady Juliette Forbes."

"You're certain she is not the woman you danced with? Couldn't you be mistaken?"

Will shook his head with utter conviction and began to pace.

"And you couldn't marry her anyway I suppose? Juliette is an attractive woman or so I've been told."

Complete exasperation and stubbornness combined settled over Will's face. "By all the gods, Robert."

Robert sighed. Once Will's mind was made up there was no sense wasting energy trying to change it.

"So you won't marry her. Few know she's been found. To those who do, put it about that there was an error. It was no one's fault, just an honest mistake. Simple."

"It would be if my father wasn't insisting that I wed her and bed her as soon as humanly possible."

"Well, bloody hell," was all Robert could manage.

Will couldn't suppress a snort. "My sentiments exactly." Will's mirth faded. "Unless I obtain irrefutable proof of deception or, better still, of treason, I'll be forced to marry her." He came to an abrupt halt mid-pace. "That's it."

Wary of the look in the prince's eye, Robert asked, "What is it?"

"We need proof of treason, incontestable, indisputable proof. You will get it for me."

"And just how am I supposed to do that?"

"I'll assign you as my betrothed's bodyguard. Get close to her as well as that creepy mother of hers and find the evidence."

Robert held up a hand. "Just so we're clear, you want me to spy on her?"

Will nodded. "For the good of the realm, yes."

For a long moment, Robert considered. The idea itself stuck him as sound, if risky. He shrugged inwardly. Regardless of the merits of the plan, there was little else to be done if they were to know the truth. "When do we start?"

****

When Jonathan failed to appear in her study at the appointed time, Rosalind waited, expecting him at any moment. Thinking perhaps some emergency had delayed him, she remained patient. After half an hour, however, her slight annoyance morphed into anger. Once a full hour had gone by with no sign of the wretched man, her anger progressed to rage.

At last, she summoned the butler.

He bowed low as befitted her station then awaited instructions.

"Where might Jonathan be, Anders?" she inquired, icy calm not quite concealing her temper.

"O-out in the fields, my lady, as is usual for him so n-near the harvest," the poor man stuttered.

Rosalind absorbed this information then fixed Anders with a stern gaze. "He received my summons yesterday evening I trust?"

"Y-yes, absolutely, Miss," he assured her.

"Very good." Rosalind rose. "You will take me to him."

"Now?"

The poor man looked so pale and sweaty she thought he might faint with shock. Well it wasn't as if she asked to be taken to a brothel for heaven's sake, she thought, with an irritated shake of her head.

"Now," she confirmed.

"But Lady Dubois never—"

"I am not my mother," she informed him. Grimly, she wondered when, if ever, people would finally no longer need to be reminded of that fact. "Be so good as to obey me. Take me to Jonathan."

****

Finding Jonathan had been a chore. With ill grace, Rosalind made the half hour journey on horseback. Just as Anders had informed her, he was in the south field, working alongside the men in the hot sun like a common servant instead of the head steward of a great house. He was tall, six-foot if he was an inch, and every bit of it muscle. Well-formed from head to toe with broad shoulders and slim hips, she couldn't help admiring his backside in particular. Golden blond hair clubbed at the nape made a woman wonder if it was as soft as it looked, topped a well sculpted face. Fine cheekbones, a strong chin and striking blue eyes were enough to make women of every station take notice. The fact that all he wore was disreputable boots and a pair of brown homespun trousers only made him more appealing.

"Shall I get him for you, my lady?" Anders asked.

She did not reply, but shook her head and continued to observe. It didn't take long to see that the men looked to him to lead, deferred to him when a decision needed to be made. Their respect was plain to see. Was it in spite of his station or because of it? Or was it the man himself who provoked such a reaction? His rock-steady, dependable, confident air reassured those under his protection. More, he was ready to assume responsibility for any choice made whatever the outcome. Even if the choice was protecting her. A rich warm thrill curled deep inside Rosalind at the thought of this man protecting her. At the idea of him doing her bidding, the thrill became just a touch illicit.

He must have felt her eyes on him at last because he turned to her, inclined his head in acknowledgement. He did not, however, curtail his conversation, but instead continued to demonstrate to one of the hands a better way to cut grain with a scythe.

Some minutes later, he approached. "How may I be of service, my lady?"

"By attending me whenever I require," she informed him, her voice and manner cool as a winter's day.

"My apologies. I assumed the summons I received was in jest. You would wish me to attend to the harvest first and foremost I'm sure."

"When it comes to estate business, I never jest. Furthermore, I have wasted the morning seeking you out. I do not intend to do so again. Is that clear?"

"Yes, miss."

She nodded her approval then continued, "I have need of your particular skills. It is time to balance the estate's accounts. Come."

"My lady, I fear I would offend you with my untidy state. I beg leave to attend you in one hour, once I've washed and changed."

An impatient sound escaped. "Oh, very well. I will

expect you in an hour, no more."

****

As promised, Jonathan arrived within the hour, washed and dressed in garments far fresher and finer than those he had worn in the field. He was impeccably garbed in light beige waist coat paired with fawn colored knee breeches. His coat was made of rich, if sober, dark brown with gold stitching edging the cuffs and collar then continuing down the lapel. Perfectly suitable attire for a steward of a noble family.

Yet she remembered him in the earlier homespun. The fact that he was comfortable in either sort of attire and could mix with both classes of people easily, intrigued her. She tried to forget the expanse of bare chest and well-muscled arms she had glimpsed before with little success. In any sort of garb or lack thereof, he was in fact, almost handsome, Rosalind reflected. Sandy blond hair freshly washed, large build, and strong features, in particular a well-crafted chin, and finally blue eyes that were always alive with one emotion or another: discovery, affection, righteous anger, compassion. Yet he was often so controlled that one would not know how he was feeling unless those eyes were watched very carefully.

She studied him a moment. "Well, I suppose the delay was worth it. At least you no longer smell like sweat and horses." She wrinkled her nose at the memory.

Jonathan bowed but said nothing.

Rosalind cleared her throat. "So, the books. Show me."

Bowing again, he proceeded to a book case at the right of the desk where she sat. From a shelf full of large, black leather-bound tomes, he pulled a newer volume and placed it before her.

"As you see, my lady, all the ledgers kept since the Dubois' first acquired the estate are housed here. This is the most recent."

She nodded. "Good. How is it arranged?"

He pointed out the columns of expenditure and income. Columns not written in her mother's hand but her father's. Some little time after her father's death, an unfamiliar hand took up the pen. "Who wrote these? You?"

"I did. Your mother disliked doing the books."

His brief answer made her purse her lips. "How did this work then? She allowed you to tally everything, all the expenses for the whole estate?"

He inclined his head. "She kept control of the money, never fear. She knew what this estate was worth down to the last farthing, I wrote it all down for her. At times I would try…"

His voice tapered off. Sensing the greater detail she craved, she urged, "Go on."

Jonathan did not answer.

"Jonathan, if we're to work together, we may as well begin as we mean to go on. When we are alone, and on this subject only, you may speak freely. In fact, it is vital that you do so if we are to be productive."

He considered this for a moment then dipped his head in acknowledgement. "From time to time I would suggest improvements to Lady Dubois. Improvements which would make life better for the tenants as well as make a profit. She…declined to implement them."

"I see."

And she did, more clearly than he might suppose.

Her mother's greatest aspiration had been to bleed every bit of profit out of the estate she could without regard to anything other than her own comfort and, by extension, that of her daughters. Overweening as it was, her ambition had been more than sufficient to accomplish this. "I am not my mother. Bring your ideas to me and I will consider them."

His eyebrows shot up in surprise. Would she have his approval? Rosalind couldn't be sure.

Either way he bowed in assent. "As you command, my lady."

****

When she woke, Juliette discovered the guest chamber assigned to her was even lovelier in the morning light. The huge feather bed covered with a forest green counterpane was more comfortable than any she had ever been in, not that she'd slept much. The intricate vines and leaves carved into the posts of the oak frame made her feel as though she were in a forest. In the right corner stood a dressing screen. Embroidered with trees, from which deer and other wildlife peeked, it furthered the pastoral impression. Beside it was a washstand made of the same oak as the bed frame which, judging by the similar designs carved into the wood, had been fashioned by the same artist. The thick rug beneath her feet was a woven rose garden. A large fireplace took up the majority of one wall and would keep the room as warm as one could wish. Never had she seen such elegant luxury.

The morning dawned bright and clear and sunshine poured cheerily through the elegant white lace curtains in contrast to Juliette's mood. She and her mother remained unexecuted and undiscovered, yet she was under no illusions. The orders for her death could come at any moment.

A soft tap at her door roused her from her dark thoughts. When she called for those waiting without to enter, the little maid assigned to her rushed in.

"My lady, the prince wishes to see you in an hour in his private dining room. If that is convenient, he says." The girl's eyes were as big as saucers, yet she managed to deliver her message.

Juliette's stomach clutched, but she gritted her teeth and steeled herself to begin what was sure to be a very trying day. "Very well. You may give him my compliments and assure him I will attend him."

The maid bobbed and hurried to discharge her duty.

****

"Good morning. I hope you slept well after your long journey."

Juliette curtseyed in answer to this basic pleasantry. "I did, your grace. The accommodations are everything I could desire."

"Good. Forgive me for asking to see you at such an ungodly hour. There is an important matter I wish to discuss with you and it would not wait."

"Of course, sire. I am an early riser so you need not worry about the hour and, as always, I am eager to do your bidding."

Will smiled then gestured for her to take a seat. "I appreciate that. As you know, this kingdom is on the brink of war. Tensions are running high."

"I am aware," Juliette assured him.

"Taking that into consideration, I must insist that you have a bodyguard."

Startled, all Juliette could do was parrot his words back to him. "A bodyguard?" Whatever she had been expecting, it hadn't been this.

Will nodded. "My dearest friend, the man I've entrusted my own life to for years, is who I have in mind for the job. I swear you will be quite safe with him." Turning to a waiting servant, he murmured an order.

Juliette's consternation increased a thousand-fold when she thought about how her mother would feel having a bodyguard underfoot every moment. Gods, she had to stop it if she could. "Sire, surely I will be safe enough here within the walls of the castle and in your royal presence. There's no need—"

"I would not ever have you worried for your own safety. On the contrary, I would instead take every precaution. Let me introduce you." He motioned to another nearby servant who moved to do his bidding and usher the prospective bodyguard inside.

There was little else she could say and even less she could she do. To object further would give the prince cause for suspicion. Beatrice would have to deal with this new development.

The man who entered a moment later was her fantasy brought to life. It was as if everything she had ever found physically attractive in a man was melded together into one being. At six feet tall and about 13 stone—every bit of it muscle—he was striking to say the least. His face was saved from being too perfect by the crooked line of his nose, broken in some previous altercation. Sleek black hair and fathomless dark blue eyes completed his good looks, but there was more to his appeal than that. His sheer physical presence, the way he moved made her belly clench. Then he turned those beautiful eyes of his on her and she couldn't look away. To Juliette it was as if he were seeing into her very soul, reaching for her very essence and she was helpless to prevent it. She hoped whatever he found there didn't disappoint him.

As she withstood his scrutiny, she gathered her courage to conduct her own perusal. If he could study her so closely, so intimately, he should expect her to return the favor. She did her own belated survey of what she could sense beyond the physical. No pretense, nothing but passionate belief, mercy but little gentleness, strength of will. All this was as clear to her as if he were made of glass.

The sound of the prince's voice jolted her back to the present. "Lady Forbes, allow me to present Lord Robert Weston. Lord Robert, Lady Juliette Forbes."

She offered her hand and started at the sharp tingle that shot up her arm when they touched. Judging from his slight hesitation before kissing her offered hand, he experienced something similar, she was certain of that down to her bones. His lips burned where they met the back of her palm, forcing her to suppress a shudder having nothing to do with fear.

What on earth was the matter with her, she wondered, all at once angry at her own reactions as well as her resulting behavior? Since he was unaffected by this casual contact, she had best pull herself together lest she forget he was there to be her bodyguard while also spying on her as likely as not. He was not there for any other reason. He did not intend to court her, still less to be her lover.

Composure somewhat restored, she offered him her

most practiced curtsey and murmured, "My lord."

"My lady," he replied in a soft rumble that had her fighting those shivers again.

Gods, even his voice had her all but melting. At this rate, how on earth would she manage to be in his presence every waking moment without throwing herself at his feet like some fool? She had to find a way, she told herself sternly. This was no time to go muddle-headed over a man she just met. It was vital she maintain her focus; stopping her mother was priority number one. He was a complication she could not afford.

****

Robert's first glimpse of Juliette was of a mass of her auburn curls on the periphery of his vision as he walked up the room. His idea of beauty had never been traditional. Women with a unique mix of features, forming a pleasing, if unusual whole had always attracted him. Serious hazel eyes set wide apart regarded him a moment, but then her gorgeous smile transformed her entire face.

If her goal was to charm, she did so beautifully. Yet, he wasn't deceived. In her eyes, in that one instant before her shields slammed into place, he'd seen enough to assure him there was more to her than mere attractive elegance. Fear had filled her. In that one flash, he'd seen it. Then he'd seen her rein it in. Her chin had firmed and she had not let her fear rule her. The strong impression of strength and vulnerability together made for an intriguing mix.

There was something else he'd seen in her eyes: attraction. She was attracted to him and he felt the same undeniable pull. Like magnet to steel, they were drawn together.

As they went through the formality of introductions his head kept spinning. She had to be the loveliest creature he had ever seen. All those beautiful curls falling in clouds about her head awed him. He wondered idly whether her hair was as soft as it looked. Then he caught himself, appalled. This outlandish scenario might still end with her wed to the prince, despite all of Will's pledges to the contrary. In which case, such thoughts made an easy path to treason. For anyone to even touch the future queen without her express consent was sedition. To lie with her was treason of the worst sort. He was to be her guard and her spy, not her lover. His own feelings could not, would not, absolutely did not, enter into it.

When she assessed him in turn, a shudder of pure desire coursed through him. That she would meet his scrutiny with her own, that she could and would meet him as an equal, made him yearn to test her to see if she could match him as well in other areas.

When he kissed her hand, a gesture he had performed with others countless times, heat shot from where his lips met the back of her palm, all through him to the tips of his toes. 'Oh, no' was all he could think. Resisting his fascination with her would not be as easy as he had, in his arrogance, supposed.

****

When Beatrice heard her daughter's long awaited footsteps at last, she rose and went to the connecting door between their adjourning bed chambers to meet her. "Juliette, where have you been? I thought you—" She broke off as she realized her child was not alone. The prince and a rather handsome stranger accompanied the girl. She lowered into a hasty curtsey. "Forgive me, sire, I was unaware of your presence."

"Not at all. We don't stand on ceremony here, Lady Dubois. I'd like you to meet Lord Robert. He will have a care for your daughter's person."

Robert bowed and Beatrice curtseyed once more. "You mean he'll be her bodyguard, majesty?"

"Just so. Either he or I will always be within calling distance. The world we live in is a dangerous place. I would not have Lady Forbes harmed for the world," Will explained. His sincere and earnest concern was evident in the way he put a protective hand on Juliette's arm.

Nothing less than a lifetime of utter control enabled Beatrice to keep her true reaction in check. A bodyguard always within earshot? Well, that was just bloody perfect. Doing what she came to do would be that much harder with this one around, she fumed. Even if he turned out to be as dumb as a post, he would still be an additional obstacle, another pair of eyes and ears that she would need to keep from seeing and hearing too much. "You've served the prince in this capacity before?" she asked when she tamped down her fury enough to speak.

Robert bowed. "And very well I might add." His deep voice continued, "My lady, I've held this position for almost eight years. I know what I'm doing and you won't even know I'm here," he assured her.

Adopting the motherly persona she still had use for on occasion, Beatrice inclined her head, let warmth fill her voice. "Of course, Lord Robert. We must do everything we can to insure my daughter's safety, even more so now, as she is the future queen. I am certain you will do quite an admirable job."

Come to think of it, he looked as if there were any number of things he could accomplish admirably, she realized as she studied him. Young, in his mid-to-late twenties, well-built and altogether attractive, she judged. Perhaps she could distract him while bringing pleasure to them both. The thought appealed. Still, there would be time enough to test that theory when they were no longer under the watchful eye of the prince.

"Good, it's decided then. I'm sure you'll be very happy with Robert as your bodyguard and I am sure I'll rest easier knowing you are safe even when I cannot be with you."

Juliette curtseyed. "You are most kind, sire. I feel as safe under your grace's protection as I could possibly be."

****

Seated behind his desk in his study, King Henry perused various letters. Most were formal written requests from his nobles for aid or justice. He was so engrossed in his task that he gave his son no more than a glance when Will, entered.

"I've little time, son. What is it?" Henry demanded.

Will took a deep breath and steeled himself. He had to play this right or the whole business, his whole world, would come crashing down. "I have decided to marry Lady Forbes."

"How very gracious of you, Will. I am speechless," Henry replied acerbically.

Ignoring his father's acid tone, Will continued, "I thought you'd be pleased. Of course there are conditions."

"Conditions?" his father blustered. "You, sir, are in

no position to make conditions."

"Oh, I think you'll find I that I am. I will marry her if and only if you say nothing to the court regarding her identity. Say that I have found the woman I was looking for, no more than that. Explain to them that we are getting acquainted and negotiating the details of our marriage settlement."

"And just how I am I to keep this woman's name a secret? Things like this have a way of coming out sooner rather than later," Henry pointed out, "Stands to reason."

"I suppose you are right. So, give the staff and any others to have contact with her strict instructions to say nothing of her particular appearance or attributes on pain of death. It will leak eventually, but this should buy me some time."

"Time for what? Not to keep searching surely?"

"Of course to keep searching. I am your son. Did you think I would just give up? No, I will find the woman I danced with at the ball. I will marry no one else."

The king considered this for a long moment. "Very well. Look for her, but you will not continue to search for a woman that doesn't exist forever. You have two months. At that time your impending marriage to the striking Lady Juliette Forbes will be announced. Two months after that you will wed. I'll not have you wasting your life or endangering the kingdom in this way. I won't tolerate this indefinitely, Will."

"And if I find her? Because I assure you, I will find her, Father."

"If you find her, so long as she is suitable, you will have my permission to wed. Agreed?"

"Agreed."

****

A few days later. Robert joined Will in the library as he did most evenings and settled into his usual chair.

"Forgive me for being blunt, but what do you think of her?" Will asked Robert.

"I think she's lovely and intelligent. I think she's got a temper which she keeps under strict control. She's like a frightened bird, but there's this steel beneath."

"Interesting," Will mused. "If I hadn't already met the love of my life... But I have. What have you learned?"

"I think, whatever is happening, she wants no part of it. As for her habits, she reads, plays the harpsichord, breakfasts alone and spends time with her mother. That woman, majesty..." Robert shook his head, as weary as an old man. "The more I see of her, the more she disgusts me and the more I am around her, the more I am certain it's Beatrice behind all of this."

Will's head came up like a hound that's caught a scent. "What makes you say that? You've found something?"

Robert shook his head. "Nothing concrete. No... it's just a feeling, a sense. Juliette is this strong yet somehow fragile creature that's caged. She's smart and I can see her searching every moment for a way out."

"Intriguing. If that's true—"

"It is true and it's our duty to help her find it," Robert stated in a firm voice.

Chapter Three

The rattle of the key in the lock woke Celina, but before she could do more than sit up, Rosalind entered.

Holding a single lantern high to illuminate the dim room, her stepsister studied her with more than her usual air of contempt. Three days had passed since she had been allowed to wash, nor had the room been aired during that time. As a consequence, the stench of her sweat and the reek of urine and excrement from the unemptied chamber pot rose like a miasma.

Rosalind set down the lantern on the small bedside table, wrinkled her nose then opened the single window. "This chamber is foul. I'll have the servants in to clean within the hour," she informed Celina in a brisk tone. "You'll also have water to wash and fresh clothes. Did she leave orders to at least feed you?"

Celina had to swallow against a dry, burning throat. "I've had nothing for three days other than a little water."

Rosalind sighed. "Oh, for pity's sake. Did my mother think to have you die of thirst and starvation? I suppose you must have meals as well."

Through parched lips, Celina managed, "Your mother left me here to rot, as, I assumed, had you. Why would you care what became of me?"

A strange look passed over Rosalind's face before she answered. "Because I am not my mother.

Nevertheless, she has left me in charge and while I am, you will be treated decently. You will have all you need: food, water, even books if you wish. You will be free to go back to your regular duties soon enough."

Upon the death of Celina's father, her stepmother had set them on a swift path to ruin. Gambling, the expensive finery, as well as a bad harvest had soon forced them into reduced circumstances. Almost all of the staff and many of the field laborers were soon gone. To keep her home from ruin after her father's death, Celina began to take over certain tasks. The front hall needed scrubbing; she sought out bucket and pail. Weeds began to take over the vegetable garden and Celina fought a valiant battle against them. No one else in the family could cook anything edible, so Celina prepared the meals. When the washing piled up, she cleaned it. Soon it was expected that she would do these things as a matter of course. She wondered who was doing such things in her absence.

Rosalind added, "Once Juliette is safely, not to mention legally, wed to the prince, things will return to what passes for normal around here."

Celina stared at the older girl in horror. So, what she had long suspected was true. Juliette was to marry her prince, her Will. Every instinct within cried out a denial.

Rosalind ignored her stepsister's distress and continued. "Think of this as a holiday, spent here," she urged, as she gestured about the tiny space. "But let me make this plain, if you try to leave, if you attempt to send any messages, if you do anything at all to disrupt my mother's plans, I will kill you. Do you understand?"

Celina's pale cheeks flushed with rage. "I

understand that you are a fool. The honorable Lady Dubois will get the prince to marry Juliette then she will kill him. After she's committed that kind of treason do you seriously think Beatrice will ever let me go? No, I shudder to consider what she has in store for me. Even if she did later free me, with Will wed, it would be too late. Please—"

"I find this conversation exceedingly inaccurate not to say tedious. You will do as I command."

Sheer desperation made her incautious. In that moment, she realized she would do anything to be with the man she loved. "I love the prince. His majesty is the only man I'll ever love and his life is in danger. Rosalind, please, I beg you. If he dies, I do not want to live."

Rosalind clucked her tongue. "Celina, you of all people should know we don't always get what we want."

She rose to shut the window. "I'll send the servants in presently." She turned back. "Oh, Celina, don't think to take your own life. If I end up with your blood on my hands, it will be by my choice not yours."

Celina studied her stepsister for a long moment. "You must hate me. Otherwise why continue with this? Why not let me go? That awful woman is gone. Much as you tried to hide it, I thought you were different. You are different."

Rosalind's eyebrows shot up, the sole sign of her surprise. "Am I? I'm not so sure about that." Saying nothing more, she took up the lantern and left.

Celina sank to the floor, all hope, like the light Rosalind took from the room, gone.

****

"I see you've ordered three meals a day brought and Celina's room cleaned each morning. You even went so far as to direct her chamber be aired twice weekly," Jonathan commented.

Rosalind did not look up from the ledger in which she was dutifully scribbling, just shrugged. "When my mother locked her in there, none of the other servants dared to go near it, aside from you. As a consequence, Celina, not to mention the room, was in a deplorable state. Mother may wish the girl dead, but it won't be of deprivation. Not when the decision is mine. You thought I wouldn't do at least that much? I told you I am not my mother."

"So you said. Yet still you keep her prisoner." The coolness in his voice was plain.

"Yes, and I'll thank you to desist in offering your opinion on such a disagreeable subject. There she is; there she'll stay and that's the end of it."

"But, my lady—"

She set down her quill, swiveled in her chair to face him. "Jonathan, you and I have come to an agreeable truce these past weeks. We've been able to work well together and I value that immensely. It's easy to see you are a man of honor and principle. My admiration for you grows daily, but do not presume that because of that admiration, it follows that we are on such familiar terms that I will do as you ask in this matter."

His face was wiped clean of all expression. "That is your final word?"

"It is. Until or unless I say otherwise." Her voice was low but admonitory. With one brisk motion, she picked up her quill and resumed writing.

A heartbeat passed during which he dared not meet her eyes. The fury and challenge in his own would be far too clear, she suspected. Best to give him a moment. She could all but hear him count to ten, and as he did, the death grip on the ledger he held eased and his heightened color faded a trifle. Visibly calmer, he sank into a comfortable wingback chair.

"The crop in the east field needs to be rotated," he began.

****

"I don't know about you but I could use a drink," Will said.

"I could also stand to get out of here," Robert replied.

"Let's go to the Boar's Head then. Let Wellman take his shift at bodyguarding."

The Boar's Head pub was one of the finest establishments of its kind in Camston. Known for its specially brewed ale, it was also a place where the prince would be guaranteed anonymity. The bar was made of dark wood and the tables clean. In the dim light, there was little chance of them being recognized. If the clientele was a bit rougher than those he usually associated with, Robert welcomed the change, as did Will.

The effect of one bottle of good Flemish wine, should not be underestimated, Robert discovered. After a few glasses he was far less reticent, several more and he became downright verbose. Verbose enough to ask the question which had been plaguing him ever since this ghastly affair started. To the devil with propriety, he decided, he needed to know so he'd ask.

"How far do you want me to go, with the spying, I

mean? Just where should I draw the line when extracting information?"

Will, more than a little drunk himself, peered blearily over the rim of his tankard. "What are you getting at?"

"I have to spell it out for you? Should I—assuming I can't get the information any other way—seduce her?"

"Seduce her?" The prince spluttered for a moment, then collected himself. "For heaven's sake, Robert, I would never ask you or anyone in my charge to do such a thing. What the devil ever made you think I would?"

Robert shrugged. "We are talking about the good of the kingdom. I could seduce her, gain her trust and get what we need."

"Your loyalty is admirable—no amazing—but, as I said, I could not order you to do such a thing. I will venture to say, however, that if you're worried about lying with the future queen, don't be. I won't be bedding Juliette. So in the end, you must use your own judgment."

Robert grimaced. "That bloody well helps," he muttered.

Will slanted a sharp gaze at his friend. "You'd do it though, wouldn't you?"

"To save the kingdom, yes. To protect you, my liege, absolutely. To shield us all from that viper Beatrice Dubois, definitely," he vowed.

"No," Will snorted. "I don't question your loyalty to this country or to me, but you're no whore, Robert. What's more, you're a fool if you think I would ever allow you to be one for my sake or for any reason at all. Now what's this actually about?"

Robert contemplated his wine for some time before answering. "Perhaps all I want is to bed her. In truth, it would be no hardship. She's beautiful, charming, witty, and I'd bet my life she's innocent to boot."

"That's better. Closer to the whole truth at any rate, but there's more. If all you wanted was to bed her, you'd have already gotten her on her back."

Robert frowned. Sometimes it was difficult to have such an astute friend. "The truth is I want her more than any woman I've ever known. I'm just not sure whether I'm going to take her yet."

It was Will's turn to shrug. "If you want her and the lady wants you in return, then why not?"

"Indeed." Robert couldn't contain a wry grin, but it was fleeting. "It's a little more complicated than that."

"When it's important, when it's worthwhile, it usually is," Will concluded.

****

The next morning dawned and with it the prospect of enjoyment. The prince—Will—as he insisted she call him, had suggested they ride through his nearby holdings. As riding was a beloved pastime of hers, Juliette agreed with alacrity. It also meant some hours away from her mother since Beatrice was no horsewoman, which made the activity all the more appealing.

As comfortable on a horse as she was on her own feet, she declined the first several mounts the well-meaning groom offered. Instead, Juliette meandered through the stable, examining each horse, some at length. Finally, she stopped beside a dappled gray mare who tossed her head at their approach. "This one will do."

The groom looked dubious. "She's very spirited, miss. Wouldn't you like something gentler?"

"No, I like this mare and—" She broke off when she heard the prince approach, not wishing to trouble him.

"Is there a problem?" Will inquired.

Juliette smiled her most charming smile, the one that made men forget whatever had been troubling their minds. "Oh, no, it's...well, I'd like to ride Chelsea here. Your groom thinks I might not be able to handle her. It is all right. He is concerned for my welfare and has no idea of my skill as a horsewoman; I can choose another for now."

"And could you handle Chelsea?"

Her smile turned reminiscent. "I learned to ride almost as soon as I learned to walk. I'd like a mare with some spirit, surefooted, fast, with good breeding and better wind. Chelsea has all of these qualities and I assure you I can manage her."

Will's eyebrows rose, but he indicated to the groom he should fulfill her request. "Chelsea it shall be then."

****

When Robert saddled his mount he took note of the interaction between Will, Juliette, and the groom. As the prince stepped away and Juliette waited for her horse to be saddled, a pleased smile softening her features, Robert caught his friend's attention. "Can she ride? If she can't, this will be a very interesting morning."

Will spared one glance at his friend. "Don't be such an old woman, Robert. She seems to know what she's doing and if it turns out she doesn't, we'll deal with it."

Robert gave a snort that was echoed by his own mount and said nothing more.

****

As Juliette stepped onto the mounting block, the distinct clip-clop of a third horse caught her attention. Lord Robert was leading his own animal forward.

"Sir, I had not realized you would be joining us today."

"We'll be riding some distance. You need more than my protection alone," Will said by way of explanation.

"Of course."

Neither by her face nor her voice did she show the slightest sign of reproach. Not for nothing had she spent years hiding her feelings. Still, she could admit being in close proximity to both men at the same time was a challenge. To stay alive she had to at least keep up the pretense of falling for Will, yet the one she found herself drawn to, was Robert. The worst of it was she had no idea how to talk herself out of it.

Mounted, they started out.

****

Much to the relief of the two gentlemen accompanying her, she proved to be a more than adept rider. Still, when they came to the edge of a vast field stretching all the way to the horizon and Juliette suggested a gallop neither was inclined to agree.

"No, this is unfamiliar ground and that horse is strange to you," Robert stated.

"The ground may be unfamiliar to me, but it isn't to Chelsea." She gave the horse's neck an affectionate pat. "Already I feel as though the two of us know each other well enough to tackle most anything."

Robert exchanged a look with Will.

Once again she treated them to her most charming smile. "Oh, come now. Surely you would not deny me one of the few pleasures open to me? I've not ridden in over a week. It's been forever."

Robert could see that Will was still hesitant, yet weakening. "You do seem competent and Chelsea is as steady and true a mount as anyone could ask for. Perhaps a short—"

"Majesty, it's far too dangerous. One slip and she could break her neck as well as the mare's."

Robert could not hold back the instinctive protest, but he was sorry for it a moment later when Juliette shot him an amused look.

"I assure you I have no intention of breaking my neck. Nor would I damage so excellent an animal. Don't be such a kill-joy, my lord," she finished, addressing Robert.

"Yes, Robert, don't be such a kill-joy," Will added with a look of innocence which did not fool his friend in the least.

Before he could remonstrate further, however, Juliette spurred her mount and, followed an instant later by Will, they took off across the meadow.

Muttering curses under his breath, Robert urged his own stallion forward.

Sweet heaven but she rode like the wind, was his first thought. Effortless and weightless, it seemed she and the mare were one being. Her skill was such that she did not have to think to exert control over Chelsea. Which meant she could enjoy the ride, which in turn meant so could he.

Presented with the evidence she was indeed an exemplary rider, he relaxed and gave his attention to his own horse. The stallion was more than ready for a run so Robert let him have his head. For long minutes he lost himself in the pure joy of the race.

As he rode up alongside, Juliette tossed a coy look over her shoulder, one that had heat pumping through his veins and pure lust washing over him. With the slightest command, she urged Chelsea ahead. Exhilaration filled him. As a rider she met and she matched him. For the first time in a long time he was interacting with a woman who challenged him. He didn't even notice when they left Will quite behind. At last they reached the edge of the clearing, Robert arriving mere seconds before Juliette.

"Lady Forbes, my apologies. I should have trusted your skill. It's been an age since I've found a rider who could keep up with me much less come close to besting me. I congratulate you." He took a deep breath, savoring the moment. "Gods, what a ride."

"A marvelous gallop indeed." Juliette affirmed, eyes bright and cheeks pink with pleasure.

The easy camaraderie of the moment was broken as Will arrived.

"Not many can keep pace with Lord Robert , as you see," he said, as with an easy smile, he gestured to indicate himself. "Did you enjoy it?"

"Very much, your majesty. I do wish we needn't go back so soon."

The very real regret in her voice was unmistakable to Robert and must have been to Will as well.

"We do not have to return this very moment if you do not wish it." With a pat he indicated two saddle bags full to bursting. "I thought you might enjoy a picnic."

At the prospect of an alfresco luncheon, she beamed and left Robert charmed.

****

After setting out a simple meal of cold chicken, brown bread, and fresh strawberries along with a crisp white wine to wash it all down, Robert took himself off to walk the horses, much to Juliette's relief.

"I hope you enjoy the meal as much as the ride," Will commented, as he joined Juliette on the soft blanket Will had put down.

"Oh, I know I shall, your grace," Juliette assured him with an amiable smile signifying nothing.

"That is my wish. I have seldom seen you so relaxed and would like it to continue."

Juliette flushed and busied herself with filling her plate. "Forgive me if I have been a less than desirable companion these last days. The stress of a new environment—"

"You have nothing to apologize for. You have been most engaging, I do assure you. I meant that if there is anything troubling you, please come to me."

"There is nothing—"

"Life at court can be perilous," he cut in. "Little intrigues can turn into far more serious matters. Be vigilant, for my father will deal with such things swiftly and harshly, as will I."

Juliette shivered almost imperceptibly, and hoped her fear was not obvious. It was apparent to her that he would protect his people against the likes of Beatrice. He gave her a moment to let that sink in then continued.

"If, on the other hand, anyone, and I do mean anyone, is causing you distress, you have only to speak of it and I will deal with them. You are under my protection now, as are all of my subjects. As my future wife, that protection of necessity will be even more all-encompassing than it might be for others. Be loyal, dutiful and truthful and no one will harm you. I won't allow it."

"I thank you, majesty, for your pains and for your excellent care of me and your realm. Camston is lucky to have such a king, as am I. If ever I am in need, I promise I'll come to you."

Will sighed loudly enough for her to hear, but let the matter drop.

****

Their conversation during luncheon had not gone the way he wished in spite of his utter sincerity. He hoped Juliette would soon come to understand and trust him enough to let him help. It was plain that she was not ready to confide anything yet, but would she ever be, and if so, would it be too late?

The return journey gave him plenty of time to mope about this state of affairs as well as to come to a much less depressing realization. His best friend was in love. There was no question of this in Will's mind. After their meal, Robert returned and they started back, his betrothed and his friend talking of the particulars of horseflesh all the while. He found to his great amusement that he needed to say very little as they had all but forgotten his presence.

"This has been a marvelous day indeed. Such days as this will be few and far between, at least for me," Will stated, once there was a break in the conversation.

"Why so, your grace?" Juliette inquired, eyes widened in surprise.

"I have many duties to attend to and much as I would like it, I cannot spend every day dallying with my bride-to-be."

"I am truly sorry, sire. I know your duty must come first above all things, but what a pity to give up such a pleasure. It's been a wonderful day."

"You needn't. You and Robert shall ride together."

He dared not look at Robert or he would never keep a straight face. It was for his friend's own good and if he, Will, were amused that was just a side benefit.

A flash of warning in Robert's eyes came and went so quickly that only Will noticed it. "I'm sure your majesty can make the time—" Robert insisted.

"I will try, of course, but I am sure I will not succeed as much as I would like, I regret to say. You would not deprive my lady of something she so enjoys now would you?"

Robert set his jaw and squared his shoulders. "If your majesty wishes it, of course, I will accompany Lady Forbes."

Decision made, the prince nodded. "Excellent. I'm sure with so much in common you will have more than enough to talk about. You'll hardly notice my absence."

****

"So have you made any plans for a ride?" Will asked Robert as they relaxed in the prince's library later that evening.

Robert poured them each a brandy before answering. "We have no definite plans as yet. Thanks for that by the way. Are you trying to throw us together like some matchmaker?" He set Will's glass on the side table hard enough that it clattered.

Will shrugged. "Maybe. Somehow I doubt spending your days with the woman will be a hardship. She is as lovely and charming as you said and, more importantly, she couldn't want to kill me any less if she were a babe in arms."

Robert's non-committal grunt was his only reply.

Undeterred, Will continued, "If that weren't enough, I am now certain she is not the woman I danced with."

"What makes you so sure?"

"Every feeling I've had since I set eyes on her confirms it, but today I was able to test her."

"How?" Robert asked.

"I mentioned something I said that night."

"And?" Robert demanded.

"She went white as a sheet. She covered as best she could after that first shock, but it was obvious she had no idea what I was talking about. The girl is terrified to put a foot wrong, worried it will mean her life. So, spend time with her. Do your best to gain her trust so she will let us help her before she does anything stupid."

"Hmm, yes I suppose there is nothing more volatile than a woman who's backed into a corner," Robert mused.

"Exactly." Will knocked back the last of his drink and rose. "I've a council meeting tomorrow afternoon. See if she wants to go for a ride," Will encouraged, all innocence.

"I am not going to sleep with her," Robert stated in a tone which left no room for argument.

Will just grinned until he was quite sure Robert was resisting the urge to hit him with great difficulty, prince or no. Deciding not to press his luck, the heir to the throne of Camston headed to bed.

****

The morning dawned and Will, Juliette and Robert met in Will's private dining room to break their fast.

Juliette had just taken her seat when Will said, "Much as I might wish to spend the day with you, my dearest Juliette, I must join my father in a meeting with the high council." Turning to Robert, he added, "Perhaps you might show Lady Forbes the south fields and the village?"

"If the lady wishes it, I would be more than happy."

He looked nothing of the sort, but Juliette could not bring herself to care. Another day of freedom out of her mother's immediate reach and on horseback as well would be more than welcome. How could she resist? Except…

"I would most devoutly wish it were it not for one thing. Might I be of assistance to you? Or, failing that, I am certain I could benefit from the council's wisdom."

"True on both counts, but this meeting is private I fear. Go, enjoy the day and I will join you for dinner this evening."

"Of course, sire."

The swooping feeling in her stomach she got whenever she thought of spending time alone with the attractive Robert was her own to deal with. That she could not imagine a better day was her own problem. One of far too many, but there it was.

"Shall I escort you to the stables in half an hour, my lady?" Robert inquired.

"Absolutely," Juliette replied.

****

Bordering on cheerful, she called to her maid to ready her emerald green riding habit as soon as she returned to her rooms.

"Riding again? Twice in as many days. Well done, daughter," Beatrice commented.

Years of training kept Juliette from jumping, but it was a near thing. Her mother occupied a deep arm chair in their shared sitting room, so she was not visible to Juliette from her own chamber. She waited for her galloping heart to slow then crossed to Beatrice and answered, "Not so well done as you might think. The prince does not join me, only Lord Robert."

"Here a little over a week and already he abandons you to his lackeys? Not so very well done indeed. What, pray tell, is more important than his future bride?"

"He attends a council meeting. I am, therefore, left to amuse myself."

Her mother huffed. "Hmm, you must find a way to attend those meetings. The information procured would be more valuable than anything else we might obtain. I wonder that you haven't already done so."

Her stomach tightened at the clear disapproval in her mother's tone. "I did try," Juliette said, crossing her arms in defense. "He did not wish my presence and I believe it unwise to push so soon into our acquaintance.

"Oh, very well. Tomorrow is soon enough I suppose. You just remember who it is you are marrying. Do not even think of that delicious bodyguard of yours."

Juliette turned and pretended to examine the book she had left on a side table so her mother would not see the blush coloring her cheeks. She hoped Lord Robert did not hear. "I'll remember, Mother."

"Be sure that you do. Now go away, I've a headache and I must rest if I am to be in top form this evening."

Feeling lucky to get off with no more than a scolding, Juliette curtseyed then left her mother to her own devices.

Chapter Four

"I'm sorry, what? I don't think I heard you correctly, majesty," Beatrice said through clenched teeth. When the king summoned her she knew nothing good could be afoot, but she had not expected such a serious setback.

Henry repeated, "She will not be presented to the court just yet,"

Beatrice could not hold back her response. "But if she and the prince are to be married, why wait?"

"The young people should have time to become accustomed to one another away from the prying eyes of the vultures that constitute my court, should they not? In two months we shall present your daughter at a grand ball. They shall wed two months later."

"But why—"

Henry's expression turned thunderous. "It is my express wish. That is all you need know."

The honorable Lady Dubois bit her tongue until she could taste blood in the back of her throat, but then bowed her head in acquiescence. For now she had little choice. "Of course, sire. All shall be as you would have it."

With the cool dignity that had ever served her well, she begged leave to go and got herself away before she used her magic to stop his heart or flay the flesh from his bones.

****

Juliette returned to find her mother in quite a state. Her forehead beaded with sweat, Beatrice paced and raved. After regaining a modicum of calm, Beatrice described her audience with the king.

"I don't understand. I'm not to be presented at court for two whole months? Nor wed for another two? Why? Does the king suspect what we've done?"

Beatrice gave her daughter a withering look. "Of course not. He knows nothing. If he did why bother feeding and housing us for months? Why not execute us this very day? No, he has some foolish notion you and the prince should get better acquainted before the wedding. Idiot."

On one level, relief threatened to engulf her. So she wouldn't be wedded and bedded in a matter of days after all. At least now she would have a chance to spend time with the prince beforehand and if the worst happened and she did indeed have to marry him, he wouldn't be such a stranger to her. On another level, however, she wondered how on earth she would survive. How could she keep up this ruse for so long? How could she resist her attraction to Robert? And how, in the name of all the gods, was she to avoid being exposed? Finding a way to escape was essential, now more than ever.

She put on her most conciliatory expression and did her best to appease her mother, all she could do for the present. "Forgive me for saying so, but you are looking at this the wrong way. You should see this as an opportunity. He likes us. He trusts us. This delay will give us more time to build up both even more. The longer he believes us, the easier it will be to do what needs to be done, what we came to do." Sickened by her own words, she tried to convince herself that in the end somehow she would save all the lives her mother wished to ruin.

"I hate waiting, but I suppose we haven't much choice." Beatrice pouted for a moment more then with a brisk shake of her head continued, "Still, we won't be idle. We will both do all we can to move the wedding date up. I will handle the king while you handle the prince."

"I am doing my best." Juliette complained, now a little sulky herself. "We are getting to know each other and I am spending as much time in his company as he will allow. I'm not sure what more I can do."

Beatrice flashed Juliette a look she could not interpret. "Have you slept with him yet?" she inquired, tone cool and matter-of-fact.

Genuine shock left her gaping for few moments. At last she managed, "Of course not. I've known him for little more than a week!"

Beatrice made an impatient noise. "The two of you are to be married. Anticipating the vows is not beyond the realm of possibility. Don't be such a prude, Juliette. Use what passes for feminine wiles with you to get him into your bed. That's the surest way to get what we want."

For a moment, Juliette thought her head might explode the tension inside it was so great. She took a long, deep breath then turned to face Beatrice. "Mother, I don't think you quite understand. He was originally intended for the church. For over half his life he thought that was to be his destiny. During that time, he more than accepted that fact, he embraced it. In all its aspects," she pointed out with particular emphasis.

Beatrice gave her a sharp glance. "Is this your way of trying to tell me he's a virgin? Even all these years after his brother's death he yet remains chaste?"

Juliette could not keep her hands still. "Well, he hasn't come out and said as much of course but I believe that is the case, yes."

Beatrice bit her bottom lip, always a sign of serious thinking. Her answer when it came was not one Juliette expected. "Hmm, so our prince is untouched. This could make getting him to tumble you either far easier or next to impossible, depending on the depth of his convictions and the strength of his drives." She set her glass down, careful not to spill even a drop of her wine. "You'll have to make sure the latter wins out over the former."

Sheer panic had her shaking. "How am I supposed to do that, being as chaste as he? I know little of men."

Beatrice's expression hardened. "Learn," she advised succinctly. "You've watched me often enough."

Juliette had and been appalled. Upon her husband's death, Beatrice had gone into deep mourning as was proper. One month after John Dubois's burial, however, Juliette, aged thirteen, had caught her mother dallying with an attractive but none-too-bright young stablehand. More than appalled, Juliette was revolted, aghast and completely horrified. Still in shock, she confronted her mother only to be slapped so hard that her face was bruised for days after.

Lord Dubois had been one of the few to ever show her and Rosalind any kindness. He had curbed Beatrice's worst excesses and soon grew to love her young daughters as his own. Had he lived so much might have been so very different, she thought with a pang. As the only father she had ever known, his death had left a hole no other could fill. Then to see her mother betray him with such callous indifference had devastated her. After that first stableboy there had been numerous others, most of them cut from the same cloth. Juliette had had no wish to know of them although from time to time the knowledge was unavoidable. Her dear father, for so she would always think of John Dubois, was an exception rather than the rule. He had been the best of men.

"I did learn quite enough from you. Nothing, I fear, that could ever be of use in my current predicament. And I'd rather not discuss the matter any further if you don't mind," she informed her mother coldly

When she turned to go, the older woman caught her arm and squeezed until pain shot up her shoulder. "Don't take that tone with me, miss. Bed him now or later, I could care less, but bed him you will. And you will have him move the wedding date up."

Juliette jerked her arm away and without another word, she stalked from the room.

****

Morning rides with Robert became routine. Each day they would explore another area of the royal holdings until, by the time a fortnight had passed, she had seen them all. At that point she had chosen several favorite paths and had only to inform Robert which one she wanted to take.

One bright day, they arrived a bit early, soon enough to observe the horses being put through their paces. Several of the grooms were mounted and taking the animals around the paddock. Juliette noted her favorite, Chelsea, was ridden by an old, rough-looking fellow. The man's weight was far too much for the high-spirited mare. What was more, he had much too heavy a hand with the bit and hurt her sensitive mouth. As a result, Chelsea was far more fidgety than she would have been in the normal course of things.

Noting the animal's distress, Juliette acted on instinct and moved forward to help. Before she reached them, the groom sliced the horse's delicate flank with a riding crop, hard enough to draw blood. She whinnied in shock and pain then reared. The groom hit her again with even more force then pulled back the reins. Her hand fisted and her magic rose up inside of her.

"Stop!" Robert's voice, full of authority, carried over the resulting din.

All sound ceased; no one moved; no one so much as breathed. Even the groom, hand raised to strike once more, froze.

"Dismount, sir," Robert ordered with a steely stare. He said nothing more, but waited to be obeyed, jaw clenched almost hard enough to break.

With obvious reluctance, the man did as he was told. When he was on solid ground, Robert addressed him. "Your name?"

"Jones, sir."

"We do not countenance such cruelty here. You would do well to remember that. You will get your things and you will leave this property within the hour."

"On whose authority?

Robert glared at him. "On the authority of the prince's bodyguard, and member of the council, Lord Robert Weston. Me."

Unfazed, Jones scowled. "You mean to dismiss me without a character, sir?"

Robert's silence was answer enough.

Jones's face, already bright with anger, grew redder still. "But, Lord Robert—"

Robert rounded on him. The temper he had, until this point, held in check was now on display and Jones blanched. "Be grateful I don't administer the thrashing you so richly deserve here and now. If I ever find you have done anything of this kind again, I will remedy that oversight. Now go."

Jones bowed his head and left.

Juliette blinked once and found her open palm glowing as blue as the summer sky. She closed it, extinguishing her magic. If Robert had not been so quick to step in she would have used her powers to throw Jones to the ground and...she knew not what else. What was wrong with her? Perhaps after so many years of witnessing similar atrocities, her heart could no longer bear it.

She would have broken a vow and, although it was one made to no one but herself, it was a principle by which she lived. She must be more careful. Control was essential, no matter the circumstance. And, even more important, she must rededicate herself to that vow. Now more than ever, it was essential she keep it. The next weeks would be fraught with temptation in abundance. There would be so many situations where she would long to use her powers, but she had to resist. It would not be a meaningful vow if it were always easy to keep. Still, she was thankful Lord Robert acted with such dispatch.

"I am sorry you had to witness that, my lady. Are

you all right ?"

"Not yet, but I will be." She took a deep breath to steady herself then went on. "I am most grateful to you. I would have stepped in myself had you not done so and the result would have been far less amicable, I must confess."

"So I sensed. For that and a plethora of other reasons, I dealt with him as expeditiously as possible. Are you certain you are all right ?"

"I am fine," she assured him. "I just won't stand by and allow such things, not anymore. It comforts me to know you feel the same."

"I understand."

For a moment, she believed he did. The thought was some consolation as she tended Chelsea herself.

****

Within a week Chelsea was fully recovered and Juliette and Robert went on another ride. When they reached their destination, a rather pretty lake, they dismounted, leading the horses as they walked.

The day was so beautiful, Juliette thought, she could almost forget all of her problems. Her worries burned away altogether in the warm sun or maybe they were floating away on the cool breeze. She smiled at the errant thought.

"You could just tell me you know," Robert suggested, his voice matter-of-fact.

All her tension rushed back tenfold with his words and all her joy in the day dissipated as though it had never been. Although her heart beat fast in her chest, Juliette replied in as casual a tone as she could manage. "Tell you what?"

He made an impatient noise. "Don't be dense.

There is something going on and I would rather you tell me than have to continue ferreting it out for myself. You might also consider that the prince and I have certain suppositions which I am sure come uncomfortably close to the truth."

As her blood turned to ice in her veins, she gave him her haughtiest stare. "I have no idea what you are talking about."

Tossing the remains of an apple he had been eating into the brush beside the path, he looked over at her. "Very well, if that's the way you want to play it. Let's start with this instead then, I know that you are not the woman the prince danced with."

"How did you come up with such a ridiculous theory?" she asked, with a nervous laugh.

"What you're really asking is how I know. Never mind how I know. I do. So does his highness."

Juliette's whole being went wild with panic. Her body went hot, then cold and she thought she might faint, but she gritted her teeth and the moment passed. "I have no idea what you are talking about," she repeated. The automatic denial sounded weak even to her own ears.

Robert inclined his head. "You refuse to talk. Very well, perhaps you will listen. Consider this, the prince and I have our suspicions as I said. If either of us believed you meant to harm him, we would never let you run free."

She dared not look at him.

He caught her arm and halted them both. "If either of us wanted you dead, you would be. Many have been executed for less. We have a general idea of what is going on, but no details, no specifics. Nor do we have anything even approaching proof. Yet. But we will have, sooner or later. We want to help you. I want to help you. Can't you see that?"

At length, she met his eyes. His sincerity could not be mistaken. Still, how could she trust him? How could she trust anyone? "I do see and I thank you, but there's no need. Whatever you think you know—"

He held up a hand. "Stop. Let us have some honesty between us at least. If you can't tell me the truth, then say nothing. It's a bit more respectful than lying to my face."

Without another word, he helped her to mount and they made their way back to the castle.

****

Rosalind decided she would begin as she meant to go on. Her mother had left her in charge and by the gods she meant to make the most of it. Where there was room for improvement, she would make it. When an idea struck her, she would implement it. To begin with, the back fields would need to be planted. Next, new horses used primarily for breeding would need to be purchased. After that...

So it went on. A fortnight and more passed so quickly for Rosalind, the time barely registered. She spent every waking moment dealing with the estate in all of its aspects. By the end of those short weeks, a solid foundation was laid for the future. Throughout, Jonathan was beside her, offering advice, arguing the merits of one plan over another, then coming up with the best compromise. By the end of the first week, he became indispensable to her.

As the month came to a close, it was time to go over the books again. For the first time, the estate operated at a loss. Despite knowing full well this was bound to occur, Rosalind could not help but be dismayed.

"Are you quite certain these figures are correct?" she asked Jonathan as she studied them.

"Of course."

Rosalind leaned back in her chair as she pressed a hand to her throbbing temple. "My mother will not be pleased."

"Hmm, perhaps not, but the cost of the improvements you've implemented will soon be recouped. Besides, she left you in charge; she can hardly complain."

Rosalind made a rather unladylike, but very descriptive noise which she hoped gave him a clear idea of what she thought of that notion.

Jonathan's lips quirked for an instant as if he were amused, then straightened. After a moment he was more somber than she had ever seen him.

"Answer me this, how do you feel about what you've done here? Are you proud? Are you confident of success?"

Rosalind pursed her lips, considering. "Yes," she finally replied. "Yes. I know the changes I've made will benefit the estate as a whole in the long run."

"Good. That's what matters."

She studied him for a moment and consulted her own emotions. "You are right. That's what matters and doing things my own way was the whole point, the one reason I even agreed to remain here. To the devil with her."

Jonathan's brows shot up at the coarseness of the expression, but he repeated, "To the devil with her."

They continued to tally and figure. After a time, Rosalind noticed Jonathan no longer wore his easy expression or even the air of intense concentration she often observed when they worked together. Instead, his jaw was clenched tight enough to break while his eyes were razor sharp and hard as granite.

"Is something wrong, Jonathan?"

"I'm not entirely sure, but the odds are," he began, hesitating a little. "I've found some discrepancies and I think someone's skimming."

Rosalind lips thinned. "Show me," she insisted.

He presented her with several rows of figures and explained, "This wool here should have been sold for a far larger amount." He indicated another sheet, "Where did the difference go you ask? Here," he told her, producing a sheet listing household expenses for each tenant and pointing to one. There were unusual purchases adding up to the twenty pounds more that the wool should have sold for.

Her mouth tightened into a grim line at the concrete evidence set before her.

"I've found several other transactions just like this."

"All proceeds ending up in the hands of this one man I assume."

Jonathan nodded.

"But this has been going on for months. Why didn't you tell me?"

"I only noticed it myself two months ago. It is a serious offense, but I didn't want to accuse anyone until I was certain.

"Of course. Well, now you have proof. He must be dealt with."

"Yes, he must be because it's worse than a mere twenty pounds. When it happened again this month, I went further back in our records. He's stolen 250 pounds total that I've found so far."

"Bring him to me."

****

In the study that had once belonged to her stepfather and which she now made her own, Rosalind faced the thief. In a few brief words, she presented the evidence against him. "What have you to say for yourself, Marcus?"

"Nothing, my lady." The man refused to meet her eyes and instead stared sullenly down at the floor.

"Nothing," she repeated. "You would say no word in your own defense?" He shook his head, gaze still locked on the ground as if it contained all the secrets of the universe. "Could you make restitution? Would you even if you could?"

Still no response. The silence stretched but, with a sigh, Rosalind broke it. "Let me put this another way," she began. "Why? If you won't excuse yourself, at least give me a reason."

This captured Marcus's attention, or enough of it at least, to have him meeting her eyes. Rosalind was unprepared for the sheer loathing in his. Between that and the unveiled defiance that surrounded him, that in fact permeated his very being, was it any wonder her mother had threatened to be rid of this one more than once?

"You want a reason? To prove your mother doesn't own me. Nor do you."

"I see. Do you know what my mother would do to you for this?"

When he ventured no answer, she'd had enough "You know and you don't care."

Decision made, she got to her feet. "Very well, tomorrow morning, I shall render my judgment for all to hear. Jonathan, have all our people gather in the outer bailey one hour after dawn."

****

As commanded, all those attached to the Dubois estate gathered an hour after the sun rose. In the center was the dreaded whipping post her mother made copious use of. A few of the onlookers eyed it with nervous, jittery gazes which never rested on it for long. Others stared upon it with loathing, still others eyed it with something akin to anticipation.

Rosalind addressed those in her charge from the outer steps leading to the hall. Jonathan she placed just behind her on her right hand and the culprit was made to stand before her at the bottom of the stairs. Gradually, stillness fell over the crowd.

"Good people, a wrong-doer stands before you. Marcus Bradford took profits from our wool trade and lined his own pockets. Evidence against him was found and he has admitted his guilt. For the crime of thievery, in the normal course of things, Bradford would receive fifteen lashes then be thrown upon his own resources without ceremony. I am not my mother, however. Therefore, I propose a different punishment today. I would give Bradford leave to go and further give him until sunset to be off Dubois lands. I dislike messiness of a public beating, yet I would have no greedy scum by me, taking the bread out of the mouths of good, honest people. Guards, please see that he leaves with the clothes on his back and food enough for a week and nothing more. Your cottage and all other personal items will be sold to cover your debt. This is my word. In my mother's absence, I am mistress here and I will be obeyed. Do not think to cross me. Any other such infractions will be dealt with more severely. That said, bring any questions or concerns to me and I will endeavor to address them. Now please, go about your business." With a gesture, she ordered her guards to lead Marcus away. Sensing Jonathan's presence behind her, she spoke to him without turning her gaze from the scene playing out before her. "See that it is done."

Jonathan gave a slight bow of assent. "All shall be as you wish, my lady." He turned to do her bidding then stopped a few steps from the door. "For what it's worth, I believe you made the right choice."

"Did I? I'm not so sure. Will they see me as weak? I don't know."

Jonathan shook his head. "Not weak. Just."

****

"You surprised me today," Jonathan said when they were once again alone in her study dealing with the business of the day. "At least on one level. On another, you didn't surprise me at all. I always knew."

"Knew what?"

"That you could act with compassion. The way you dealt with Marcus... I'll say again you made the right choice."

An unfamiliar feeling swept through her. An emotion so foreign, it took a moment for her to give it a name. It was pride, she realized. Flustered, she busied herself with the papers on her desk. Still she could not stop herself from asking the question foremost in her mind. "Is that really how you see me? As someone who acts with compassion?"

Jonathan nodded. "Right now, yes. Of course you are so many things from one moment to the next. A man has to use all the faculties at his disposal to keep up."

"Thank you, I think," she replied.

****

Throughout the next week, they worked late into the night to finalize their plans for the next season.

"Well, there we are then. Done." After seven long days, Jonathan finished writing the last of the letters Rosalind had dictated with a flourish.

"What? Done?"

"Yes, unless there's something more, my lady." He leaned back in his chair a satisfied expression apparent.

"No, I can think of nothing we've left out. So we're finished. Truly?"

"Truly."

"Oh, Jonathan, we've done it! Now no matter what mischief my mother chooses to do, this year at least, our people will eat and well. And what's more, the estate will prosper, perhaps not this year, but soon, I am certain. We've done it!" Filled with an excited, triumphant exuberance, she grabbed his hand, brought him to his feet. She took both of his shoulders in a firm grip, let him go, then wrapped her arms about him.

She'd never thought her laughter was infectious, yet he joined her. As he did, he pulled her close and spun her around. She gasped, then giggled.

When he lowered her, however, her merriment faded as she became aware of his nearness. Almost every inch of her was pressed to every inch of him so the essential maleness of him surrounded her. All at once, realization of his greater physical strength burst upon her. Throughout her life, she'd been vulnerable for many reasons, but for the first time her vulnerability felt distinctly feminine and not at all unwelcome.

But it wasn't until she looked into his eyes that her entire being shook to its core. He wanted her. Such a look from a man was unmistakable; she'd seen looks of that kind before, never from him, though, until now. It was plain to see and for one moment she couldn't catch her breath. She was utterly captivated.

Neither of them moved a muscle, but even as she watched, his face closed up, shut down and his desire was veiled almost as if it had never been. What a pity, was her first coherent thought.

With infinite care, as if she were made of some peculiar volatile material that, when brought into contact with his own was dangerously combustible, he stepped back from her. He cleared his throat, as if it had all at once gone quite dry. "Well, I'm sure you must be tired. I'll bid you good night."

"You won't stay and have a drink with me? You've worked as hard as I, harder. Join me, I wish you would."

"I thank you, my lady, but I must make an early start tomorrow. The grain must be brought to market."

"Of course. When can I expect your return?"

"Two days. Three at the outside, depending on how well negotiations proceed."

"Very well. Safe journey."

Once again, it took her a bit of time to put a name to the feeling that overwhelmed her: disappointment. She had become far too used to spending her days with him, she lectured herself. Desperate, she tried to conceal the distress which would embarrass her were Jonathan to ever know of it. He did not appear to notice. In fact, he said nothing more, but bowed and headed to his rooms.

****

Lying in his bed that night, Jonathan found sleep eluded him in spite of his exhaustion. Gods, he was still shaking. What just happened? For one second he could have sworn she wanted... Jonathan shook his head to clear it. Whatever she, or for that matter he, wanted, was moot. Perilous thoughts about a perilous woman would do no one any good. Things were going well and now was not the time to allow his body to respond to hers. Oh, but he wanted to. What we want is not necessarily good for us, he told himself.

Jonathan's stomach had churned as he had obeyed his new mistress and brought Marcus to face her judgment. The man's actions, while reprehensible, hardly deserved the punishment he had been sure she would mete out. Then again, one of her most fascinating qualities, as it turned out, was her ability to surprise him, as she had that morning and as she had just now. He found her unpredictability as captivating as it was infuriating, yet his main objective was to do the best he could to protect the people of the estate and Celina in particular. If he had to use her high and mightiness Rosalind Forbes to do that, work with her to do that, then he bloody well would, no matter how uncomfortable it made him. Keeping things strictly platonic was the way forward. He'd not complicate matters any further by touching her, he vowed.

Then another thought occurred to him. What on

earth would he do if she came to him? If she offered herself, how would he handle it? His wayward mind helpfully provided details of what such a scenario might entail. For just a moment, he couldn't stop the vision of her over him, under him, enveloping him. With sheer brute force, he checked himself. He would have to refuse her no matter how difficult it was, no matter what the enticement.

He would do whatever he had to do to keep everyone safe. He swore to himself Celina would be freed. He would see to it.

****

Tossing and turning got Rosalind no closer to sleep, so near dawn, she gave up the attempt. How could she rest? He wanted her. There was no mistaking that flash in his eyes. Yet, until that moment in the study she'd had no idea. Most men could conceal little from her, certainly not their desire, but Jonathan had. They'd worked together for weeks without him raising the least suspicion. A man who possessed that degree of control intrigued her.

Even more fascinating was the fact that, for the first time, her own desire was ignited. Those who wanted her had thus far, left her cold. Not Jonathan though. With him it was so different and so unfamiliar as to be unprecedented. That was the only way to describe it. In essence, he made her body yearn.

Heart and soul, however, were another matter. Those would remain untouched, if they even still existed somewhere deep within her. She could satisfy the demands of her body without undue concern over her non-existent heart, couldn't she?

Now, while there was no one to gainsay her, would

be best, in her view. From all she ever observed, sooner rather than later might also be wise, before her desire and his petered out. Besides, she was 28 and it was high time she lost her virginity. She ought to have handled the matter long ago, but none of the men she came into contact with had appealed. Not so now. Relishing the thought, she allowed her lips to curve just a little in the dark since there was no one to see. As she didn't ever intend to marry, a scathingly passionate, downright scandalous affair with the gorgeous Jonathan was called for.

Decision made, impatience, strong and immediate, filled her, but unfortunately, her would-be lover was already gone. Well, a few days would force her to take a least a little time to consider before she acted. At any rate, if she was still of the same mind in three days' time, she would approach him. Glad to have the matter settled and lulled by imagined scenarios, she slept.

Chapter Five

There would be an informal dinner and dance tonight with members of the family in attendance. Beatrice had informed Juliette that morning, much to her dismay.

Warm brown velvet beneath rich forest green satin made up her gown. Soft red-gold tresses, just a shade darker than the silk fabric she wore, were piled high atop her head into an elegant chignon of the latest style. Pearls of the first water given to her by the prince fell just above the plunging neckline and matched the comb in her hair. The fit of the dress was outstanding and subtly, elegantly defined every line and curve. The fashionable new pagoda sleeves with three wide ruffles of lace falling from the elbow suited her.

Transformation complete, Juliette stood before the full-length mirror in her room and sighed. How much longer would she be forced to endure this torture? Wondering whether each day might be her last and wishing, in some small part of herself, it would be. If it were, she would no longer have to deal with her mother after all. Yet a much greater part of her wanted to survive. A knock disturbed her gloomy reverie and she bid whoever it might be to enter.

"Your mother wishes you to attend her, my lady. She says she is more than ready and..." Robert's voice trailed off.

"What? What's wrong?" When he said nothing, just continued to stare, she asked in a tone she hoped was sharp enough to snap him back to reality, "Robert, whatever is the matter?"

"Forgive me. You are a vision. Words fail me." He brought her hand to his lips, his eyes on hers all the while.

Unable to prevent the blush which rose to her cheeks, she decided, why try? Instead, she let his admiration wash over her. "Well, those words are quite lovely and will do very well," she assured him.

For one glorious instant, she thought he might kiss her. The look in his eyes made her almost believe it. The preemptory knock on the door made them both start. By the time her mother entered, Juliette was at her dressing table and Robert was on the far side of the room looking out of the window at the pitch-black night, all innocence.

"Are you ready yet, Juliette? We'll be late if you don't hurry along," Beatrice complained.

"I'm ready. Shall we go down?" Without a backward glance, she followed her mother out.

****

"I must mingle, speak with important men and discuss affairs of state. They'll be no more dancing for me tonight," Will informed Juliette some time later in the evening.

"How very tedious. Still, I am no dancer, so it is of little matter." Yet, she sighed to herself. Whirling across the floor with Will had been an unlooked for pleasure. In general, she was a passable dancer at best, but with Will leading, she hadn't had to think, just glide about.

"No, no you must continue to dance, I insist. No need for everyone's evening to be spoiled. Robert, would you take my place?"

Disappointment morphed into full-fledged panic in an instant. How could she dance with her all-too-handsome bodyguard under the watchful eyes of the entire royal family, not to mention, her mother, and not give the entire game away?

And what her prospective husband could be thinking the gods alone could tell. A flash of insight had her narrowing her eyes, fixing them on Will. First he encouraged them to ride together and now this? Will wanted Robert as his stand-in for more than one activity, but why? No fool, he must see what a wretched idea this was yet, here they were thrown together again by their prince. Could it be a purposeful decision on his part? If it was, she would have his head long before the king could put hers on the block, she vowed.

All this passed through her mind from one flicker of a candle to the next, so when Robert bowed before her, she was ready. Steeling herself, she took his offered hand and permitted him to lead her to the floor. Shrugging, she tried to be resigned. It was not as if she hadn't put on an act before. Nothing must show this time, that was all. She would conceal her true feelings and no one would suspect, least of all her mother. Her life depended on it. She must not fail.

****

Robert wondered if it was permissible to assassinate a future monarch on the grounds of said monarch's obvious insanity. Reluctantly deciding that it wasn't, he contented himself with hissing 'Bastard' under his breath in Will's general direction before turning to the woman waiting with her hands folded before him.

"My lady, would you do me the honor?" The question was asked with admirable smoothness and Juliette replied in the same vein.

Mere seconds later, she was beside him and they were heading toward the other dancers readying themselves to go through the motions of the waltz. With her arm tucked securely under his, and their bodies so close together, it was impossible for him to ignore the fact that her every muscle was locked tight.

"Breathe," he whispered. "Better still, relax. If you don't, people will think something's amiss."

"Relax!" She all but spat the word. "With every eye on me? When I should be dancing with my betrothed, not you? Little chance of that. I have no idea what the prince was thinking, suggesting this," she muttered through clenched teeth.

Deciding now was not the time to divulge his own theories on that subject, he gave her hand a gentle, encouraging squeeze. "Who can know the mind of royalty?" he quipped with an easy smile. "Besides, there's no help for it now so why don't we make the best of it? I am a rather good dancer as it happens." With that almost cheerful observation, he spun her onto the floor.

As they whirled he thought of the moment he had first seen her tonight. In that instant, all thought left him and the power of speech utterly deserted him. Before they had been interrupted, he had wondered if her mouth would be as soft and warm as it looked, longed to know whether her skin would feel like silk. Suddenly, he couldn't bear not to touch her, not for another moment. He had lowered their still joined hands and taken a step toward her, leaned into her. She did the same until they were a mere whisper away from touching. He had tilted up her chin and could all but taste her lips when her mother almost caught them. Well, at least now he had her in his arms and the pleasure of a dance.

****

Waltzing with Robert was like flying. He gave her wings and she soared. She was a passable dancer with the right partner, but for the first time, it was effortless. For little more than one blissful moment, for the length of a song, there was no one else in the world but the two of them. With his strong arms about her and his beautiful eyes looking straight into hers, she had never felt so safe or so elated.

As they spun then glided to a halt the illusion shattered. They stopped near her mother and Beatrice's cold gaze froze every bit of the life and joy of the past few moments right out of her. Oh, gods, what had she done?

****

Robert sensed her returning tension. Even as he searched for the source of her distress, a chill went up his spine. Hunting for the cause of his own uneasiness, his instincts soon honed in on Beatrice. The dreadful woman stared daggers at them. Glancing over at Juliette, he noticed she could not stop gazing at the elegant Lady Dubois and the look on her face was one of pure terror. He had seen people in battle react like that. Her delicate hands began to shake. "Take it easy. I won't let her harm you," he promised.

Juliette gave a slight nod, and trembled, but she

held her head high as they joined her mother.

Robert had no choice but to deliver Juliette back to Lady Dubois, as was proper and appropriate. Never had he wanted to do anything less. Helplessness threatened to engulf him until he realized that he could guard her at least. So he watched over her with an impassive, rather intimidating air.

****

Halfway through the evening when Will tore himself away from his diplomatic duties and joined him, Robert gave the prince a cool look. "What on earth made you do it?" he demanded as he took a glass of champagne from a passing footman then began to pace.

"Made me do what?" the prince asked.

"Insist I dance with Juliette. That viper is suspicious now."

"So what if she is? Let her be. She does not hold all of the cards here. It's time she knew that, don't you think?"

"Not at Juliette's expense I don't. There's no telling what that woman will do to her now." The suppressed violence in his voice was something Robert could do nothing about.

"You are her bodyguard. You have my leave to protect Juliette from any and all threats, including Beatrice Dubois. In fact, I command that you do so."

Robert stilled. "Using whatever means necessary?"

Will inclined his head in assent.

A part of Robert went cold and deadly determined. "The task will be my very great pleasure, majesty."

****

"You made quite an exhibition of yourself with that bodyguard of yours. Whatever possessed you to dance with him, Juliette?" Beatrice demanded.

"The prince ordered it. I could not refuse."

Beatrice's mouth tightened. "You ought to have found a way to decline without giving offense if you're so very clever. What concerns me even more is that you appeared far too familiar with Lord Robert."

Juliette's heart pounded so fast and so hard, she thought it would jump right out of her chest. "I'm not sure what you are getting at. Lord Robert and I spend a lot of time together since he is responsible for my protection. It is natural that we feel easy in each other's company."

Beatrice's eyes narrowed, a sure sign of impending temper. "Lying, especially to me, is never smart. Anyone with eyes can see the two of you are attracted to each other. Don't try to deny it. You'll just make yourself look ridiculous."

Burning embarrassment and ferocity took precedence over fear now. "What would you have me do? He's a very attractive man. I am only human and to request a change of bodyguard now would rouse too much suspicion."

"Get yourself under control. All those thoughts of bedding him, those sweet little daydreams of what it would be like, put them out of your mind. The prince expects a virgin and a virgin he shall have. Or I'll give you to my guards to rape, do you understand?"

Swallowing sick dread along with her wrath, she managed a curtsey. "I understand, Mother." She turned away to watch the dancing, but took in none of it.

****

Late one evening some days later, Robert heard Juliette. Her voice was low and fierce, so different from her usual measured tone that it stopped him in his tracks. Riveted, and sensing an opportunity to learn more of Beatrice's endgame as well as Juliette's part in it, he concealed himself behind the half open bed chamber door, ready to watch and listen.

"We can't go on like this," Juliette protested in a strident tone growing louder with every word. "I won't be presented as the prince's future bride for another two weeks. It's clear the king has reservations. Already the prince suspects and he won't stop until he has proof."

"Proof he'll never find," Beatrice countered. "You will continue to do as you are told. If you even think of telling anyone, remember you are as deeply involved in this as I am and you will be charged with treason just as surely."

"Mother, I can't marry him. I won't."

When he heard the unmistakable sound of a slap, he moved forward to defend Juliette before the thought even registered, but her calm, level voice stopped him.

"Nothing you do to me will change the fact that we will be caught."

Another, harder slap rang in the air. "You had better do your very best to prevent that."

Enough, Robert decided. The sight of Juliette pressing her palm to a reddened cheek made him half blind with rage. He crossed the room in two long strides. In another he grabbed Beatrice's upraised wrist, restraining her. She stood, mouth agape, stunned he would dare lay hands on her.

"It is treason to touch the person of the future queen in that way. Perhaps, as she is your daughter, you are unused to such restrictions. All the same, this is your one and only warning." Tightening his grip, he continued, "Hurt her in anyway ever again and I will tear you apart with my own hands and I will enjoy every moment of it, I assure you." He released Beatrice's wrist with a jerk. "Now leave us."

With one fulminating look promising vengeance, she left.

Juliette crossed the room then lowered herself into a nearby chair. Once her mother was out of ear shot, she said, "I'm sorry you had to see that. I'll be fine now. Thank you."

"Do not apologize," he replied, voice sharp as a razor. In far gentler accents, he continued, "You have nothing to apologize for." To give himself time to calm as much as to help her, he fetched a cool cloth to clean her split lip. As he tended the cut, he asked, "That wasn't the first time, was it?"

Her every muscle went rigid. "I won't discuss this with you."

"Juliette, please, I can help you."

The look she gave him was full of pity. "So you've said. Much as I know you would like to and much as you honestly believe you can, Lord Robert, you can't help. No one can."

Perhaps she was right, he thought, as he withdrew to the antechamber he occupied, leaving her alone. Much as he wished it, he couldn't save her; she had to do that herself.

****

The circumstances were not perfect for an escape, nor was the night. She touched the little box in her pocket and smiled. The money the prince had given her for her own personal use would be enough, with it she could run. Juliette knew it was now or never. She could see no other way to end the nightmare. With Robert getting closer to the truth by the day and her mother implementing her evil plans, little time remained. So it would be tonight.

Food enough for the journey, check. Money enough for lodging, check. Traveling clothes and shoes packed, check. All she had to do was wait until her mother slept and she could be away.

She adhered to her usual daily routine, but found it more and more difficult to keep up the pretense as the afternoon wore on. So with infinite relief, she bid her mother goodnight and retired to the relative privacy of her chamber.

Blissfully alone at last, her determination increased. She was Juliette Forbes and by all the gods, she had her own particular brand of magic, far stronger than that which ran in her blood: a belief in true love. She would find the man meant for her, the man she could give her heart to. Perhaps she already had, she thought, as an image of Robert flashed through her mind.

Either way, she would not be executed for treason, not if she could help it. She would escape. Escape Beatrice, her sister and even the prince, who was kind enough, but whose heart belonged to another. She would find the courage to make her own destiny.

****

At first, Robert heard nothing and wondered what could have wakened him, but then a soft scraping sound reached his ears. Body on full alert within seconds, he moved without a sound to the doorway of the adjoining room, Juliette's bedchamber. Nearer now, he heard the same distinctive noise once more. Could be anything, he reasoned, which, in itself, was a strong argument for going in armed without loss of another moment. Soundlessly and with infinite care, he reached for his sword then opened the door. He found Juliette, trying to force open a window and getting nothing more than a sharp creaking for her pains. Small distressed sounds came from her as she tried yet again.

Without troubling to lower his sword, he entered and took a deep breath. "Explain yourself, my lady."

****

She gasped, whirled then stifled a shriek of alarm at his unexpected nearness. "Oh blast," she swore, when she had use of her vocal chords again. At that moment, the window popped free. She struggled to evade him and go through it, afraid of what might happen if he got his hands on her, but even more afraid of what might happen if she failed to escape. So when he reached for her, she fought like a wild cat.

He let out a satisfying whoosh of breath when her elbow connected with his stomach, but he did not loosen his hold. Instead, a soft but heartfelt curse reached her ears and he strengthened his grip. "You aren't going anywhere so you may as well stop fighting me," he advised.

"I'll be damned if I will," she shot back. "I will save my sister, Prince Will and the kingdom if I possibly can and you won't stop me," she vowed.

"What does your sister have to do with this?" he asked.

Even in the dim light she could see his eye widen in genuine astonishment.

When she tried to wrest away from him once more, his grip on her tightened. "Enough. You are staying right here until you tell me all of it. Stubborn woman."

"There isn't time."

His expression softened not one iota. "Make time."

Realizing she was beaten and that it would be faster to simply tell him what he wanted to know than to continue to argue, she explained. "The shortened version then, if you insist. My stepsister is Celina Dubois and she is the lady the prince danced with at the ball. I swear on my life, Robert, I had no idea until we arrived. My stepmother locked her up, did a little magic on the slipper when it came round, the bloody shoe fit me and we ended up here."

"Why perpetrate such an elaborate ruse? And why take such a risk?"

Juliette shook her head. How could anyone be so naïve? "My mother wants the throne. She will use me to get it then she will kill me, Celina, the prince, the king and anyone else who gets in her way. She will not stop until she is crowned. I, however, am not sticking around to see my mother's plan come to fruition. Why on earth would I remain when this can only end with us both charged with treason or worse, with that demon on the throne? I have to release Celina and warn her, and you can do me a great service and warn the king. I vow I am no traitor. Now let me go so I can do what I came for."

Redoubling her efforts, she fought as hard as she could. She used every trick she knew, every scrap of her strength, every skill she had to hand except her greatest, magic. Watching her mother abuse the gift every day, she had vowed at the age of eight to never use what she was to harm. In fact, she swore to use it not at all if she couldn't control it. Yet here she was pushed to the brink. "I don't want to hurt you, but I will unless you let me go," she warned, desperate.

"I have no doubt you can and will do exactly that, but letting you escape is not an option. For the good of the kingdom as well as your own, please let me help you."

Everywhere he touched her would be like touching an open flame, she knew and she regretted it, but she had no choice.

"Stop," he commanded. "I believe you. Damn it, I said I believe you!"

Well, he had her attention now. Her gasp was audible and while she remained stiff in his arms, she stopped struggling and the fire within her cooled.

"Let me help you," he entreated again.

His voice, little more than a soft murmur, nevertheless penetrated through her bones to her very soul. She closed her eyes against the wave of sheer longing that swept through her. To lean back into his embrace and let his strong arms enfold her was something she wanted almost as much as she wanted to breathe. Here was safety and strength, but... "No one can help me," she whispered.

Again his grip firmed, this time not to restrain, but to reassure. "I can. I will, if you'll let me."

Gods, how she longed to believe him. "Tell me how."

"We'll speak to the prince. All he wants is his kingdom safe."

"But how could he ever trust anything I say?"

"As I told you, even before tonight he suspected your mother of some treachery. Prove your desire to help, and you'll be fine. In addition, if you reunite the prince with his one true love, he'll forgive you anything."

Juliette shook her head. "No, he'll never believe me without proof and even if he does, there's my mother, not to mention my sister Rosalind, to be reckoned with. You have no idea what they are capable of. It's best if we leave now. Better still if I go alone."

"No. we'll see the prince in the morning, explain everything then go from there. It will be fine."

Despite his utter sincerity, Juliette was not at all reassured.

"Stop worrying," Robert insisted. "The king will deal with Beatrice and Rosalind and anyone else who might stand in the way. If you let him, if…you let me, help you."

Too tired to fight the inevitable anymore, she nodded.

"Swear to me there will be no more escape attempts, at least until morning and we've seen the prince."

Smiling in spite of herself, she replied, "Very well, I swear."

She waited while he searched her face for a moment. Then she allowed him to lead her back to her own chamber.

Chapter Six

The next morning, Robert arranged an audience with the prince as promised. Even getting her mother out of the way had been relatively easy. All it required was a little lie. Juliette told Beatrice the prince required her, Juliette's, presence and her presence alone. What could her mother say after all? How could she protest?

It was harder to face her prince, but it was long past time she grew a backbone. Life was about action and consequence, something her mother had never understood and would never learn. She would do far better to learn that lesson now.

She took a deep breath, entered the prince's receiving room and bowed her head. "Majesty, I cry for your mercy. I crave your pardon for the terrible treason I have committed. I beg only to be allowed to live long enough to make things right in some small way by taking you to your true love, my sister Celina."

"So all Robert has told me is true then?"

Miserable, Juliette nodded.

"So I believed from the beginning. I sensed something was wrong as soon as we met. I knew damned well you were not the woman I danced with and had hoped you would come to me sooner. Well, that's done. I do have one very important question. Your sister Celina is the one, you are certain?"

"Yes, very certain. My mother spelled the shoe to

fit me because she knew it."

"Lady Dubois would have kept her from me and you knew all along. You would have helped her."

"Not willingly, Majesty. I tried to stop her but—"

He made one small gesture and her voice died in her throat. "'Tis fortunate for you I have seen that woman in action, else…well, others have been executed for far less. As it is, if you take me to Celina and she is unharmed, I will owe you a debt."

Juliette's legs, weak as water a moment before, firmed. "I will deliver her safely to you. Upon my life I will. All that aside, it is high time my mother was thwarted."

"I quite agree," he replied, voice cold, eyes colder still. In quite a different tone he continued, "Now, let's talk logistics."

"My mother cannot know of any of this. If she even suspects—"

Robert took her hand in a firm grip. His touch helped her fend off a wave of panicked hysteria.

"She won't. We'll leave in secret, under cover of darkness as soon as she is asleep. That will give us as much lead time as possible."

"I set the watch and I can make certain those on it are the ones easiest to get past," Will pointed out.

Juliette shook her head. "We'll need to do more."

"What did you have in mind?" Will inquired.

"I will dose her with a sleeping potion insuring that she won't hear me when I depart and indeed won't stir until morning."

"A good plan unless she figures you out."

"She won't." Steel filled her heart and soul then determination crowded out the last of her fear. For the first time since the whole dreadful business started, Juliette began to hope she might come out of it alive.

****

"Show me a little bit of magic," Robert urged.

The request was not entirely surprising considering her lapse the day before and the fact that they were alone, taking their usual daily ride to avoid suspicion. So, Juliette had her answer ready.

"Absolutely not, nor will I discuss it further with you."

"Now that's a pity as you fascinate me. You have such an amazing gift."

"It isn't a gift. It's a curse." The words were out before she could stop them.

"It doesn't have to be. I realize I haven't known you long, but in my estimation, you are beautiful. How could the magic inside you be any different? Don't hide it." He whipped his stallion into a canter and continued down the path, leaving her to her thoughts.

He'd surprised her after all, she mused. No one had ever called her beautiful. No one had ever spoken of her soul or her body that way. Nor had anyone ever taken that view of her magic before either. Few outside of her family knew of course, so that might explain it, and yet, she suspected his perspective to be uncommon to say the least.

The very idea of doing magic at all had cold perspiration prickling at the back of her neck. Forget trusting Robert so completely, a thing she was far from prepared to do, how could she trust herself? Still, in his eyes, she was beautiful. What a lovely thought. Too lovely to dwell on, she decided, and spurred Chelsea forward.

****

It had to be done now and it had to be done with speed. Her mother napped each afternoon until she dressed for dinner and this was the only time Juliette could be certain of where Beatrice would be and where she would not. The laudanum she habitually ingested before bed each night was in its accustomed place in her dressing room well within reach.

Shaking, Juliette perused the contents of the table until she found what she was looking for. The large bottle was well labeled and at three-quarters full, the added sleeping potion would not noticeably change the level. She prayed the dose was right. Too much and it could induce a comatose state Beatrice might never recover from. Too little and her mother might wake to thwart their plans. Even so, it was more than worth the risk and besides, there would be no mistake. Heart beating like mad, she added the concoction.

Done, she replaced the stopper on the flask of laudanum and made sure all was as it had been. Pocketing the vial, she started toward her own room, but didn't take one easy breath until she reached her chamber and barred the door. Phase one was complete. If the gods were good the rest of the plan would go as smoothly.

****

Before retiring for the night Will and Robert had a drink as usual in the prince's library. It gave Will a welcome opportunity to examine his reactions to the day's events.

"I can't tell you what a relief it is to know the woman I fell in love with has a name and that she, Celina, isn't a figment of my imagination." Will could admit this to his friend as he could admit it to few others.

"Yes, well, we haven't found her yet," was Robert's dour reply.

"Cheer up, man." Will clapped his friend on the shoulder. "We will soon find my woman and yours has begun to trust you. Life is good."

Robert let out an exasperated breath. "How many times do I have to tell you? Juliette Forbes is not mine."

Will grinned. "Until I believe it or until you decide to save your breath, whichever comes first. I've seen the way she looks at you, and what's more, I've seen the way you look at her."

Robert shot his friend a glance then leaned against the doorjamb. "How does she look at me?"

"Like she wants you. Like you are her rescuer, her friend and her lover all rolled into one."

Robert couldn't help but gape.

Will shrugged. "Well, you asked."

"I must confess part of me thought it was purely my own wishful thinking."

Will raised his eyebrows. "This was not at all the reaction I expected. The woman favors you. What could be wrong with that? More importantly, why does this downright infuriate you?

"I can't afford to be distracted right now. Not until we finish this."

Will scoffed. "You can't stop living your life. Besides, she's to be with us for quite some time and she still needs your protection. Why not let nature take its course?"

"I'm not looking to become entangled with anyone, not now," Robert complained.

Will took a contemplative sip of his brandy. "When my father insisted on holding that ball, I would have done anything to get out of it. I had no interest in the marriage mart. I had even less wish to even consider marrying and producing an heir, despite my advancing age of twenty-eight. I was furious with my father for arranging it. Why would I want to spend my evening scrutinizing vapid women as if they were chattel?" He shrugged once again as his lips curved slightly, unconsciously. "Then I saw her. The moment I set eyes on Celina, everything changed for me. After that, all I wanted was her."

"But what if you saw her and couldn't have her? What if she belonged to someone else?"

"Hmm. You still feel she belongs to me or at least not to you, in spite of everything. And then there's the fact that her head could be on the block at any moment to boot, right?"

Robert just closed his eyes. "Yes. It's so bloody complicated."

"So it's complicated. So what? That doesn't necessarily mean you turn your back on it."

"Maybe. The truth is I'm not sure I could walk away now even if I wanted to." He shifted, sighed, "We should rest. We'll leave in a few hours."

****

Heart in her throat, stomach churning, Juliette waited. Her customary bedtime rituals performed, she had to continue the charade by retiring at her typical time. Slumber was, of course, impossible. Not only because she was terrified she would oversleep and miss her rendezvous, but because she had to be certain her plan worked. What if her mother decided not to take her usual dose of laudanum? What if she somehow discovered a sleeping potion had been added? Juliette lay awake, eyes wide and staring, head spinning with all of the things that could go wrong.

She kept her ears open for any sound which might indicate disaster, but all she could hear was the normal sounds of her mother preparing for bed. Silence reigned for some minutes then deep rasping snores could be heard clear across the suite of rooms. Juliette giggled with relief before she could stop herself, then put a shaking hand to her mouth to muffle the sound. Get it together, she lectured herself silently.

On stocking feet, she tip-toed to the door of her mother's room to see the results of her handiwork. Sure enough, from the doorway, she could make out the half-empty bottle on the nightstand. If that weren't confirmation enough, her mother lay on her back, hair tousled, the drool dripping from her chin glistening in the moonlight.

Satisfied, Juliette backed slowly out of her mother's chamber and shut the door. Not a moment too soon either. A bare instant later someone tapped on the outer door. With great care, she opened it.

"Did it work? Are you ready to leave?" Robert whispered as soon as she opened the door. "We've got horses and are all set if you are."

"It did work and gods, yes, I'm ready to leave. Just let me get my things." Once she retrieved a small saddlebag containing food, drink and clothing from its hiding place, she rejoined him.

****

On horseback they approached the south gate. Soon enough the expected call of 'Who goes there' from the watch halted them.

"Lord Robert and two companions," Robert called back.

"Who's with you, my lord?" demanded one nervous fellow, indicating the two hooded figures alongside.

"No one of import, Charlie. Now let us pass."

"Sorry, I can't do that until you tell me who these two are. King's orders."

Will let his hood fall back then gave the man a moment to process just who it was he was detaining. Then, he leaned down and spoke in a conspiratorial tone. "Look, Charlie, I have to leave the castle, along with my companions, in spite of the King's orders. It concerns the safety of the realm and I can't tell you more than that. The less you know the better. Now, will you allow us through?"

"I can't, sire. I'm sorry." Charlie opened his mouth to call the rest of the watch.

Without warning, before he could utter a word, the boy coughed, choked then drew in a deep wheeze of breath. His left hand clutched at his throat while the other held the hilt of his sword in a convulsive grip.

Shocked, Robert asked the boy if he was all right .

"He'll be fine," Juliette said, strain clear in her voice. "I've just made it impossible for him to speak. It's temporary."

Robert whipped his head around to stare at the blue glow emanating from her lifted hand. "You're doing that?" he asked. The question struck him as inane and perhaps unnecessary, but he had to ask it.

"Yes," she confirmed with a curt nod. "Now let's get out of here. I can't hold this spell for long."

Without further comment, Robert dismounted and strode into the gate house. It took a moment for him to obtain the key to the sallyport. Fortune is fickle, however, and he was evidently out of favor with her. Or so he thought when he heard the unmistakable sound of footsteps on cobblestone.

"Put down the keys, my lord."

It was all Robert could do not to wince. Before him stood Roland Thorston, the captain of the guard. Whatever he had done to offend the lady Fortune, he hoped she would soon pardon him. Lifting both hands, keys still clutched in his right palm, he did a slow pivot and faced the captain.

"The king ordered the prince to remain within the castle walls yet here the both of you are, defying your sovereign's express command."

"Roland, I can explain," he began in his most placating tone.

"Sure you can. Tell it to his majesty."

"We won't be telling his majesty anything," Will announced from the doorway.

The prince's stance was firm. Hand resting lightly on the hilt of his sword, he confronted his old friend. "What are you doing here at this hour, Roland?"

"Doing my duty, sire. With everything that has been going on of late, I thought I ought to keep a close, careful eye on things. It's good I did. There's no need for this to get ugly. Let's just head back inside. Quietly."

"As I explained to Charlie out there, this is a matter of the safety of the realm, one which my father refuses to acknowledge. So let us pass and I'll forget the discourtesy along with the sad state of your troops."

Without a word, Roland placed his hand on his sword hilt, waited.

"Be reasonable. Don't make this harder than it has to be." When the man just stood there, unmoving, the very definition of implacable, Will's own jaw tightened. "This is no game. The stakes are too high. You have no idea. So if I have to hurt you, Captain, I will. That's the last thing I want to do, but I will."

"You must do as you see fit, sire, and so must I," commented Roland, his expression impassive.

"Well, damn it." With a sigh, Will drew his sword.

Robert followed his prince's lead.

With a sigh of his own, Roland released his blade from its scabbard.

Honest shock held Robert in place. After a moment righteous indignation loosened his tongue, however. "You dare to show steel before your prince?"

"As I explained, I am acting on the express orders of the king. Even so, I will not strike first. Turn around and go back inside and I'll forget this ever happened."

Robert stood, sword drawn. "We can't do that I'm afraid. Let us pass."

In response, Roland blocked the entrance with his considerable bulk, sword held at the ready.

Robert straightened his stance and shrugged. There was no help for it. He lunged forward.

As steel clashed against steel, he prayed the noise did not wake the entire castle. Roland was older and perhaps a fraction slower, but he made up for it with experience, a longer reach and amazing strength Robert soon discovered.

The entire castle was not roused, but in mere moments, the rest of the guard appeared from the upper look out to investigate the noise. Five young, able-bodied men as well as Roland against the two of them; Will and Robert were no match for that many. Robert and the prince each fought three, but they were losing. In defense, they tried to maneuver so they might fight back to back, the only way they'd stand a chance, but could not manage it.

Robert found himself blocked at every turn until at last he ended against the far wall with a blade to his throat. There was no time for his life to flash before his eyes, just time for torchlight to glint off the blade and for him to think 'Son of a bitch' as his opponent raised an arm for the killing blow.

"*Arreste!*" cried Juliette in a deep, commanding voice.

All motion ceased. Roland and the other guards were unable to stir an inch. Only Will and Robert alone could still move of their own volition.

With infinite care, Robert sidled to his right a few steps, all but hugging the wall, until he was no longer beneath the point of the sword. With that done, he gave Juliette one fierce, searching look, but all he said was, "Thank you."

She nodded, but dropped her own gaze. "We should go."

Robert opened the door and the three of them rushed out into the night.

****

When they stopped to make camp for the evening, Robert waited long enough for the prince to settle in then he questioned Juliette. "Why didn't you tell me? I had no idea you had that much."

"That I had that much magic? I didn't tell you

because I rarely use it. Magic is capricious and more; it can come with a terrible price. Use it too often and it can change one's very nature. So I try my best to steer clear."

"But you used it back there."

"It was instinctive and it was to save your life," she informed him, her tone curt and dismissive.

"What else can you do?"

"I can freeze people and move objects as you saw. I can heal with the right herbs and incantations. I dream and sometimes my dreams are prophetic, but my particular gift is knowing another's thoughts. I can even sense strong emotions left behind in a particular place."

He shook his head, not in negation but in wonder. "Amazing," he murmured. "You were born with it?"

"It runs in my family," she confirmed.

Now Robert grimaced. "Your mother has it."

"And my sister does as well. Rosalind is more naturally gifted and far more accomplished than either of us. My mother can move objects with her mind which are too heavy for a person to lift. Rosalind is most gifted in two areas, spellcasting and mindreading."

"Fascinating," he said, more to himself than to her. "Forgive my inquisitiveness, it's just I'm curious about your abilities. I wouldn't still be here without them after all."

"I haven't properly thanked you for saving my life."

She would not meet his gaze. Juliette looked at the fire, at the night, at the torn hem of her skirt, she let her gaze fall anywhere but upon him. She turned her face away, he suspected, in the hope that the dark would be deep enough to hide her blush.

Robert grasped her hand in his. "I'm supposed to be your bodyguard and yet you saved me."

"You've helped me more than anyone ever has," she said. "I could hardly let you die. I did what anyone would have."

"No, not anyone. Please know I greatly appreciate what you did."

She all but squirmed under his steady gaze. "It was nothing."

He shook his head. "You saved me at great personal risk. Let me thank you."

****

Well, she thought, if that was what he wished, who was she to deny him? She held her breath as, without moving a muscle he gathered her in. No words came from his lips; there was no need for them. A mere moment later, he kissed her.

There had been that one moment before the ball, but she had never expected such a thing, not until an instant before it actually happened, yet even so she didn't question it. She only accepted. His gratitude, his passion, all was there for the taking. How could she ever reject such a gift? There had been so little joy in her life, shouldn't she grab onto what she could? Yes, came the answer from every part of her being.

So she opened her arms to him and when he coaxed her, she opened her mouth for him as well. When his tongue immediately entered, forceful and unhesitating, she shivered. As he stroked, she responded with a similar, though tentative movement. His encouragement was clear and unambiguous. He took her straight into heat and passion, but most of all into a coming together.

****

When he finally pulled away his breathing was heavy. "I won't say I'm sorry for that," he stated in as decisive a tone as he could manage.

"Good, nor will I," she informed him, her tone as firm as his.

He blinked then his lips twitched as he tried not to let a deeply satisfied smile spread across his face. "Well, so long as that's settled." He bowed. "Good night."

As he walked to his tent alone feeling virtuous, his mind remained full of what had just happened between them. For an all too brief instant of forgetfulness, he had allowed himself to simply enjoy her, to enjoy also the very fact of his continued existence. He literally reveled in his condition. Alive and well and still able to appreciate the softness of a woman's lips and the warmth of her body, he'd all but basked in the moment.

In truth, he owed it all to her, he reflected. Had she not acted as she had, he would be quite dead. That deserved his everlasting gratitude. More, it deserved some sort of reward. On that score, he had done his best. With that last thought running thru his brain, he settled down in his solitary bed and was asleep in moments.

Chapter Seven

The morning light shining directly in her face woke Beatrice. As she sat up, she groaned and pushed hair out of her eyes. Peering out of the window at the source of the offending sunbeam, she got quite a shock. It was well into mid-morning, in fact the time was quite close to noon. She never slept so late, not even after a night of sport. What could have caused such a thing? After her nightly glass of wine laced with laudanum, she slept remarkably well, too well perhaps. She pondered over the rest of the events of the evening and could find nothing else to raise suspicion. Drugged she most certainly had been, she concluded. The question was by whom and why?

As if to confirm her surmise, the world spun when she sat up and reached for the bell pull. Gritted teeth alone kept the vicious wave of nausea at bay. Tightening her jaw as far as teeth would allow she rang for a servant. Just from walking the few steps to her wash basin, beads of sweat broke out on her forehead, but she splashed her face, blotted with a nearby towel, and felt moderately better. Moments later her maid arrived.

"Summon my daughter, then return to help me to dress," she ordered. With a brusque gesture, she dismissed her.

Upon hearing these words, the poor girl went white

and just stood there like cornered prey.

Frustrated, impatient and still feeling far from well, Beatrice demanded, "What on earth's the matter with you? Do as I say."

The maid went even paler, if that were possible, and wrung her hands. "I'm sorry to have to tell you this, my lady, b-but she is gone."

"Gone? What do you mean, gone?"

"Lady Juliette , the prince and Lord Robert are all gone. D-discovered missing this morning they were."

For several long moments her mind refused to process this simple sentence. When its meaning penetrated, the rage that welled up nearly choked her. Agonizing effort and years of self-control alone kept her from flying out in a terrible temper. It was a near thing, but she managed to pull herself together enough to demand an answer to her most pertinent question. "Have they begun a search? The world is a dark and dangerous place for everyone, but it is all the more so for one that is unprepared."

"His grace started out about two hours ago when it became clear they were nowhere to be found on the estate or in the immediate area."

Two hours. The search had only been going on for two hours and the gods alone knew how far her daughter had gotten during the night. The words screamed through her abused brain. Now there was barely enough time to catch the search party, even if she could pick up their trail. "I see. Send a message to the stables. I want my horse saddled and ready within this quarter hour."

The unfortunate girl bobbed a swift curtsey and raced away. Beatrice shrieked then further relieved her feelings by flinging a pretty ceramic ewer at the wall opposite. As water dripped on shattered fragments, she grabbed for the accompanying basin, and chest heaving, she rested most of her weight on it as she fought off another wave of nausea.

Within half an hour she was on the road in pursuit of the search party.

****

Coming at that hour, the knock startled him. Jonathan almost didn't answer, tired as he was from his journey, but thought some urgent matter might require his attention. Even more astounding was the woman he found when he opened his door. For a moment all he could do was gape.

"Well, don't just stand there, let me in." Rosalind ordered. Both her tone and manner were brisk, as if she came to his rooms each evening.

Belatedly, he took a hasty step back, allowed her to enter. "Forgive me, my lady, I had not expected you here so late. How may I serve you?" The familiar words were innocuous enough, not so his tone. That bordered on insolent and he was well aware of it. To speak so to her was a risk, he knew, but the risk of being alone with her in his private chambers was far greater. She knew this as well as he and that she would come in spite of it, made fury start a slow burn in his chest. What on earth was she playing at?

She did not leave him to wonder long. "Lie with me," she said without preamble.

He blinked. "I'm sorry; what?"

"My virginity is an encumbrance. I want you to rid me of it."

The fact that she was still untouched rocked him.

Not that he would ever label a woman unchaste, but her free manner, her unrestricted ways, had convinced him she was no innocent. He'd have sworn it. Well, he'd been wrong about her before and would be again. With a mental shrug, he brought his mind back to his present quandary.

"Sit down," he commanded. When she turned up her pert nose at the order and raised a haughty brow, he repeated, "Sit down. We'll have a drink."

As he poured two glasses of decent whiskey from his private stock, she said nothing, but did follow his instructions. Once she was seated, he handed her one goblet, then settled across from her. "Since you could care less that it is more than my life is worth to even have this conversation, I'll start by asking what the devil you are thinking."

"As I said, I no longer wish to remain a virgin." She shrugged. "Since I'm inexperienced, not blind, I've seen the way you look at me. Forgive me for thinking you might be interested."

How could he deny what they both knew to be true? He wanted her. But his every instinct for self-preservation was screaming at him to run, not walk. His body on the other hand...his body was telling him something very different. He examined these conflicting impulses for a moment then chose his next words with immense care. "If I refuse?"

For the first time, she touched him. Leaning forward, fingertips traced a light, shivery path from his neck, over his collarbone, to his chest, rested there. "Now that would be a great pity. It's your decision, of course. I could not force you, nor would I wish to. But please believe that I'll find someone else if you say no.

Think of it this way, Jonathan, this would be your choice as so few things in this life are."

"True." For one split second, he toyed with the idea of backing off, backing down but couldn't. He just couldn't bring himself to give a damn about any consequences. All he cared about right at the moment was his own selfish desire for her. In spite of all the vows he'd made to himself over the past days and all the very good reasons he had to leave her alone, he simply couldn't let her go. He would never allow her to harm Celina or his people so what could it matter if she spent the night in his bed? He had wanted her for years, yearned for her from afar for what felt like decades and here she was offering herself to him. Why shouldn't he seize all she offered? It would take a stronger man than he to say no. He downed the last swallow of his whiskey then vacated his chair.

"Very well. Come to bed then."

He took her hand, helped her to rise, but got no farther. Breaking the spell, she all but jerked her hand from his. "Wait. I didn't say I wanted to do it here. We'll go to my rooms."

"Rosalind, if you seek to rule me, let me disabuse you of that notion right now. What did you think, woman, that you'd have it all your own way? Did you really believe you'd have me as your steward to run things to your precise specifications during the day and as your tame stud in your bed at night?" Her cheeks flamed with temper and he realized this was what she had thought. His own temper rising, he assured her, "It doesn't work like that. In this sphere we are equals. Besides, you came to me so we'll do this now, here, before I come to my senses, or not at all."

For an instant charged silence reigned. Then she replied, "Very well." She echoed his words of a moment ago before then offered him her hand and followed him to his bedchamber.

Never taking his eyes from hers, he kicked the door shut. In an instant, in a blink, she was in his arms and he pressed her back against the rough wood of the closed door. In another he ravaged her mouth. Her lips tasted as he'd always imagined, hot, with just a hint of spice.

All, his body demanded frantically. He had to have all of her. To satisfy his craving, he started by releasing the buttons of her gown. He had it off her before either of them had time to think and she was standing in just her chemise. The fine silk was little barrier to the sensation of his skin to hers once he pulled off his shirt.

Like a cat, she rubbed against his bare skin then reached down, grasped the hem of her chemise and pulled it over her head. Stunned, he drank in her beauty. She possessed the body of a goddess and had no problem, despite her ingenuousness, putting said body on display. In that moment, he swore only he would see her like this. Not merely gorgeously naked, but completely, gloriously free on every level. No matter what it took, he would make her his in every way

****

She had chosen well, was her sole coherent thought. If his kiss and his touch were any indication, she had chosen excellently. Then he set her head spinning. Her skin burned at all the places his lips touched and he wanted them everywhere. They raced along her arms, traced paths along her neck, lingered at the rise of her breasts.

The way he looked at her made her tremble and for the first time she wondered if this had been such a good idea after all. Desire she had fully expected to see, but this reverence shook her. His gaze made it clear she was his, his to worship, his to take. It was not just his adulation which rocked her, but the possessiveness. Shaken deep in her soul, far more frightened than she had been seconds before when she removed the last of her clothing, she kissed him, immersed herself in the pleasure of his body to the utter exclusion of all else. The effect was instantaneous and electrifying. He devoured her body just as he did her mouth.

Yet when she reached for the tie of his breeches, some sense reasserted itself. "Wait," he gasped, "The bed."

"If you insist." With no regard for modesty, she all but leapt on him then wrapped her legs around his waist. Taking a firm grip on her bottom, he got them both to the bed although she never quite figured out how he managed it.

He followed her down, never breaking their kiss. Returning to her original goal, she again reached for his pants. Before she could free him, he trapped her hands with his. Rising, he loosened the ties himself, let the garment fall then stepped out of it. Standing before her, naked as the day he was born, he gave her the chance to take a good look at him while he did the same to her.

She expected him to cover her as he had for that one blissful instant and finish but instead, he lay alongside her. With his head propped up on one arm, he ran his free hand over every inch of her then paused at the apex of her thighs.

"What are you doing? Aren't you going to…"

Wishing her voice was sharp and commanding, instead of coming out breathless, she clung to him.

Despite the fraught situation, he shot her a wicked grin. "Oh, believe me I am. But this will make it easier."

One warm finger slid into her and she shivered.

"I'll make sure there will be only a little pain, then nothing but pleasure," he promised. As he added another finger, simultaneously pressing his palm into her very center, she moaned. "When I'm inside of you, it'll feel even better. Trust me."

Having no inclination to do otherwise, she put herself into his keeping. In return, he lavished unimagined sensation on her.

After a time, she sensed it all coalescing, every part of her body gathered, readied for a leap into some sensual void. "Jonathan, what's going on?" she gasped, bewildered. She hadn't realized her body could be so out of her control. Despite the glorious physical sensations coursing through her, she wasn't sure she liked feeling so abandoned.

"Exactly what's supposed to. Just let it happen. For once, just let yourself go. Let it take you. Let me take you."

Every last bit of her resistance faded and she knew she would take him at his word. And yet… "Come with me."

****

Her whispered words echoed in his head.

No request but a sensual command, one he had great difficulty refusing, but somehow he found the strength. Managing to shake his head, he promised her, "I will. Soon. For now I want to watch you." She was beautiful, skin luminous in the warm light of the fire and as she shivered with the strength of her climax, she was like a flame. He had to burn with her.

As soon as the last tremors died, he positioned himself atop her. "If you want me to stop, tell me now."

"No. I want this."

"Thank the gods." he breathed. The prayer was impromptu but fervent. "This may hurt," he warned. With one thrust, he was through her barrier and lodged deep inside of her, where he'd wanted to be from the first time he'd seen her.

As much as he tried, he was unable to prevent all of her pain. The sudden rigidness of muscles formerly loose kept him in check. Fighting to remain still, he drew in a shaky breath, rested his forehead on hers.

As the seconds ticked past, Rosalind spoke. "Jonathan?"

"Mmm?"

"There's more. Show me." She was seduction incarnate as she arched up to take him deeper.

He gritted his teeth against the shot of pure pleasure that ran through his veins. "Rosalind, wait. I don't want to hurt you. Oh, gods," he swore as she moved against him again. "Damn it, woman."

"You won't hurt me. Even if you do, I don't care. Now show me," she demanded.

No longer able to fight her and himself, he capitulated, submitted, surrendered. "Your servant, my lady." Easing out just a fraction then back left him breathless.

Rosalind moaned and arched once more, as tempting to him as any siren. "Again," she ordered.

He obliged, but this time he made his withdrawal

almost complete then rocked back into her even more deeply. With every thrust, he could feel her body easing around him, welcoming. When he laved her breast in sync with his movements within her, a breathless cry resulted. A heartbeat later, her inner muscles tightened involuntarily around him causing a searing wave of ecstasy to roll all the way from where they were joined to the tips of his toes.

Jonathan could barely think. All he could see, all he could feel, was her. His world had contracted to include the two of them, no one else. Higher and higher he climbed and as he did he fought, desperate to make sure she was right there with him. Until he realized he wasn't fighting anymore, he'd never needed to.

Wherever he went, she followed. Or she tried to lead. And that was so new, so exciting and so unexpected in one so little versed in such matters that it fascinated him, enticed him, intoxicated him and even tempted him to let her have the reins. When he did, briefly, he realized that in truth she was no more in control than he, but that they were propelled by a force stronger than them both. Surrendering to it at last, he let himself go and they went over the edge together.

****

"Are you all right?" he whispered quite some time later.

Not the words she'd pick, Rosalind mused, but she nodded. She doubted she could form a coherent sentence in any case.

"I didn't hurt you too much at first?" he asked, as he stroked her hair.

Rosalind kept her eyes closed, focusing on the soothing motion of his hand and shook her head. "It was as you said. A little pain, then only pleasure. And you? Are you well?"

His reply was an affirmative rumble from deep in his throat. She found the strength, though her limbs were still boneless, to raise her head to look at him. "I suppose what I mean to say is, was I satisfactory?"

"I never pegged you as one to need reassurance about your performance, but, yes, you were more than satisfactory. In fact, I'd go so far as to say you were exemplary."

She discovered he was capable of movement even if she was not. Although she could only just manage to lift her head, he could and did turn enough to nuzzle the scented spot beneath her ear. Inordinately pleased, but just as determined not to show it, she nevertheless asked with what casualness she could muster, "So, you wouldn't mind doing this again?"

He stilled, then drew back to look her straight in the eye. "Not at all and at the first opportunity." He paused a moment then continued, once again choosing his words with great care, "I did wonder whether if, having divested yourself of your virginity, as you so uniquely, not to say colorfully, put it, you would wish to repeat the experience."

"Before tonight, I wondered the same. Now, I have no doubts, no misgivings. I'd do it again without a qualm."

"As would I. In a heartbeat," he reiterated, as he stroked a hand down the length of her body.

A sound of surprised pleasure burst from her when she felt him, hot and hard at her entrance. "So soon?"

"Apparently. Still certain?"

"Oh, yes."

****

They made love a third time in the pre-dawn light. He slipped into her, waking her to pleasure, rocking them both to completion and then letting her drift into a warm cloud of sleep.

It soon became clear she cared nothing for her own reputation. It was not until he mentioned the consequences to his own standing if they were discovered that she got out of his bed. Despite her protests that they had time enough and the bitter complaints about the early hour, he helped her into her clothes and escorted her back to her chambers before the servants were about. After which he proceeded to fall into a deep sleep for another two hours.

He woke well rested and ravenous at his usual time and hastened down to breakfast. As he enjoyed a cup of strong coffee he tried to ignore the little ball of tension tightening his belly. Every other muscle of his body was relaxed due to the night's activities so why this sense of unease?

Plowing through a plate heaped with bacon, eggs and toast, he considered the question. He was nervous. How would they relate now they were lovers? She'd indicated she wanted to continue sleeping together, but what if she changed her mind? Whether or not she did would have a great effect on how they would go forward. Either way, how was he to treat her? She was his mistress in both senses of the word now and one sense could conflict quite spectacularly with the other.

These and other similar questions circled round and round in his brain until the little knot of strain grew and a headache started behind his eyes, spoiling his post-lovemaking glow. Enough, he told himself. Ultimately they would have to deal with each other and now was as good a time as any to face the music, as it were. He pushed back his chair and headed to her study.

****

When he left her, she'd gotten into bed, but had been quite unable to sleep. Aside from some slight physical discomfort—her body was sore in places she'd never known existed—she couldn't stop replaying the events of the evening over and over again in her head.

She had a lover and a skilled one at that. A man willing to overlook her many faults, accept her just as she was, and who was keen to continue.

Promptly at nine, his particular rap reached her ears and she bid him to enter. He bowed and as he straightened, his gaze found hers. In those fathomless orbs were a million delicious recollections and all of them, each and every one, traveled from him to her.

All of these new and foreign reactions left her disconcerted and perhaps even a little uncertain. Uncertainty was a feeling she was unaccustomed to and thus, had never been comfortable with, so she decided to come straight out with the foremost worry in her mind. "I'm not at all sure how to behave in such a situation as we now find ourselves. Should we talk about what happened last evening or pretend that it didn't?"

"That all depends," Jonathan began.

"On what?" She urged him to sit, gestured to his accustomed chair, but he remained standing.

"On whether you meant what you said last night. That you want it to happen again."

"I did mean it." That was one thing she was quite certain of.

The tense lines of his face relaxed a fraction and he sat. "In that case, I see no reason to pretend it didn't happen. In fact that would be counter-productive."

Relieved, she drew in a deep breath. "Nor can I. Still, as you pointed out, your reputation as well as mine would sustain irreparable damage if anyone were to discover the new...tenor of our relationship."

He shrugged. "I don't give a damn one way or the other about my reputation. The people that matter to me won't care who I sleep with so long as I'm happy. Yours, on the other hand? I'm not so sure about that and I would never wish to cause you grief."

"I could care less what people think of me. Judgmental, self-righteous bunch in the main anyway. Even if they were not, the days when others could dictate my life are over. Added to that, whom I sleep with is no one's business but mine. Still, we should probably conduct ourselves with a modicum of decorum; else we'll never get any work done."

He chuckled and the sound was like a caress. "An astute observation given recent events."

He relaxed back into the comfortable arm chair, fully at ease for the first time since she'd left his bed. "So we'll be mindful during the days, circumspect even. But the nights..."

"The nights will be ours," she confirmed.

"Good."

His answer was one word only, yet the look he gave her was enough to sear her bones. It sent a delicious shiver through her and it was one full of anticipation and promise, she decided. Promises he was more than capable of fulfilling, she now knew firsthand. With the greatest reluctance, she let him go and focused on the household tasks needing her attention, but when they completed their duties for that day, she found him as agreed.

****

When she joined him in his rooms that night, Jonathan wasn't sure who kissed whom, all he could fathom was that they came together by mutual impulse. Desire fueled them and nothing more. At least that's what he told himself as they shared his bed a second time. He said nothing; he merely took Rosalind in his arms. Even knowing full well it wasn't a good idea, he couldn't seem to stop. Still less did he want to stop.

Sometime later, they lay sated in the aftermath and they both felt better than they ever had.

"I could get used to this," she commented, as she drew lazy circles on his chest with a delicate fingertip.

"Hmmm?"

"No mother to order me about. People taking orders from me instead of her. You in my arms each evening," she clarified.

"Rosalind?"

"Hmmm?"

"Be quiet." To ensure she would do just that, he kissed her indignant pout away.

****

Another fortnight was gone in the blink of an eye, time passed so pleasantly for Rosalind after that. Pleasantly enough until her pretty new world all came tumbling down one morning. The day began like any other. Waking with Jonathan was her favorite part of the day, second only to their nights alone together. Later they would meet in her study after breakfasting separately.

The post arrived as usual and Rosalind sifted through it idly, wondering how early in the evening she might seek Jonathan out. Then midway through the pile, she recognized her mother's hand. She went cold all over and bile rose in her throat. Her vision blurred and she stumbled the few steps to her study then lowered herself into the nearest chair. Could this missive be to announce her mother's return? She choked back her nausea and forced her numb fingers to fumble the letter open.

Daughter,

I hope this letter finds you well. Things here do not progress with the swiftness I had hoped for. It will be at least two-and-a-half months more until I return. I trust you are caring for things in my absence as I would myself. Be certain to make our guest as welcome as possible so that she will be inclined to remain. Your sister sends her love and I am, as ever,

Yours,

Mother

With shaky hands, she refolded the sheet then she closed her eyes, breathed. Beatrice would be gone for another 10 weeks, thank the gods. For that brief space of time, she would remain safe. For one awful moment, fear had gripped her. The mere thought of her mother's return had knocked her to the floor. The terror she had sworn would never rule her again even for an instant, had filled her. Now embarrassed anger over her reaction heated her cheeks.

Get hold of yourself, she ordered with a stern mental shake.

Jonathan's distinctive rap broke her reverie. She placed the letter in a drawer of her desk and tried her best to smooth her features into a relaxed expression. "Come in," she called.

Her efforts must not have been successful because the moment he got a look at her face, Jonathan became concerned. "What's wrong?"

"Nothing." She offered him her politest smile and hoped he would take her at her word. After he gave her one long, searching stare he shrugged.

As they worked she couldn't help but make a surreptitious study of him. Her mind kept coming back to what would happen when her mother returned. She couldn't lose all she had gained. How she would hold on to it, on to him, she had no idea. She knew only that she would. She had to.

All at once the night appeared much too far away. Need filled her and would not be denied. Every moment she could steal with him was abruptly vital. Before she could give herself any more time to think, she rose and locked the study door.

At the click of the latch, Jonathan's head came up from the tedious ledger he was studying. He fixed his gaze on hers, regarded her a moment, then commented, "I thought we would be circumspect during the day."

Rosalind started toward him. "We were, but I can't wait until tonight to be with you."

"You can't wait? Really? Are you falling for me, Lady Forbes?"

All trace of easy anticipation fled and she froze where she stood. "Love is for fools. I have no intention of making myself a fool over you or any man. You'd do well to remember that." She spun on her heel and would've let impulse carry her right out of the room if his voice hadn't stopped her.

"Who said anything about love?" As she turned back to face him, he rose. "I'm talking about desire." He had her backed against the conveniently locked door. "I'm talking about wanting my hands on you. About you wanting the same. That's all. Right?"

"That's right," she agreed. So what if her throat was dry and constricted? So what if her weak and shaky knees were barely holding her up? It only meant she craved him, nothing more.

"Well then, let's not waste time. Let me give you what you came for."

Against a door again, she thought in the dim corner of her mind that was still functioning. He would take her as he had their first night together but this time there was no bed they could adjourn to. A little frantically, she tried to corral her scattered wits into some sort of order, at least enough to point out a flat surface for him to lay her down on.

He noticed her distraction. "What is it?"

"The desk or better yet, the settee. We should go—" she choked out.

Jonathan just shook his head, a movement that was all but imperceptible.

Her eyes widened with surprise which turned quickly to enthusiasm when she realized. "Here? Like this?" she asked, unable to believe it.

"Yes. If you wish it."

"I do. How?"

Reaching down, he grasped a handful of her skirts and lifted them until his hand met bare thigh. Beneath she wore the thinnest silk which he soon dispensed with. His hand worked between them to unfasten his britches until he freed himself. Then, at last, he buried his face in her hair just as he buried himself in her.

Her gasp of shocked pleasure, almost a groan, could not be contained. He slid inside her so deeply, so smoothly, so utterly that she nearly came right then and there. As he pressed into her, then out, she was surrounded in the best sense. She could feel the wall firm at her back and every inch of him just as firm in front of her.

He picked up on her every nuance, matching her every motion, meeting her every rhythm. He appeared to know her every thought despite the fact that she was careful to keep her mind shielded from his. The moment the thought crossed her mind, it became a thousand times harder to keep those shields from crashing down. Desperate, she closed her eyes and focused on him, on the physical fact of their joining.

"Look at me," he commanded. "I want to see your eyes when you go over."

She obeyed. How could she do otherwise? When he changed the angle of their joining and stroked an exquisitely sensitive part of her, she shattered. When she came back to her senses, she found herself tangled with him in a heap of limbs and half-on/ half-off clothing in the middle of the study floor.

"Are you all right now?"

She made a contented sound deep in her throat. "Oh, I'm more than all right."

She sensed more than saw the smug smile on his face.

"Good, but I meant that I could tell you were upset before. What happened?"

Loose muscles and relaxed limbs stiffened in a heartbeat. She sat up then made to disentangle herself and rise, but before she could stand he surged up and his arms came around her in one swift, smooth motion.

"What happened?" he repeated, his tone gentle but intractable.

"I had a letter from my mother," Rosalind admitted.

Now she could feel his muscles stiffen. "Ah."

"Yes, ah," she said, and the words tasted bitter on her tongue. "She writes that she intends to stay for another two-and-a-half months and not to expect her return until then."

Jonathan scratched his chin. "Well, you could have had worse news, that's certain."

Rosalind inclined her head in agreement. "I'm well aware. I should be overjoyed at the prospect of two months and more of freedom. Instead all I can think is, Seventy-four days, 1,776 hours, 106,560 minutes until I'm back in a cage. I won't go back, Jonathan. Not ever."

He offered her no empty words of comfort; instead he gripped her hands more tightly in his. "Tell me how I can help. I am yours to command. What would you have me do?" he murmured after a long moment.

It was then that she realized. He was prepared to do anything, absolutely anything at all for her. The tightness in her chest eased an infinitesimal fraction and she could breathe again, if shallowly. "I'm not sure yet. I have a few ideas, don't you worry."

"I've a few of my own as well, so don't you worry."

His lips curved against her hair and she was relieved out of all proportion considering the gravity of their current situation.

She tilted on her axis, turned within the circle of his arms. "Until then..." she murmured. Then she kissed him and let him hold her world—crashing down around her—at bay at least for a little awhile.

Chapter Eight

"Is Celina well?" Rosalind asked casually as Jonathan entered her bedchamber on a fall evening some weeks later.

Jonathan stilled. He hadn't realized she knew he'd tried to get in to see Celina. In retrospect, he ought to have. Nothing happened on the estate without Rosalind knowing about it. It had been arrogant of him to assume he could hide anything from her. "Well enough I'm told but I haven't been allowed to see her for over a month, not since your mother left, as you well know." Clamping down viciously on his frustration, he steadied himself, took a deep breath. "Rosalind, let me see her," he all but pleaded, though to do so galled. "Better yet, release her. Your mother is gone. You have everything you say you want. Why not just let your stepsister go?"

He argued the point as well as he could, with all the passion he could muster but it was clear none of it reached her or made one iota of difference.

"I will, after Juliette marries the prince. I'll be more than happy to be rid of her then. Not before. Now, come to bed."

For the space of a breath he tried to resist, but, after some slight hesitation, he gave up the attempt. He was persuaded that, given time, she would trust him enough to let her guard down, to let him see Celina. If he could see her even once, then he could help her escape and put an end to all of this.

Then another thought occurred to him. What on earth would he do if Rosalind continued in this vein, willing to support her mother, thereby destroying Celina, himself and their people? His answer could only be 'whatever he had to'. Should that include refusing to take her to bed? Should he use that, the promise of his body, to try to force her hand? More importantly, did he have the stomach for it? No, he decided, he did not. It was bad enough he was using her desire to influence her in his favor. He would not make lovemaking between them a commodity.

In that final instant of lucidity before he let himself take her, he decided that he was through lying to himself. No matter how he might try to convince himself he was doing this for the greater good, the simple fact of the matter was, he was doing this for one reason and one reason alone. He wanted her and it was long past time he admitted it. He would never have come near her otherwise.

In any case, he was already damned anyway, so what difference would one more night with her make? Or so he tried to believe as he closed his eyes and let his body take over.

****

At last, she'd left the keys where he could get to them. As quietly as possible, Jonathan removed them from the top drawer of her dresser, left Rosalind sleeping and headed straight to Celina's tower room.

His luck held; those guarding the room were ones he knew. It took some serious convincing, but he managed to get them to turn a blind eye to his unauthorized visit.

As quickly as the old, heavy locks would allow he twisted the key and opened the door. After his eyes adjusted to the dimness, he could just make her out, where she stood facing the single window.

Celina turned and gasped. "Jonathan! What are you doing here? I can't believe Rosalind let you see me."

Jonathan's smile was crooked and rueful. "She didn't, precisely. I've come to help get you out of here."

"What? You can't. What about my stepsister? She'll know. She'll sense it. Her powers are formidable."

"She won't. She'll be distracted. Leave it to me."

"What do you mean she won't? How do you plan to…" Her voice drifted off as she studied his face. "I've seen that look but once before, please tell me it does not mean the same thing now as it did then. Jonathan Andrew Stot, please tell me you haven't—"

"Lain with her? Sorry, I have. I have been with her every bloody night for the past month."

Her pale face went a bit green at the edges. She swayed then sat on the small cot. "What on earth were you thinking?"

"I don't know to be honest," he replied. "We'd been working together for about three weeks, managing fine. I was attracted to her just as I've always been, but I was handling it. Then one night she offered herself to me. I was free to refuse, she made that quite clear, but somehow I found myself taking her to my bed. Once I started, I couldn't stop." He closed his eyes a moment fighting the bliss and guilt of the memory. When he opened them again, he turned his steady gaze upon the battered young woman beside him. "But I swear,

Celina, I've also never stopped looking for the opportunity to free you. Tonight she dropped her guard enough to leave the key where I could get to it."

He knew his words did little to comfort Celina. Instead of looking pleased, she paled further. "Are you saying you lay with her in order to convince her to free me? Because Jonathan, I would never want—"

"No," he hastened to assure her. "Freeing you was in the back of my mind of course, but it only gave me permission to do what I always wanted to." He worked up a smile for her from somewhere. "Look, the last thing you need worry about, especially now, is my virtue. Just take this key, await your moment and escape from here."

"But—"

"No buts. Head for the palace, seek an audience with the king and sort this out. Be happy and at peace, my dear girl."

"How can I be either when my heart is so full of worry? What about you? What if she suspects you?"

Jonathan laughed and the sound was full of bitterness. "If? Once she finds out you've escaped, she'll know. They'll be no question. I'll deal with it. Now go."

Enveloping him in a tight embrace, she whispered into his ear, "Thank you."

He clung to her a moment. "Godspeed." He kissed the top of her head then let her go.

****

The door opened with a creak loud enough to wake the dead. Or so Celina thought until she discovered the snoring guardsmen at the bottom of the steps on her left. The one on the right, also asleep, muttered something unintelligible and subsided. Bolstered when after five minutes of observation no sign of their waking presented itself, she dared to open the door wide enough to slip through.

Padding down the corridor in her stocking feet, taking with her nothing more than the clothes on her back and the sturdy boots in her hand, she headed down another flight of stairs.

Once near the kitchen, she glided into a servant's passage and slipped on her boots. Since it was there, she also commandeered a cloak against the cold. Fastening it and her bootlaces securely, she slipped out into the servant's courtyard, grateful it was deserted at that time of night.

Once she reached the inner bailey, she had a fleeting but fierce longing for her old horse, Perry, but with deep regret, decided any attempt to take him would not only brand her as a horse thief, but be discovered for sure. That was the last thing she wanted. Wincing at the thought, she decided she would have to make the journey on foot.

With all the stealth she could muster, she crossed from the inner bailey through the outer to the gate. This feat accomplished without incident, her luck then proceeded to run out. Guards at the gate, and not ones she knew well. They were men who, on the contrary, acted always in accordance with her stepmother's wishes.

But perhaps luck was on her side after all. The shift was changing and one of the men arriving was a childhood friend. Francis Weeks had been a playmate and companion until her father's death when she was eleven and everything changed. In fact, in those first terrible weeks and months, he had been the only one, aside from Jonathan, who had treated her with kindness. So much had changed since then, but perhaps, just perhaps, he would help her now.

Heart pounding, she approached. Before she could speak, however, a harsh voice demanded, "Who goes there?"

"Francis, it's me, Celina."

"Celina?! What are you doing here? We haven't seen you in weeks. You are confined to your rooms. How did you get out? I'd better take you back before Lady Rosalind finds out." He got hold of her arm and propelled her in the direction of her rooms before she could even blink.

Desperate, Celina planted her feet. "No, please, I can't go back there. I won't."

"You must. You know how Lady Dubois is. If she finds out, may the gods help you and me for that matter. C'mon."

"Absolutely not. Francis, I'm in love and she's trying to kill him. And it isn't just any man who loves me, it's the prince."

Dragging her a few more feet, he scoffed. "You're jesting."

"No, I am not. I swear."

Since this caught his attention, at least enough so that they were no longer moving, she hastened to find the right words, frantic to convince him to let her go. "I went to the ball a few weeks ago. I wasn't supposed to and it doesn't matter how I managed it, but I did. While there, I met the prince. We danced, he kissed me and my heart will always belong to him. When I had to make a rather ungraceful exit, I left behind my glass slipper. Beatrice found the other. As you are no doubt aware, the prince promised to marry the woman who fit the shoe. When my stepmother realized what happened she was able to spell its mate so that it would fit Juliette instead. She means to pass off Juliette as me, have her marry the prince—*my* prince—and then kill him, along with the king himself more than likely. So, you see, I have to escape. I have to warn him. If Will dies…" Her lungs seized and her chest tightened. All of her breath gone, she could not speak, just gasped in a panic.

Seeing her escalating distress, Francis placed a gentle hand on her shoulder. "All right, Celina, just breathe. Everything will be fine. All will be well, I promise."

She shook her head. "You have to help me. Please." Wheezing like an old, ill-tempered bellows, she groped unseeing for his hand.

Francis acquiesced. "I'll help you. We are friends, if I don't help you now, I don't think I'll be able to live with myself. "

"You'll let me go then?" she asked a moment later, winded but just about able to force the words out.

"Yes. I must be crazy, but yes, I'll help you. In fact, I think I know a way we might both get out of this alive."

Without waiting for a reply, he conducted her to a small door in the wall, which, by all appearances, had long since gone into disuse. Bending to push back the vines which covered it almost entirely, Francis told her, "Your father used to send covert messages to the king. They communicated back and forth often during the war, but when the war was over, there was no more need. When your mother died and then your father, the door was forgotten."

"How do you know about it then?"

Francis grinned. "My uncle told me. He served with your father, even carried those secret messages from time to time. Anyway, I believe I am the only one who knows about it. Lady Dubois and Lady Rosalind don't, I'm certain. Far as they are concerned, you disappeared, like magic."

Celina couldn't help but grin back.

The door opened onto a small copse of trees. Through them was the field which surrounded the castle on every side.

"We're on the west side of the gate. If you go across to the trees and follow them, you'll reach the road." He dug into his pocket for a small loaf of bread wrapped in cloth and thrust it into her hand. "For your journey. Bonne chance."

And then he did something that surprised Celina. He kissed her. It was just a sweet, swift meeting of lips, hardly more than a peck, but when it was over she could do little more than goggle up at him

Francis ducked his head and even in the semi-dark a faint blush rose up his cheek. "Forgive me. I've always wanted to do that and I realized all at once that I might not get another chance."

Celina cleared her throat and gathered her wits. "No apology necessary. You are saving more than one life tonight and I am sincerely grateful. You are very brave and will make some lucky woman a wonderful husband someday."

"Thanks for that. Now go."

She did as he bid her and raced out into the night.

****

Celina ran through the forest until her body rebelled at the prospect of taking another step then she kept on running. She ran farther than she thought she could, farther than humanly possible, but she had to get away. She was, she knew, running for her life, but she would not stop until she reached some haven of safety or died in the attempt.

When the light in the distance reached her eyes, she almost wept with relief, but she knew she could not afford the luxury of tears, so she stifled them. Who knew how long it would be before her disappearance was discovered? Who knew how close any pursuers might be? There was no time to indulge in tears or weeping, only time enough to elude her hunters if she were strong. She'd been on the move for hours but the day was fading and this place, whatever it was, was a godsend. Taking heart, she staggered as she walked as swiftly as she could toward her deliverance.

For a moment Celina stood, took in her surroundings. The place was warm if a bit threadbare ramshackle. No rich establishment this, nor even a comfortable country inn. The place was one shaky step up from disreputable. Still, she was in no position to quibble. Determined to make as decent an impression as she could, she smoothed her skirts then ran a hand through her disheveled hair, braided it, hands flying. There was nothing she could do about the cut across her check or the welts on her arms left from her struggle through the forest. Satisfied it was the best she could do, she strode over to find the proprietor.

The middle-aged man at the bar was the most probable candidate in her humble estimation. "Sir, if I might have a word?" she began. Her voice was breathless and low, but that was as much as she could do.

He didn't turn to face her or even look up from the glass he polished. "A room is thirty pence a night. Forty pence if you plan to take your meals here," he grunted in a bored tone.

"Of c-course," she stammered. "I've enough for one night and the price of a meal but I'm not sure I can quite…" Her voice faded and her vision wavered.

The bar-keep straightened, set down his glass with a clank. "Look, miss this establishment don't run to ladies' maids or baths or much else come to that so—" He took a good look at her. "Marianne, over here!" he barked as he rushed around the bar to keep her from landing on her face.

The last thing Celina heard was his order to find a room for her then the world went black.

****

A thunderous pounding woke her at dawn. Muttering curses and imprecations, Rosalind shrugged into her dressing gown and opened the door. "Something very important had better be ablaze for you to waken me at this hour."

The hapless servant stood still, too terrified to speak. Impatient, Rosalind snapped, "What is it?"

"My lady, I'm sorry to tell you this, but Celina is gone. She escaped sometime during the night."

"That's ridiculous. There's one key to her room and I have it." Rosalind walked the few short steps to her dressing table, opened the drawer where she kept the key. While someone had taken pains to make it look otherwise, judging from the other items which had been disturbed, it was obvious the key had been used then put back. For the first time in her life, she knew what true rage was. The edges of her vision blurred red. As if it were the finest crystal, she closed the drawer and turned back to her servant. "I want all able-bodied men on this estate after her within the hour."

The servant, rushed away to carry out her orders.

With infinite care, she shut the door behind the man. Only then did she turn to look for Jonathan. He came into the sitting room, wearing his pants but no shirt or stockings, with his hair still mussed from her bed.

"You took the key and released her didn't you?"

He remained silent. "You took the key and released her didn't you?" she repeated. "I want to hear you say it."

At his utter lack of response, some small portion of the fury inside of her boiled over. The slap across the face she gave him was hard enough to get his attention, as well as convince him of her seriousness. She hoped.

"Yes," he admitted at last. "I took the key and I released her. I'd do it again."

"Where is she?"

"I don't know, not exactly. Even if I did I wouldn't tell you. Does it matter? She's long gone from here."

"How could you? When the prince comes looking and he will, will you tell him where to find her too? Because don't ask me to believe that you have no idea at all where she plans to go. Or is it enough that you helped her escape?"

"She was my friend. We grew up together. How could I let her remain a prisoner? How could I ask her to watch while the love of her life marries another and is then murdered? I begged you to let her go and when you wouldn't, I helped her."

"Was it all a lie, then? Was everything between us just a way to distract me while you concocted a way to get her out?" The thought left her cold, so very cold.

"You know better than that. Distracting you was just a bonus."

In a heartbeat, she was no longer cold and her fury burned white-hot. What other response could there be to a statement like that but another slap? As it was more than deserved, she gave him as hard a blow as she could.

When he did nothing more than stare at her, her hand rose again. His lifted to stop hers in mid-air.

With a jerk, she freed herself from his hold then took a step away. "Well, I'll just have to find her first and bring her back."

With amazing swiftness, Jonathan moved to block her path. "No, you aren't going anywhere."

"Unhand me."

"Or what?"

As she gazed up into his handsome face, Juliette noted the dark amusement that filled his eyes and the smug grin that covered his features.

"Or I'll make you," she threatened.

His arms restrained her, yet it was the force of his personality which held her entrapped. "Believe me when I tell you, you aren't going anywhere," he repeated.

"You won't hurt me," she stated with absolute certainty.

"Nor you me so I'd say we are at an impasse."

Judging her to be subdued at least for the moment, he released her then sat down. "Do you really think

Lady Dubois will let either your sister or your stepsister live? Once Juliette marries the prince, she is of no further use and is, therefore, dispensable. Beatrice will make sure the king, the prince, and Juliette are dispatched. As for Celina, she's as good as dead once the prince's nuptials have taken place. You do realize she'll have you do it, right? You are here as your stepsister's jailer and her executioner."

Rosalind could feel the color leech out of her face. "No, you're wrong. Once the prince is dead, why kill Celina?"

Jonathan shrugged. "She's a loose end, as are you. As soon as you have served your purpose, Beatrice will dispose of you as well."

Rosalind had to sit. He told her all he knew to be true with a gentle insistence she would have appreciated under other circumstances. As it was, the awful reality of her situation was sinking in at last.

"Do you honestly think she'd leave you here in possession of all of this? Once you've done her dirty work…" He grasped her hand. "I do not want to see that happen," he confessed. In a very different, far gentler tone, he continued, "This is an opportunity. This is your chance to be the woman you are meant to be. The kind, passionate, intelligent woman I've come to know well in the past few weeks. The truth is, if you want to capture Celina, you will find a way and nothing I say or do will stop you. But, Rosalind, is that what you wish? Is this what you want to be? A murderer? Give the matter some serious thought, I beg you."

For a moment she could see compassion in his eyes but he was nothing if not implacable.

His expression hardened and his tone was cold

when he spoke to her again. "If you live by the sword, you will die by it, to that I can attest. Right in this moment, though, you have a chance to choose us. More than that, you have a chance to do what's right for the realm, for your family, and most of all for yourself. Consider well before you decide."

With that final piece of advice, he left her.

Chapter Nine

After Jonathan's moving speech, Rosalind debated for all of five seconds then she pushed his words to the back of her mind. She would not let sentimentality get in the way of her duty.

So she rode as though the devil were after her. Or perchance it was the other way about, perhaps she herself was the devil, ready to bring down Armageddon upon the world. Like some hunter in quest of prey, she cast all other cares aside to let one thing matter, finding Celina.

After hours of searching, a young groom called them all to a halt.

"Why have we stopped?" she inquired, voice unmistakably cool.

"The trail ends here, my lady," the man explained. "Where she has gone we know not, nor can we follow."

"Is that so?"

The man nodded and her thoughts whirled for a time as she considered. Whatever happened next, whatever else she might do in the future, she would not let her stepsister go. To hold on to what was hers, she would do anything. Why not start now? There were innumerable gifts at her disposal and she would use them all. With a gesture, she called for silence. Words of an ancient tongue learned long ago were well within her recollection. Power surged within her, like a lover, hot and familiar, rich and welcome. She gave herself over to it and was mistress of it simultaneously. As ever, she embraced the paradox, reveled in the magic, then focused.

"Power of vision broaden my sight
That I may know my stepsister's plight."

Seeing was one of her strongest gifts. Years of her life had been devoted to channeling, refining, and honing this ability. Yet the vision when it came was uncontrollable. The images came one right after the other with the force of a physical blow.

Her mother, holding a beautiful stranger captive while Juliette looks on. Desperate, her sister tries to free the green-eyed man but fails.

Celina dying in the arms of the prince.

The king poisoned at his daughter-in-law's funeral meal.

The prince attempting to kill Beatrice and barely avoiding a knife to the gut for his pains.

The prince dying in battle, head cut clean off.

Jonathan kissing her then racing away, deliberately jumping into a ravine to escape.

Juliette and Beatrice in some final epic battle.

And in the end, her own death at her mother's hand with the same knife Beatrice tried to use on the prince.

Too much information, too many feelings, so much death. Her world, which had been a kaleidoscope of colors, went black.

****

Jonathan heard the clatter of hooves in the forecourt and raced to greet the returnees. His heart tripled its beat, knowing lives hung in the balance, knowing he would soon have answers and would soon be privy to what fate would bestow did nothing to slow it.

Whatever he had expected, it was not an unconscious Rosalind.

"What in god's name happened?" he demanded as he stumbled forward the last few steps to examine her.

"We lost the trail. When we did, she tried, I think, to call up a vision. It worked. For several minutes together she was unresponsive then she fainted," the guard holding her explained.

"Give her to me," Jonathan ordered. The man handed her down with alacrity. "Fetch Sally. She may know what to do."

"I'm here, sir," Sally piped up.

She took in the entire situation with a swiftness he admired. "I've seen this before, though never so serious. Sometimes a seeing will affect her thus. If she's carefully tended, she should be all right, but there's no time to lose. Please bring her to her bedchamber. Be slow and careful and do not jostle her. I'll need willow bark tea."

"Fintan!" Jonathan shouted. "See to it."

With the greatest vigilance, mindful of her delicate state, he carried her through the hall and to her bed.

****

Awareness came to her not all at once, but in waves. First sound, then touch, followed by sight, then at last, Rosalind's brain fully engaged and she realized that she was home in her own room.

"Sally, what happened?" she croaked as the familiar face of her nurse wavered above her.

"You had a vision that was too much for you," the older woman stated, her tone matter-of-fact. "You fainted."

"I fainted? I swooned like some weak female? Over a vision?" Horrified and more than a little embarrassed, she tried to piece together the jagged edges of her memory, but try as she might, she accomplished little.

Sally nodded. "You fainted dead away. Quite the dramatic performance I'm told."

"How long have I been here?"

"About an hour. Why?"

"Because I want to continue the search, of course," she said. Her tone was sharper than it might have been, but she could not regret it, not when there was so much at stake. "Unless Celina's already been found?"

Sally shook her head. "No luck, I'm afraid."

She winced as she did her best to sit up. "In that case, I must get back out there. I can't give up." When Sally put a firm hand on her shoulder and tried to force her to lay back, she resisted. "You do not understand. I have to find her, especially now. Perhaps if I find her she won't...I have—"

Rosalind broke off when a wave of dizziness overcame her as she attempted to rise. It was not residual bodily weakness from her previous ordeal, but renewed emotional and physical distress which prevented her. The vision hit her again with just as little warning as before and as much intensity. The same images passed before her eyes, but somehow her body coped better with them this time around, leaving her mind to bear the brunt of the upheaval.

"My lady, are you all right? What did you see? Was it another vision?" Anxiety covered the middle-aged woman's face as she peered at her charge.

Shirley McCoy

"It was the same one, yet this time I was able to absorb more of it. Sally, I...I died."

The nurse's face paled. "What? What do you mean, you died?"

"There were many images, but the final one was of me taking my last breath as my mother stabbed me, over and over. Do you believe in visions, Sally? Can it be true?" Desperate, she fumbled for the older woman's hand.

Sally's careworn face was more serious than Rosalind had ever seen it.

"I believe those things you see are warnings. Nothing is set in stone. Nothing. You've been given a great gift, the means to change the future. If you know what's to come you can alter the result."

"But what if I can't? What if all I have is the knowledge? What if nothing I do can stop the inevitable? Then my visions are no gift; they are a curse. Oh gods, Sally, what if I have already seen my unalterable fate?"

A work-hardened hand reached up to gently smooth her hair, mussed during her ordeal. "Child, I've known you since you took your first step, and you are the stubbornest, strongest, creature I have ever encountered. If anyone can alter a purportedly unalterable fate, it's you. For now you must rest. Regain your strength."

Rosalind leaned back on her pillows with a shaky sigh. "Live to fight another day?"

Sally made an indistinct noise of agreement and bustled around making her mistress comfortable as best she could by smoothing the sheets, fetching cool water for her to slake her thirst and plumping the pillows.

Despite the pleasant atmosphere of the room and bone-deep exhaustion, Rosalind was certain it would be a long while before she drifted off to sleep. So much emotion churned within her, more than she'd ever experienced before and little wonder. How did one come to terms with death by one's own mother's hand? The sound of a knock caught her attention and brought her out of her reverie. The door creaked opened and Jonathan walked in.

"So you're awake at last," he commented by way of greeting. "I've taken the liberty of calling off the search. Celina has yet to be found and I won't pretend I'm sorry."

Rosalind surged up onto her elbows. "You called off the search?! How dare you!" The anger that had given her strength was short-lived and seconds later she collapsed back into the soft mattress.

"I did and, by all the gods, I would do it again," he assured her. "The gods also know there are times I like you better silent. Stay that way and recover."

She did not have to obey of course, but, all things being equal, she decided it might be best if she did as she was told and clamped her mouth shut.

****

Celina's first realization was that she was warm all the way down to her bones. When she could be bothered to open her eyes, she discovered the room was an unfamiliar one, however. Panic seized her and she sat bolt upright. Dark spots danced before her eyes and she sank back onto the pillows again.

"Relax, love. You've been awfully ill with fever and chills since you arrived last night."

When her vision cleared, she saw the voice

belonged to a woman perhaps some ten years older than herself. Possessed of brown hair, thin build, and a ravaged, yet still pretty face, the stranger put a cool cloth to her head.

"Where am I?" The words cost her the last of her remaining strength, but she had to know.

"You are at the Crossroads Inn, halfway between the palace and Tansey Village. Don't worry. We'll take care of you," Marianne reassured her.

Exhausted and somehow sure she was in good hands, Celina slept.

****

The next morning with her strength returned, Rosalind called Jonathan to her. "You believe all that you said to me over the last few days?"

"Yes."

That one simple word sealed everything for her. "Then we are in agreement."

"You mean you'll do it? You'll let Celina go?"

When she nodded, his relief was so palpable she could feel it in her own skin down to her bones, as if she were now inextricably bound to him. "I'll do more than that. We'll help Juliette find her and put her on the throne."

Never had she seen a man so shocked as Jonathan was in that moment. If the situation hadn't been so deadly serious, she might have laughed at his gob-smacked expression.

After making a visible effort to pull himself together, he managed to ask, "What's changed? Not that I'm complaining mind you."

"What you said yesterday, coupled with the vision I had altered everything," she clarified. Then she told him all she'd seen.

"But that's only one possible future. So help me, I am determined that it will not come to pass. I'm no saint, Jonathan but there are two things I know. One: Juliette and Celina will not die by my hand. They will not die at all, not when I can prevent it. The second thing I am sure of is I will not be used."

"Good. You won't regret this, Rosalind. I swear it."

"Well, that remains to be seen. Doing the right thing does not come naturally to me. Who knows if I'll have the strength of character to continue?"

"You, Rosalind Forbes, are the strongest, most obstinate, woman I know. If you put your mind to it, you can accomplish anything. Besides, there are certain…incentives that come with doing what's right."

"Incentives? Really?" Shivery heat filled her at the thought and kicked up a notch as she drowned in the possibilities evident in his eyes.

"Mmm-hmm. Shall I show you?"

Her answer was an unequivocal yes.

****

With the dawn their horses clattered into the forecourt, bearing company as expected to those within as it was unwelcome. Will didn't give a damn. After a day and night of riding, all he wanted was to clap his gaze on Celina and wring Rosalind's pretty neck, preferably in that order. They entered the outer bailey unheralded. Yet to their credit, the servants of the house reacted with speed, taking the reins of his horse as he dismounted.

"I am Prince William Rutherford and I need to see Lady Rosalind Forbes right away. If you would inform her that her sister and I are waiting," Will ordered the steward who came to greet them.

The man, who introduced himself as Jonathan, bowed low. "Majesty, if you give me a moment, I'll see your horses are tended to and that light refreshment is prepared."

"That is not necessary. All I need is to see Lady Rosalind. Now."

It was rare for him to speak with such authority, yet he had done so more in the past few days than he ever had. It felt good. In less time than Will expected, but more than he wished, they were ensconced in the front parlor awaiting the lady of the house.

"Where is she, Rosalind?" Juliette demanded, once her sister appeared. She did so far more gently than he would have done, but so long as her method got results it was of little matter.

"She escaped just two nights ago," Rosalind admitted, the picture of reluctance.

"Why should I believe you?"

Rosalind tossed her long braid over her shoulder in a dismissive gesture. "Believe what you like, but it's the truth."

Will took an involuntary step toward her, but before he could take another, Jonathan got between them.

"Lady Forbes is telling the truth for once. I sent Celina to find you, majesty. She'll head south."

"First you imprison her then, according to you, she escapes. How can you expect me to believe anything you say? How can I trust what I do not see with my own eyes? Am I supposed to take your word, for whatever that is worth? Let me assure that I will not. If you've harmed one hair on her head you will all answer for it with your lives. Take me to her. Now."

Jonathan stepped closer then restrained Will. "Touch her and I swear you'll be dead before you can finish the blow."

Everyone went still. To lay hands on royalty meant death, as everyone was well aware. To threaten to harm a prince of the blood was unthinkable. "You dare to lay hands upon your prince? Step aside," Will commanded. His voice was soft but lethal.

"Forgive me, your grace, but I will not allow any harm to come to this woman. I have sworn to protect her, just as I swore to protect Celina. I am also loyal to you as my rightful prince. Please don't make me choose."

Will strode forward, the move an instinctive challenge to the other man, but Jonathan stood his ground. Calling on every iota of his self-control he managed to stop himself stepping any closer. "You've done a pretty poor job of defending her so far, wouldn't you say? Now take me to where you are holding her."

"Celina is gone. Pardon me, sire, but we have told you the absolute truth," Rosalind informed him, her tone flat and expressionless.

Before Will could tell Rosalind precisely what he thought of that notion, Juliette cut in. "As much as I might wish it were otherwise, she is my sister and this is Jonathan, one of the best men I know. If he says Celina escaped, then she did."

"I can show you where we were holding her, but wouldn't your time be better spent going after her?"

Will gave him a look. "My time is my own to waste. Show me."

"Very well."

Jonathan led the way to Celina's tower room.

"You might be interested in this, your grace." Jonathan went to the small armoire and after rooting around in the back came up with a tattered piece of velvet. "She said it would mean something to you. She insisted that this was proof she was the woman you danced with."

Will took the item when the other man offered it to him. When he pushed back the cloth, a beautiful pin with a crystal butterfly at its base was revealed. For a moment, Will stared at the delicate object in his hand. It was just a hair pin sporting a unique silver and diamond design, a small thing in all, but concrete evidence that she was real and that she had been there.

"Truly, I am sorry, sire. I know what it is to love and be denied. I sent her to you; I swear it on my life. You might still catch her."

Saying nothing, he enfolded the clip in the velvet again with great care and placed it in a pocket of his doublet. Addressing Robert and Juliette, Will ordered, "We ride."

****

They mounted and took off at speed and her sister had not so much as looked at her. As quickly as they had come, they were gone.

Rosalind was numb. "Are you satisfied now?" she asked Jonathan, lips so cold it was difficult to form words. "It's over and no matter what else I believe, no matter what happens now, my mother will kill me for this."

"She'll try," Jonathan agreed.

"She might well succeed. Can you live with that?

I'm not sure if I can, but at least it appears I won't have to for long."

****

"So what now?" Robert inquired as they rode away. "Celina could be anywhere from here to the coast. What is worse, anything could already have befallen her."

"One problem at a time. First, we do our best to track her. You and I were good at that sort of thing once."

Robert wasn't sure whether he welcomed his prince's cheerful assurance or wanted to wipe every trace of it away. Whichever it was, giving in to his annoyance and smacking the back of Will's hard head would accomplish little. So instead he sighed.

"I know it won't be easy, but we can at least make a start."

"I may be able to help with that. Can you lead me to her most logical starting point? To the edge of the forest perhaps?" Juliette asked.

Robert nodded. "Most likely we can find the spot where she went into the woods, given a bit of time. Our tracking skills are a bit rusty and we've never tracked a girl before." He cocked his head, peered at her. "What did you have in mind? Do you think you can sense her?"

Juliette shook her head. "I can't make any promises so I won't tell you what I'm planning to do until I'm sure it'll work. Just get me there and I might be of some assistance."

"All right."

****

"Well, that's it then, I've lost the trail," Robert

announced some hours later.

Will crouched down to join his friend at the river's edge. "You're certain? What if we back tracked? Are you sure she came this way?"

"She came this way right enough, but from what I can tell, she didn't just cross the river and continue. She walked in it for the gods alone know how long to cover her tracks. Smart, actually. It's what I would have done and it also shows that she was well enough and her thinking was still clear."

"At least at this point," Will muttered. Continuing in a normal tone, he asked, "What now? Walk along to see if we can pick up the trail?"

Robert shrugged, "We could. Whether it'll do any good, I couldn't say."

A little desperate now, he turned to Juliette. "What about you, Juliette? Can you tell us anything that will help? Are you getting anything?"

"It's not like a faucet I can turn on and off at will," Juliette snapped. "I'm sorry," she added after an instant. "Forgive me. I didn't mean to speak so sharply to you, your grace. Give me a little space and time and I'll try to sense something."

The two men watched, fascinated, as Juliette closed her eyes and waded into the middle of the river.

****

The water at its deepest point reached waist-high. Juliette let the liquid froth and bubble and rush about her, billowing her submerged skirts. Fingertips skimmed lightly over the surface as she chanted, the water slowed, then stopped.

Every part of her flowed then went quiet. Flashes of woods. Branches stinging her arms. Breath coming in sharp painful gasps. Celina! The part of Juliette's consciousness that was still her own recognized and rejoiced. A light flickered and she hurtled toward it. As she proceeded, the trees thinned and a clearing spread out before her. At the far edge was the source of the light, a small inn not very well-kept. The place did have a sign, a rather unique painted circle bisected by a cross. The Crossroads Inn.

The crash back into the present, the rush back into her own skin made her light-headed, but she managed to stay on her feet. Awkward due to her skirts dragging at her heels, she stumbled up onto the bank where Robert was there to catch hold of her.

"She's at a place called the Crossroads Inn or at least she was last night. It's less than half a day's ride from here."

Will nodded. "Good, let's move out." As they were mounting, he added, "When we find her, and I know in my bones that we will, I won't forget the part you played. Thank you."

****

The loud crack of a twig woke Will. As he came to full awareness, he noted Robert, who had the first watch, already had his sword unsheathed and stood ready. At a sign from his friend, Will moved, swift and silent, to grab his own sword which lay beside him. At the sound of another blade unsheathing, Juliette awoke.

The three waited for a full five minutes until Will had had enough. "We know you're out there. Show yourself."

To say that it was a surprise when Jonathan and Rosalind stepped into the dim light from the dying fire would be an understatement. Rosalind found herself with a dagger to her throat while Jonathan faced a sword pointed directly at his heart. But Jonathan had an arrow pointed at the prince's and Juliette stood poised to strike with her magic.

The frenzy of movement faded and they all stood, waiting to see who would make the next move. Still cautious, Jonathan lowered his bow.

"What are you doing here?" Will demanded.

"We want to help you," Rosalind said.

"Really? After holding your own stepsister captive, you expect us to believe that?" Robert spoke for the first time, capturing the attention of them all.

"Things are different now," she insisted.

Juliette eyes widened, her utter disbelief clear. "Rosalind, go home. You've 'helped' enough."

"Things are different now," Rosalind repeated. "I'm different now, I swear. Juliette, please listen. I had a vision and it changed me."

She described her vision.

"Our mother killed you?"

Rosalind nodded.

"That must have been awful, but I find it difficult to believe that that one moment changed you. It's not just all you've done, it's who you are."

"It wasn't just one moment, but a lot of moments. Mother left me behind and in charge. For the first time I was free. I've been working with Jonathan and it was liberating in so many ways. Things have altered for me. The process was a gradual one until the vision. It was an ending or maybe a beginning, I don't know. I'm not making much sense."

It happened fast. All Will could do was watch as, without warning, the eyes of both women went opaque for a moment and their minds linked.

"I see," Juliette murmured.

"So, what's the verdict? Should we dispatch them both? Execute her perhaps?" asked Will.

"No, sire. Within the link I could feel the change in her. It goes deep and it is real. She does wish to help," Juliette said.

"A moment, my lady, sir." Will drew both of his friends aside so they might have a small modicum of privacy. "You may be certain of her newfound loyalty, I am not. That said, I would sooner have her where I can see her than out of my sight where she can wreak havoc. Therefore, we will all watch her, as well as her steward. Agreed?"

"Agreed," Robert replied.

"I had my doubts until I linked with her. She won't harm us, but as it is your majesty's wish and it could not hurt, I see no reason why we shouldn't proceed with caution," Juliette said.

Will spoke directly to Rosalind now. "Very well, you and your companion may accompany us, but if you step one toe out of line, if you harm Celina in anyway, I will end you."

Chapter Ten

Celina packed her few things with brisk, efficient movements. It was long past time for her to leave this place and she wanted to be gone as soon as possible. Although she had avoided any would-be pursuers, the prince was still in grave danger and she had lost days. In addition, the more she saw and heard of this house, the more she was quite convinced it was more than just a tavern. 'Brothel' would be a far more apt description. She had tarried here long enough.

A knock at her door did not cause her to cease packing. "Enter," she called out as she continued placing her few possessions into a small valise.

"Getting ready to go I see," Danvers, the owner of the ill-reputed house, observed.

"Yes, it's time I went on my way. I am grateful for all of your kindness, but I have things to see to."

"Well then, I think it's time to discuss the subject of payment."

"I'm to marry the prince. You have no reason to believe me of course, but I give you my word. Now that I'm well, I should be able to make the journey in a few days at most. I'll send more than enough money to meet your price by the next mail coach. Will that suffice?"

"No, it won't."

Celina stilled. Something in his tone sent a chill down her spine. She knew she would not like the rest of what he had to say. "I'm sorry; what?"

"We've spent some days nursing you, feeding you, clothing you. Not to mention the profit lost since Marianne had to tend to you and not the patrons. And Marianne is one of my best girls. She's so good you'd barely know she was a whore. Anyway, you'll need to cover the cost of her little impromptu holiday and until you do, you aren't going anywhere."

"You want me to sell myself," she stated in a voice so soft she could scarcely hear it.

Danvers laughed. "That's a polite way of putting it. Yes, you will whore for me until your debt is paid."

"Never."

Danvers was beside her in two long strides. He grasped her by the back of the neck and she stifled a cry of pain. "Maybe I wasn't clear. This is not a negotiation. You have no choice." He released her then turned to go.

Blind instinct had Celina racing for the door. In spite of her best efforts, she wasn't fast enough and her world went bright with pain, then dark.

For the second time in as many days she woke in a strange place. Her head was pounding fit to burst and she had no idea where she was. Her blurred vision at first told her nothing, then her brain re-engaged and she knew she was still in her room at the Crossroads.

But now she wasn't alone.

****

Raucous laughter carried on the clear air to where they crouched in some underbrush at the edge of a small clearing.

"Are you sure this is where the trail ends?" Will asked.

Juliette could see how anxious he was, even in the twilight. She pointed. "I am positive. That is the place from my vision. She went in there and she hasn't yet come out."

"You've found her. Marvelous," noted Jonathan.

"That's good enough for me," Robert commented.

"Good. Let's go."

The prince made to rise, but Robert stopped him with a hand on his forearm.

"Hold a moment, majesty. Shouldn't we have a plan?"

"You've got thirty seconds to come up with one otherwise I'm storming the inn without you."

Robert shook his head. "Ha, ha. Just because it's an inn not a castle doesn't mean we don't need a plan. Permit me to scout around and see what the situation is before anybody storms anything."

Juliette waved a hand to get everyone's attention. "That won't be necessary."

While the three men stared at her, she set her bag aside then turned to her sister. "You know what to do if there are any problems."

Rosalind aimed a cool gaze in Juliette's direction. "I haven't forgotten."

For a moment Juliette stood quiet, centered herself, then she left her body behind. She flew over the rooftop of the small inn and savored the sights and sounds of the night before she altered her course and went inside.

The scene that met her eyes was worse than almost anything she had imagined. Three men pinned down her stepsister. A slim man and a burly one held each arm while a third knelt between her legs, unbuttoning his breeches. She didn't need to see anymore. Utter terror had her rushing back and into her body then covering her mouth to stifle the shriek which wanted to escape.

"Breathe, Juliette. Just breathe." It was Rosalind's voice, calm and steady.

She focused on it until she became secure enough in her own skin and it no longer seemed as if she had left a part of her soul behind. She came all the way back.

"Will she be all right?" Robert demanded.

"Yes, in a moment," Rosalind replied. "She returned to her body too quickly that's all. She should know better," she muttered.

"I do know better. There wasn't time. They're about to rape Celina! She is on the second floor, in the first room on the right. We've got to get in there. Now!"

Without another word Will ran to the inn.

"Wait, majesty. Will!" Robert called out to no avail. "Jonathan, you go around, see if there is a back door. Rosalind, stay and look after Juliette."

As quick as that, the other two men were off.

For a moment Rosalind remained where she was, crouched on the ground, gaping, then she demanded, "Can you walk? We have to help."

Juliette nodded. "We've come this far. Besides, we can't let the boys have all the fun." Feeling stronger by the second, she grinned. "Let's finish this."

****

"Stop! In the name of the king!" Will shouted as he broke down the flimsy chamber door.

For a moment, the three men froze. Then the bald one on top of Celina, yanked up his trousers and looked

159

over. "I'm not sure who you think you are, but we've bought and paid for this whore. She's ours to do with as we please. Leave us."

The prince put the tip of his sword to the man's neck. "You are addressing the crown prince of Camston and unless you want to die right here and now, you will release her."

The man snickered. "Right. Whatever you say." He carefully rose as Will lifted his blade. "I don't care if you are the king himself. This girl belongs to us, at least for the next few hours, and unless you want to die, I suggest you back off."

Then he grabbed a discarded sword from the nearby table as his burly companion released Celina's right arm. Immediately the slim man pinned both down.

The burly thug and the bald thug advanced on Will. "You might want to rethink this since you're alone and there are three of us," the huge man said."

Will's grin was just a little wild. "Who says I'm alone?"

****

Robert sprinted inside and quickly pressed his sword against the slim man's chest. "Hello there. Back away from the girl."

Shrugging, the man obeyed. Then he grabbed a sword from somewhere and attacked.

Robert noticed he favored his right side, leaving his left vulnerable. "Enjoy your work, do you?" he taunted. "Do you like letting fiends terrorize then rape ladies? Make no mistake, I will to cut you to ribbons just for enjoying your work."

The other man's arm came down like a scythe. Robert blocked then countered the blow with one of his own. He thrust. The thug stepped back, his face red with rage then suddenly rushed forward, right into the path of Robert's sword. Reflexively, Robert stabbed him.

****

Intent as the men all were on pummeling each other half to death, none of them noticed Rosalind and Juliette enter the room.

Juliette gasped when Robert was wounded by a slim man who was bleeding. Going on pure instinct, riding on unadulterated rage, she conjured a sword of her own out of thin air. The man was so focused on delivering a killing blow that he never saw her until she blocked his sword with hers. Stunned, he shook his head to clear it then shifted his entire attention to Juliette.

With no choice, she used all of the power within her to defend herself and the man she loved. Her adrenaline spiked and with her magic clear and cold inside of her, she parried and ran him through.

****

Jonathan approached the burly man, taking in his massive size and taller height. Then he threw the hardest punch he could. The blow landed squarely on his opponent's jaw but the man didn't even blink, and aimed a blow that would've knocked Jonathan cold had he not dodged it. Opting to leave his sword on the table, he grabbed Jonathan in a wrestling hold, lifted him right off of his feet then proceeded to squeeze the life out of him.

Desperate and about to pass out, Jonathan grabbed a large vase and hit him in the head. The burly man blinked and went down like a stone taking Jonathan with him.

"Ugh," he grunted as he pushed. Someone he could not see pulled the thug's body off him and he took a deep, relieved breath.

****

Thoughts focused and razor-sharp, Rosalind ripped a very burly man away from Jonathan before he could do serious damage. With a raised hand, Rosalind flung the man's sword 10 feet away. One moment the rapier was against her lover's heart and the next it hit the wall.

But she did not stop there. By her power alone, she lifted the stranger, hurled him head first into the same wall and held him trapped.

While the man gasped, Rosalind circled him. "If you must go to a whore, make sure that at least she's willing. Added to that, you just did your best to kill the wrong man, you swine. You should've been more careful." She shrugged. "Ah, well. Too late now."

She lifted a hand to finish him and found her wrist trapped.

"Rosalind, leave him," Jonathan murmured.

"What? No! He tried to kill you."

Jonathan nodded. "He did, but you saved me. He and the rest of the men are done. Let the local magistrate take care of him."

Rosalind studied the helpless man under her control and for one moment the desire to end him burned within her. But Jonathan's other hand was firm and warm on her shoulder, reminding her that the man she loved was alive and whole, no matter what this reprobate's intentions had been. She released the fool with one last none-too-gentle jolt, making sure his hard head connected with the wall, then turned to Jonathan.

"Are you hurt? Did he hurt you?" she demanded, searching for any injury, any wound.

Jonathan shook his head. "No, I'm fine thanks to you. I feel pretty damned good, in fact." Without so much as a by-your-leave, he pulled her close and kissed her soundly.

For one instant, she was startled. A heartbeat later she was with him, her fury transmuted into a wild, fierce joy that they were both in one piece.

Trying to regain a modicum of self-possession, she pulled away. No words came to her. What could she say after all? Instead she squeezed his hand and turned back to her friends and the battle.

****

Will crossed swords with the bald man, who surprisingly handled a blade well.

Then he backed away and grabbed Celina, placing his dagger under her upturned chin. "Stop!" he bellowed. "Stop all of you or I swear I'll cut her throat."

The melee died down, all movement and sound cut off. Everyone, including Will, froze.

The diametrically opposed instincts clashing inside of him almost tore him apart. He longed to rip the man limb from limb for daring to threaten his queen. But he also knew the thug was more than prepared to make good on his threat if anyone moved a muscle. He would not risk Celina's life for anything, and never for something as foolish as wrath or pride. Destroying the man slowly and painfully would have to wait until Celina was safe. Never breaking eye contact with the man, Will set his sword at his feet. "Let her go now and I promise you'll die quickly."

He guffawed and all but sneered. "You think I believe that? 'Sides, I don't want to die at all."

"Persist in this madness, and I can assure you, you won't die quickly or easily. That is no threat, but a promise from your prince."

The man's eyebrows shot up. "No one's dying here today except maybe her and you. Yeah, definitely you."

"Really? Stop hiding behind a woman's skirts then and fight me. Kill me. If you can," Will challenged.

The ruffian threw Celina into the arms of his now conscious burly friend, then reached for his sword a few paces away.

Parry and thrust and clash soon filled the small space. Will had been trained in sword play since before he was strong enough to hold one and he called on everything he had ever learned as he faced his opponent. It was plain that Baldy, whoever he was, possessed more than a modicum of training.

Will's entire being was set on keeping Celina safe. The man in front of him brandishing a sword was an obstacle in his way, nothing more. One he realized he would cut to ribbons with no compunction whatsoever. He slashed and thrust until finally the man went down.

Beating the man to a bloody pulp struck him as a very good idea. Will sheathed his blade then began to use his fists.

Somewhere in the red haze, he sensed her gaze on him and looked around. Celina watched him with an expression growing more horrified by the second. With a supreme effort of will, the prince halted. Taking a deep breath, he cleared the mental haze and restrained the bald thug with the leather ties meant for Celina.

****

Though the remnants of chaos still reigned all around her, Celina registered none of it. She could not take her eyes off of Will as he stood over the last of her foes, his back to her, taking long deep breaths. It was all she could do not to slide right to the floor. It was over. She was safe thanks to him. All at once she found the strength to hold out her hand and stumble a few steps in his direction as simultaneously he turned, reaching for her.

In a flash, she found herself engulfed in a fierce embrace, then almost a second later he nudged her back just enough to examine her from head to toe. "Are you injured?"

She shook her head. "Some pretty nasty bruises and a split lip, otherwise, I'm fine. They did hit me in the head rather hard and I saw stars. For a moment I thought I was imagining you. I m-mean I thought I'd snapped. Are you real? How is it you are here?"

That beautiful smile, the one she fell in love with, lit his face. "I am real. I promise."

The one brief, gentle kiss he bestowed on her went a long way to convincing her. Still, she clung to him, not at all ready to let him go.

"I'm sorry for not getting here sooner. You have my deepest apologies for what almost happened. As to how I am here, you can thank your stepsisters, but it's a long story."

Surprise penetrated her shock, but she decided she would let it go for the moment. It was too much to deal with just now. She would sort out how she felt about the presence of her stepsisters later. For now her general gratitude would have to suffice. "Thank you all."

Addressing Will, she said, "If you hadn't come, if you hadn't found me…" Tears of reaction spilled over and she sobbed.

"Shh, I found you. I would have never stopped until I did. I'm here. It's all over."

For a long time he held her close while murmuring comforting words from time to time and making vague soothing noises. After a while, however, it was clear they would have to move. To stay in such a place was too dangerous, especially with Beatrice tracking them.

"We aren't safe here. We should go now," Robert urged.

Rosalind agreed, "He's right. My mother can sense when magic's been done. We need to be as far away from here as possible before she finds this place."

"Very well," Will replied. "Do you think you can walk a little? Sit a horse?" he asked Celina as he gave her hand a gentle squeeze.

Celina nodded, eager to be gone. "The sooner I see the back of this place, the better."

Chapter Eleven

Sometime later, after hours with no sign of civilization, they found an abandoned barn.

"This should suit our needs. We can stop here for the night." Will said.

"Shouldn't we go a bit farther?" Rosalind asked.

Will did not deign to look at her. "Not tonight. We're all exhausted, Celina in particular. We'll camp here."

Soon enough they were settled, with horses tethered, fire built, and bedding unrolled.

As they completed the last of the preparations, Will drew Robert aside. "I'll take the first watch. I'd like you to take the second."

"Of course, sire. Do you expect trouble from our companions or some other quarter?"

"I'm not sure, but best to be safe, no? In my view, trust must be earned not given unquestioned and loyalty must be proved. Rosalind in particular must demonstrate hers."

"As you say, majesty."

Will snorted. "As I say? Hmm. Come now, Robert, you know me better than that. What's on your mind? Speak freely."

Robert's shoulders relaxed a fraction. "My first priority is your majesty's safety, second to that is Celina's. Third is Juliette. I can admit to your majesty

167

as I could to few others that Juliette's well-being has become vital to my own. If Jonathan or Rosalind interfere in any way with those priorities, I won't hesitate to do whatever it takes to remove them. What your majesty wishes to do otherwise, matters little to me so long as they don't get in my way."

"Fair enough."

Robert nodded and made to turn away, but Will took his arm. "Don't let Rosalind or Jonathan out of your sight, but be as subtle about it as you can. I'd rather not force a confrontation, not yet anyway."

"Of course."

"You needn't worry. Neither of us is looking for a confrontation either. I promise you," came a voice out of the dark.

Unobserved by either of them, Jonathan had approached.

Will gave him a calm, steady look. "Good. Please understand, while I will never forget that the two of you were instrumental in Celina's rescue, the situation is precarious to say the least."

"I do understand. Know that Rosalind has changed. She is a different woman now and her intentions are nothing but honorable. Besides, I won't let any harm come to Celina, or indeed anyone here." He shrugged, "Talk is cheap, I know. All I ask is that you allow our actions to speak for us."

"You speak for her do you?" Robert inquired

Before Jonathan could respond, Will held up a hand. He acknowledged the other man's statement with a slight inclination of the head. "I am willing to do that, but when it comes down to it, I'm not the only one the two of you have to convince, not by a long shot."

"True words, majesty. Well, good evening." Jonathan bowed and took his leave.

****

Celina had no desire to fully wake just at the moment. Continuing to drift in that world halfway between sleeping and waking was just fine. She couldn't quite remember why staying asleep would be such a good idea, but the answer teased at the edge of her brain and the one thing she was quite sure of was she did not want to know. Her recollections of the ten-mile ride of the night before and their arrival at the barn that served as their camp were sketchy at best. She wanted to keep it that way.

Still, when her stomach grumbled at the smell of bacon frying, she admitted she would have to get up some time. She opened her eyes to see Prince William's face. The heir to the throne juggled a plate piled high with various edibles as well as a fragrant cup of coffee and she thought she must still be dreaming. Then it all came flooding back. Memories of her servitude, her recent captivity, her precipitous flight and her subsequent rescue played themselves over in her head at top speed.

"Good morning." He greeted her with a tentative smile as he set the makeshift tray down beside her. "How are you?"

"Well enough. Better now that you're here and bearing breakfast no less."

"You are hungry then? That's a good sign." He gestured to the tray before her. "Eat," he commanded.

Instead of beginning her meal, she gathered her courage to ask the question uppermost in her mind. "Why did you come after me?"

"Truth?"

"Truth," she confirmed.

He set the plate aside and took her face in his gentle hands. "Don't you know? I care for you more than I've ever cared for any woman before. I would have no harm come to you."

"Oh. Well now that's lovely since I care about you too," she replied, just a little shy.

Feeling glorious, she dug into the simple—yet in her estimation—fabulous, breakfast before her. With the sharpest edge of her hunger curbed, she took a moment to consider the man beside her. He'd saved her, but what next? "So what happens now? Do you send me back to my stepmother? Am I to go back to Dubois manor?"

"Perhaps, but understand, you live under my protection now. She won't hurt you again."

"But—"

He placed a finger to her trembling lips. "Shh, shh. Not to worry. We'll work out the details once you've rested a bit more. It's still early. You should sleep. That's an order from your prince."

Sometime later, Celina rose, unable to ignore the demand of her bodily functions any longer. Stepping out into the brisk morning air, the sound of familiar voices stopped her in her tracks. Familiar my eye, she inwardly snorted. Voices which, in truth, she would know anywhere and would not forget until her last breath. Her stepsisters.

And her stepsisters were alone. The two women sat near the small fire; the men were nowhere about. They must have sensed her watching them, however, for they turned to see her approach and waited for her to acknowledge them.

"I see you are both still here. Since neither of you thought how distressing such an eventuality might be to me, I suppose the least I can do is point said fact out. I have no desire to consort with the woman who imprisoned me or the woman who aided and abetted the attempted murder of my king, not to mention the man I love. As this is the case, you will do me the courtesy of leaving at the first opportunity."

"But, Celina—" Juliette said.

"I no longer wish to be in your presence. Not ever again. Both of you will go. As a favorite of the prince, I command it, in his name." She spoke with an authority nearly impossible to argue with.

Juliette started first. "Celina, you don't understand. We can't just leave. It's more complicated than that."

Celina shook her head. "No, it is very simple. You will leave."

Rosalind gestured to Juliette as well as herself, "We cannot just show up at the castle. That's where we have to go. To stop Beatrice, we need to be near her and we need a plan. It's for your protection as much as ours."

"My protection!" Celina all but spat the word her fury was so great. "Neither of you were thinking much about my protection when you, Rosalind, held me captive and you, Juliette, tried to take my place," she stated. "I can do without that sort of protection; thank you very much."

"If we hadn't offered you our help and protection last night, you would not be in a fit state to order us about right now."

"Dearest Rosalind, my gratitude to you and Juliette

171

for your actions last evening has no bearing on our present situation or the fact that I no longer wish to see your lying face!" Her voice rose steadily in volume. Celina took deep, calming breaths until she was certain she would not scream again before she continued, "Now I suggest you follow my instructions. I'm through being used and I'm through taking orders. Now I'll give them. Get. Out."

Juliette held up a hand to forestall Rosalind's angry retort and stated, "No."

"No?! How dare you. Do you think because I do not have magic, I am so very helpless? I could kill you both with my bare hands." Celina's hands curled into claws.

****

"Stop this." Will's voice was composed, cool, and commanding, so much so that the three angry women paused.

"Give me one good reason!"

His gentle Celina was unrecognizable with her teeth bared, her hair mussed and her cloak askew.

"I can give you several but the most important is that you must save your strength for the real enemy. Beatrice."

Jonathan, who had Rosalind by the arm, stepped closer and gentled his hold ever so slightly. "The prince is right. It's Beatrice we must concentrate on here. What she did to all of you, was awful. Please, don't let her win. Don't let her damage the three of you any more than she already has."

"Besides," Robert said, "don't you think it would be satisfying if you all defeated her together? That's something I'd like to see."

Although Rosalind in particular stopped to consider this diverting idea, none of them backed off in the least.

"Can we agree, at least for the moment, to not kill each other?" Will asked. When the stone-faced women peered up at him he sighed. "Very well. I'll make it an order then if that's what it takes. You are not to harm one another, on pain of death. This is my word and you would do well to heed it. Now, all of you sit down." When no one moved, his face hardened. "Sit!"

With great hesitation, the three women sat down on separate logs.

"Celina, since your injuries are arguably the most acute, we'll start with you. Know first that I will never allow any harm to come to you again. Second, regardless of what went on before, understand that your stepsisters were both instrumental in your rescue. Without them, we would never have found you. Third, to hang on to resentment at this stage serves no purpose. I say this last to all three of you." After a pause, Will went on. "Beatrice Dubois is formidable. It will take all of us to best her. Since that is what we all want, I insist that the three of you form a truce against our common enemy. Time will take care of repairing your relationship with each other or it won't. Either way, this is my command."

For a time all three ladies considered this. Then Juliette spoke. "Celina, we mean you no harm. In truth, I am glad to be well away from Beatrice's treasonous plots with my head still intact and Rosalind had what we'll call, for lack of a better term, an epiphany."

"Really? You'll forgive me if I don't believe either of you," she shot back, addressing both women.

Juliette sighed. "Show her, Rosalind. Let her see the vision."

Rosalind stepped forward, grasped Celina's head in both of her hands and let her sister see.

****

The vision flashed before Celina's eyes in points of light and swirls of color. For good measure, Rosalind added just a few of her memories of the last weeks with Jonathan. She let Celina experience just a small fraction of her feelings for the man she was coming to care for. More, she allowed her stepsister to see how those feelings changed her.

Done, Rosalind stepped back and took a careful breath. "So there's that and, apart from anything else, no one deserves what you were about to get."

As Rosalind disconnected, a great whoosh of air escaped from Celina's lungs. "I see, but this changes little if anything. It doesn't change the years of servitude, or the pain I suffered at your hands, at Juliette's, and at your mother's. That sort of thing doesn't just get erased in an instant. I meant what I said earlier, I won't be used anymore."

"We're not asking that." Juliette assured her stepsister. "Just let us help you now. Please. We can't let this go on any longer. What my mother did to you, to me, to Rosalind, what she tried and is still trying to do to Will, to the king, to the very realm, we cannot let that stand. We can't let her win."

Rosalind added, "The prince is right, you know. It will take all of us to best her. If you never believe anything else I ever tell you, please believe I want Beatrice dead. I always have. Let us at least agree to work together until that is done even if we can't be of the same mind regarding the past."

Celina studied both of her stepsisters. "We'll cooperate until Beatrice is thwarted. Nothing else is settled."

****

"Couldn't sleep?" Celina looked up as Juliette joined Rosalind and her beside the dying fire that evening.

Juliette shook her head. "How could I sleep? I'm free." Her heart was so full of the sensation, she could not contain it.

"We all are," Celina concurred, her tone one of sheer elation.

"I know the feeling. Isn't it glorious?" Rosalind said. "We'll none of us get back those lost years and it isn't over yet by any means, but by all the gods at least we're out from under her thumb for now."

"Yes, we are and thank the gods for it."

"And I will finish it soon." Rosalind promised. "Even if it means my death, I swear I will not stop until it is done. I do this for myself, but also as my recompense to you." She looked at Celina as she made the vow. To seal it, she bared her arm to the wrist, made a shallow cut across her palm.

"We discussed it at length; all the terror, all the pain, all the wasted time. We could've done something and didn't. Now we will. This is our vow to you," Juliette lifted a hand, scored her palm with the dagger she carried.

"You would do this for me, both of you?" Celina watched her stepsisters' blood spatter into the flames and trembled. "Why now? After all of these years?"

"Everything has its time," said Juliette. "Beatrice's

is done. Ours is just beginning. We will be so much more than we have been. What I had before was empty, so empty. It was all I thought I would ever, could ever have. Now, for the first time, I have a life. I will not lose it. Added to that, now I can atone in some small measure for the pain I have caused. At long last I can strike her down, bind her where she can do no further harm. We do not expect your forgiveness nor your trust. All we ask is to be allowed to help. We know well that we cannot rewrite the past, but the future is in our hands. It will be whatever we make of it."

Celina held her silence for a long time. The thoughts and emotions swirling around inside of her were far too varied and complex to be given easy expression, but eventually she cleared her throat, tried to give voice to some of them. "I cannot say whether I will ever be able to forgive the two of you; whether that is possible for me, only time can tell. What you both did cannot be atoned for." She stared into the flames for a moment then continued in a far gentler tone. "One thing is clear, however. Both of you were victims too, as I was. And young, so very young as you both were when it all began, I cannot blame either of you for those first years. We were all little more than children then. What came after that is a different matter. Even so, I wonder, what would it have done to me, to my soul, to know it was my own mother doing such things to me and others? Still, I can say that your willingness to make this gesture means more than you can possibly know. A common aim and a common enemy help as well. Perhaps we should focus on moving forward. Let forgiveness come later, in its own time, if it comes. Agreed?"

"Agreed," both women replied.

After a time, Juliette commented, "Rosalind, you do seem different, kinder. I noticed it right away."

Rosalind shrugged. "Over the last few weeks, with our mother gone, I've been allowed to be who I truly am. I find I like it very much. Then there's Jonathan, of course. He made me see that by adhering to Beatrice's plan I would gain nothing. He treated me like a human being, not someone to be used then tossed aside. It made me think. Then after the vision, I decided I was done letting Mother exploit me. She's tried all of my life to make me a monster and it was clear she would end by killing me. Well, no more. I answer to no one. I'm free."

Looking a trifle less solemn, Juliette added, "So are we all. As a bonus, we would see you united with your prince, Celina. We will do all we can to help that along, but a large part of that is in the hands of fate and the two of you."

Celina inclined her head. "Of course."

"Well then, now that's settled, perhaps we all ought to retire," Juliette suggested. "We leave at dawn and this might be the last good night's rest any of us see for a while. I'm for bed at any rate."

"As am I," Rosalind agreed.

Celina murmured her acquiescence and with awkward nods all around, they took their leave of one another.

Chapter Twelve

With the dawn, Will called them all together beside the fire kindled against the morning chill. "We must decide on our next course of action. Run or go back."

Robert chewed, then swallowed his last bite of biscuit before answering. "I will pretend you did not say that and forgive the insult considering all that you've been through and all that's at stake."

Will sighed at the look on his friend's face. Determination did not begin to describe it. Stubborn, intractable, obstinate and perhaps tenacious came closer to the mark. Still he had to try to dissuade him. "All of you are well away. I alone must go back. I cannot leave my father nor the kingdom unprotected."

"If you think I will allow you to go back unguarded—" Robert began, his tone full of heat.

At the same time, Jonathan spoke, "I don't mean to walk away from this."

"And who will guard my princess? Who will guard her stepsisters?" Will demanded, hoping this plea would somehow get through.

Juliette held up a hand. "Who says any of us are running? If things had gone differently I might be facing the gallows or the block now. I am not helpless, nor have I ever been. You must not forget, Rosalind and I have power you could never dream of. I would use that power to end her."

"She stole from me, enslaved me for years and now she wishes to kill the man I love. I'll not sit by. I'm done running," Celina put in.

"And you?" Will inquired of Rosalind.

Rosalind shrugged, a casual gesture which did not match the hard look in her eyes. "Me? I've never run from a fight in my life. I'm with you, my prince, but with you or without you, I won't stop until it is done."

"I can see you are all quite determined." It was clear he had little choice in the matter short of a royal edict, one he was disinclined to issue. "Since that's the case, we must decide how to proceed."

As they finished their meal, ideas and tactics were tossed about, their merits considered and any holes patched until a refined, cohesive plan was formed.

"So, Robert, Juliette and I will return to the castle. Celina, Rosalind and Jonathan will return to Dubois Manor. There you three will await word from me of the impending nuptials. There is an engagement ball already in the works and that is when we will make our move. We'll present Celina instead of Juliette as my bride and trap Beatrice."

Robert took up the tale. "In the meantime we keep up appearances at the castle and you keep up appearances at Dubois manor. The element of surprise is essential."

"Too right you are." Rosalind commented. "If she catches even a whiff of what we have planned…" she shook her head. "Let's just say that eventuality would be disastrous."

"That means the three of us will have to come up with not just one but several plausible excuses for our absence these past few days," Robert said.

This caused another round of suggestions to be brought forth, examined then summarily rejected.

"One thing is certain," Robert stated, "the last thing we want is Beatrice knowing the real reason we've been gone."

"Clearly," Rosalind replied, in a sarcastic tone.

"Well, you know her best, suggest something she'll believe," Robert shot back.

She considered. "Something she'll believe," she mused. A moment later, the look of concentration faded to one of distinct grimness. "I can think of just one scenario she might accept, but none of you will like it any more than I do."

"Tell us. Then we'll decide," Will commanded.

"A tryst. You, Robert, and you, Juliette, planned a romantic assignation. You, sire, discovering their intent, went after them. They both begged your forgiveness and you, being the merciful prince that you are, obliged and you all returned to the castle forthwith."

"Rosalind, for heaven's sake," was Juliette's shocked exclamation.

"Oh, do stop playing the prim and proper lady, Juliette. You and I both know this is the only way. From what you've told me, this is the one story that might convince our mother that we haven't spent the last several days doing our level best to rescue Celina and circumvent all of her plans."

"That's a debatable point which we are not done discussing," Juliette conceded. "But what about the king, your father?" she asked, addressing Will.

"Hmm, with him the wisest course will, I think, be to stick as close to the truth as possible. I'll explain that we found Celina, the woman I danced with, the one I wish to marry. If he presses me further I'll tell him that Beatrice is dangerous. We'll just have to hope he believes me. So we're all agreed then?" Will demanded.

Juliette gazed at him then her sister for a long moment then nodded her assent. "There is no excuse Mother will buy, but this one might at least come close," she admitted.

Jonathan, Celina and Rosalind readily agreed. After a miniscule hesitation, Robert did as well.

"Then we are as one at last and we will defeat her." Will filled their glasses all around and raised his in toast. "To Beatrice's defeat and the safety of the realm."

****

Once the others were busy breaking camp, Rosalind took her sister as well as her stepsister aside. "Do you have any reservations about what we are about to do? I realize I was somewhat selfish before, longing for vengeance at any price, no matter the cost to you. She is our mother after all. It is one thing to consider all of this in theory it is another thing to act."

"Rosalind, if you are asking whether I can kill our mother if it comes to that, I don't know. Even after all she has done, I just don't know," Juliette admitted. "Could you?"

"It is my fervent hope that I can, without hesitation, especially since there is no other choice. Because, mother or no, that woman has to be stopped and we may be the only ones powerful enough to manage it. The prince said it very well."

"On that we concur."

"What do you think, Celina?"

"The woman locked me up, made me a servant in

my own house, but that wasn't enough for her. Now she wants the throne. To get it she plans to murder me, the prince, her own daughters then take the kingdom into a new dark age. We have to stop her. I don't want her blood on my hands, because by the gods I've had my hands dirty long enough for that woman, but we can't allow this to go on. In truth, I just want to watch the show whether that involves her death or her suffering. It may be selfish, I may even be a coward, but there it is."

"Not at all," Rosalind assured her. "In fact, I rather like the idea of her suffering, terribly and for a very long time. Perhaps we ought to think of some ways to facilitate that outcome."

"So we are all of the same mind then? Whatever it takes to stop her?"

"Whatever it takes."

"Yes, whatever it takes."

****

A long day of riding followed. Once they stopped for the evening they continued to refine the details of the plan. When these were rehashed and sufficient improvements were made, the men retired, leaving the ladies to their own devices. The women found, to their surprise, that little awkwardness remained between them. Their common purpose, to destroy a common enemy, had helped. A bit of wine took care of the rest. So for a time, they were able to coexist in relative peace.

"I didn't mention it before, Juliette, but you seem different too. Could it have anything to do with that handsome bodyguard of yours?" Rosalind teased.

Juliette flushed to the roots of her hair. She couldn't help it. Powerless to prevent the reaction of her traitorous body, she did her best to ignore it. "He's not mine. Not in the way you mean."

Rosalind grinned. "I wouldn't be so sure of that. It's obvious he's here for you."

"He isn't," Juliette protested. "He's here for the realm, for the prince. He's just very noble and chivalrous. He thinks of me as his responsibility."

Rosalind shook her head. "When you aren't watching, he looks at you as though he'd happily die for a moment in your arms."

"Honestly?" It was more than Juliette dared hope for. Could it be true? Could he have feelings for her? "He did kiss me. It was to thank me for saving his life, true, but..."

"But?" Celina leaned forward.

"I felt that kiss clear to the tips of my toes and I am pretty sure he did too."

The three girls giggled and sighed.

When their laughter subsided, Rosalind observed, "Hmmm, I'm not surprised. He looks as though he knows how to kiss a girl, among other things."

The mention of 'other things' had Juliette blushing all over again, but she cleared her throat and remarked, "Jonathan seems the same."

Rosalind's expression was the definition of smug. "You could say that."

Her sister referred to far more than kissing, Juliette realized. Shocked, she could not help but gasp. "You mean you let him...?"

"Indeed I did," Rosalind admitted. "Although, I'm not sure 'let' is quite the way he or I would describe it since I went to him."

Celina and Juliette fixed fascinated gazes on

Rosalind. "What is it like?" both girls asked at once.

For a moment or two, Rosalind stared into the fire, wearing a look that was not exactly dreamy but close, and considered the question. "Lovely. It's like being surrounded by a tidal wave of pleasurable sensation. The only solid thing and the source of all that pleasure is him. I can't say it's like that for every couple, each person is unique, but that's how it is for me."

"That sounds amazing."

"It is. You and Robert ought to try it."

"Rosalind!"

Her elder sister looked over then grinned, a wicked gleam in her eye.

"Speaking of, it's time I joined Jonathan. Goodnight, ladies."

Juliette marveled at Rosalind's bold confidence and wondered where she might acquire some.

****

Despite their perilous situation, Rosalind was almost cheerful as she packed her things next morning. Thinking of the night before, of Jonathan reaching for her, offering himself to her, body and soul, something indefinable raced through her. The silly smile she had not even been conscious of wearing, faded. At first Rosalind could not put a name to the feeling, but in a sudden flash she recognized the emotion for what it was: love. She was in love with Jonathan. Sweet gods, she had to sit. When the earth shifted under her feet, she lowered herself to the ground.

Since her vision so much had changed, her entire perspective had altered. Her worldview had been transformed and her very foundation had crumbled beneath her on that day. It was fascinating to realize that the one thing which had not altered was her feelings for him. He was the one rock-solid thing in a world gone mad. She was in love with him. Thank the gods she had the sense to recognize and admit it now, at least to herself.

But would he feel something for her? Could he? Would he, the one man to know her, heart and soul, inside and out, be able to love her? A better question might be whether she would have the courage to find out. Before her epiphany, she'd believed love a refuge for martyrs or fools. Now, it was the one thing she couldn't live without. How ironic that the one inevitable, unchangeable force of her life was also, conversely, the most liberating choice she would ever be granted. She could walk away from it, from him, or she could take a risk. She could reach for happiness or push it away.

She was never one to refuse a challenge, still less was she one to let go of anything she'd ever wanted. This would be no different. She would win Jonathan's love no matter the cost. Damn the consequences. Difficulties or no. And she would try to be good to him, even if it killed her. Despite her bone deep fear that she would lose herself in the process, she would endeavor to deserve him.

"May I speak with you?" Juliette asked.

Distracted as she was, she had not heard Juliette approach and she returned to the present with a jerk at the sound of the younger woman's voice. "For certain," Grateful for the diversion , Rosalind rose and dusted off her skirts. "I'm all but done packing. Feel free to talk to me as I work."

"How can I move things forward?"

"With Robert, you mean?"

"Yes, of course with Robert," Juliette replied with a toss of her head.

Hiding a grin, Rosalind thought of all the things she wished someone had told her about men and women. "It comes down to this: trust and love are the essentials to any relationship. If you have those, it's very simple. Be honest. If you want him tell him. At the very least, ask him how he feels about you. In short, be yourself, but be bold."

"I see." She contemplated this advice for a moment then grimaced. "It's just, he's been avoiding me."

"Don't let him. Talk to him. Make him talk to you."

"But—"

Rosalind cut off her younger sister's protests. "No buts. Now, I've things to see to before we depart. Go along."

****

Juliette did not want to go back. After they parted ways with Jonathan, Celina, and Rosalind she had plenty of time to be sure of that. So she knew she didn't want to be anywhere near her mother. Her first instinct was to run, but she fought it. Hadn't she promised herself she was done running? So what if bone-deep fear filled her?

"Are you all right?" Robert asked. His voice carried over the noise as they rode, but only just.

"Fine. Just tired."

Robert made an impatient noise. "Don't do that. It's more than tiredness. What's wrong?"

She sighed, not sure whether to be irritated, unsettled or relieved he knew her so well after so short an acquaintance. "I'm not certain if I can bear going back to Beatrice. Being in her presence... I thought I was done with her for good. I'd hoped never to see her again in fact. I want it to be over. I need it to be over."

"It will be soon. I promise."

Not soon enough, she thought, but held her peace as they approached the castle gate.

****

The moment they were spotted heading toward the gates, the king was informed. As a consequence, when they entered the castle grounds, a messenger was waiting, one who stepped forward as soon as Will dismounted.

The young man's bow was brief but precise then he spoke. "Your grace, your father wishes to see you in the audience chamber straightaway. He specifies that you are not even to wash off the dirt from your journey before coming into his presence."

He turned to Juliette, helped her from her horse. "Very well. Lady Forbes, Lord Robert and I will be along presently."

With a very clear wince, the boy shook his head. "I'm afraid his majesty insists that you come alone. Lady Forbes is to be conducted to her chamber. Lord Robert is to wait in the antechamber until called."

Before Robert could interrupt the boy and tell him in great detail and in no uncertain terms what King Henry could do with that idea, Juliette caught his arm, giving an almost imperceptible shake of her head.

Will looked none too pleased either, but his only option was to answer in the affirmative. "I see. Very well, we will be there in a moment."

The boy bowed and rushed off to deliver this

answer to Henry.

Robert began to protest before Will could even get his mouth open. "I'll not leave her unprotected."

"She won't be. I'll send…" He looked about and spied a likely looking page going about his duty. He strode over, clapped the boy on the shoulder. "Ben here can fetch Jason. You know we can trust him to guard her with his life."

Robert wavered. Jason would be his third choice to defend Juliette, after himself and the prince. "I know. It's just—"

"Jason will be quite acceptable, if you'll forgive the interruption. You are speaking of affairs that concern me after all."

Her tone was cool and her bearing was downright regal, making it difficult to refuse her, but Robert tried anyway.

"No, I won't send you alone to that woman. I can't."

"I won't be alone, I'll have Jason. I'll be fine."

"But Jason doesn't understand the situation. He has no idea how dangerous Beatrice is."

"But I do. Nor am I helpless. I will be all right; I promise. Do as your king bids you now."

In spite of all her reassurances, a cold trickle of fear skittered down his spine. Speaking through gritted teeth he said, "I don't like this. At all."

"You'll be with me soon. Do not worry yourself so."

With no other alternative, he bowed low over her hand and took his leave.

****

Will entered the main audience chamber with

trepidation. Convincing his father not to put him under armed house arrest would not be easy. Coming up with a plausible reason for his absence, one that his father would believe, that was not the precise truth would be even harder. With little choice in the matter, he bowed low and hoped inspiration would strike or at least that the gods would be merciful and watch over him.

"Where have you been?" his father demanded. "You went against my express wish that you remain within the castle walls. I assume you have a very good explanation."

Will took a deep breath. "No, I do not. Not one which you would believe."

"Since several of my guards were injured whilst you were making your getaway, I think you had best try." When his son remained silent, Henry added, "It's obvious you went looking for her. You are back so you must have found the woman you think you danced with at the ball. Yet she isn't with you, so the question becomes, where is she?"

The silence remained unbroken for several long seconds then his father slammed a fist against the arm of his throne. "I see you are determined to try my patience so I'll ask just once more, where is she and what are you planning? Where is she, Will?"

With the utmost reluctance, he admitted, "I can't tell you. To do so would put you, her, and even the kingdom itself at risk. Forgive me, Father."

The king looked at him with eyes as well as instincts sharpened by years of rule. "At risk how? Or should I say from whom?"

Will studied his father's wary face. Considering his father's expression, coupled with his words of the moment before, he decided a risk of some sort was in order. "I think you know or at least suspect Beatrice Dubois. She is a dangerous woman."

"Of that I am very well aware, as I have observed her these last months and am not a complete dolt. Have a care, Will. She is a viper, a harpy of the worst sort who won't hesitate to do whatever she can to damage you if she even suspects you mean to thwart her. Just how do you intend to do that by the way?"

Will shook his head. "At this point, the less you know the safer you will be, as I said."

Rising to his full and considerable height, Henry stared down at his son. "I am the king. I have a right to know and I order you to tell me now."

"I can't, Father. Please, will you trust me, just this once?"

The sincerity of his appeal must have gotten through. His father's expression softened by one infinitesimal degree. "Will, you are my son. I have always trusted you." Henry laid a firm hand on Will's shoulder in reassurance. "Now go before I change my mind."

Will nodded and turned to leave but his father's voice stopped him. "Try not to get yourself killed."

Will grinned, saluted and left.

****

"You've ruined everything! Where were you? Were you with his majesty?" Beatrice asked Juliette as soon as they were alone. When her daughter's mouth remained closed, Beatrice decided she'd had enough of such obstinacy. "Maybe a slap or two will loosen your tongue."

Juliette stood her ground against the threat. "I

already told you. I went for a walk and got lost. I don't know the woods hereabouts. Then I fell into a shallow ravine and sprained my ankle. It took me this long to get back. I wasn't with the prince."

"I've never heard such a ridiculous falsehood and I don't believe you for a minute. I want the truth!"

Juliette had the audacity to smile. "Oh, you want the truth? Very well, I was not trying to rescue Celina, nor was I with Prince Will. I was with Robert. We slept together. In fact we barely got out of bed for the entire time we were gone. I had nothing to do with Celina's escape."

"So you just wanted time alone with the bodyguard?! You had the whole of the king's guard, not to mention the king himself after you. I myself spent an entire day searching for you. You even drugged me and for what? You risked everything for some man who's good in bed? Then you let the prince catch you?"

The rage that filled her now was cold and deadly. Without another thought, she raised a hand, called her power forth then flung her daughter into the opposite wall.

Juliette's gasp of pain was like the most beautiful music to Beatrice. When her daughter could speak again, Juliette said, "We never meant for anyone to know. We thought we'd slip away and be back before anyone was the wiser. We just couldn't help ourselves. How was I to know the prince himself would come after us and tell no one, still less that he would disobey the king, his father? But perhaps it was a good thing. The prince now knows our marriage will be one of convenience. He understands."

Beatrice stepped close to study her daughter's

expression. The utter desperation there was caused by more than a simple desire to save her own neck, more even than a mere attraction. "Or perhaps you just didn't care. Perhaps you feel something deeper for Robert than a simple if inconvenient desire to share his bed?"

"No, I—"

Beatrice slapped her harder than she ever did before. "That's for lying. I don't care whether you love him or whether you take a hundred other men to your bed. You will not cause any more problems. He understands, you say? Some men do. Maybe he's one. For your sake he'd better be." For emphasis, she let her power whip across Juliette's face with the force of a blow.

Calmer now, Beatrice walked to the side board to pour herself a restorative glass of wine. Such incidents always left her quite parched. "Soon or late, there will be a war. Accidents can happen in combat you know," she mused. "With the prince's penchant for being on the front lines, it's quite possible he could die." She bent close to Juliette, who lay in a heap on the floor. "If Robert were to also pass away, defending the prince in battle perhaps, who would question it? Who would care? Any more of these problems and that's what will happen." She rose then placed her empty glass back on the side board. "Clean yourself up. Luncheon's in an hour."

****

As soon as he stepped into the room, Robert knew that something was wrong. He'd known all along it wouldn't end well, but his supposition became a definite reality when Ben rushed to tell him that Jason was out patrolling the border and Juliette had insisted on meeting her mother alone.

As soon as King Henry finished with him, he raced to her rooms to find his worst fears confirmed. For a start, Juliette's chambers were quiet when he entered. This was unusual in and of itself. Even when the chambers were all but empty, they were rarely silent. There was always one servant girl or another going about her duties. But now, nothing stirred. Then there was the table. The little table was several feet from its usual place. But it was only when he walked forward that he discovered her lying between the sofa and the hearth.

She struggled to rise and he hastened to her aid. Taking her arms in a gentle grip he helped her to the sofa, but all the while his hands were shaking with fury he found difficult to conceal or contain. "Juliette, oh gods, are you all right? I knew I never should have left you alone. That woman will pay for this. I will kill her with my bare hands, slowly and painfully."

"I'm fine, or will be. Soon my mother will never be able to hurt anyone else again. You know, when she injured me this time I did not register the pain, all I could feel was rage. I knew if I pushed her, if I said just the right things, she would tell me what I wanted to know and she did."

Robert held up a hand. "You mean you deliberately provoked her? For pity's sake, Juliette, she might have killed you."

"She didn't. She did exactly what I wanted her to do. She told me how she intends to be rid of the prince. She means to arrange his death in battle; his and yours."

"May the gods be merciful," he muttered

"Taking a bit of a beating was worth it to discover

this, don't you think? More, I now know without a doubt that I am stronger than she will ever be. I could have stopped her today at any time, but it would have been temporary. Soon, we will stop her for good. I can't tell you how wonderful that feels."

"Good." It was all he could manage to say considering the many and varied impulses roiling round inside him. On the one hand, he was prouder of her than he could say for outwitting Beatrice. On the other, he was furious she had done so alone and over it all was an icy coating of fear. She had put her very life in jeopardy, a thing he would not soon forget.

"There is one other thing. You may not be pleased when you hear of it. I had to tell her we slept together. I had to tell her that's what I was doing instead of helping Celina. I'm sorry."

"You don't need to be sorry. You did as we discussed. What's more, I'm glad. I care about you and she ought to know it. I'm not sure how much longer I could hide my feelings in any case."

With a gentle, feather-light hand, he smoothed her disheveled hair back then touched her bruised cheek. As much to give himself something to do and time to settle as to tend her, he fetched a wet cloth and held it to her split lip to staunch the bleeding. Getting her to her feet and leading her to her bedroom was a good idea as well, he realized.

"I can't bear seeing you like this. Is there anything I can do? Can you heal yourself? Should I call a physician?"

"No, there's no need," she answered with a weary sigh. "My own healing power should suffice." When he looked doubtful, she added, "I promise you, I can heal myself well enough, although I doubt I'll be up to dining in company this evening. Will you make my excuses?"

"Of course."

"Thank you."

He studied her white face as she rested back against the pillows. "Isn't there anything more I can do?"

"There is one thing you could do for me."

"Name it."

"Stay. Until I'm healed and I can sleep."

"There is nowhere else I'd rather be."

The simple truth of that statement didn't shake him as he had expected. She was his just as surely as he was hers. More than anything in the world he loved her, this woman he hoped would be his wife, and so he stayed by her side as she used her power to repair the damage her mother caused. When she finished and fell into an exhausted, but with any luck, restorative, sleep he held her.

****

"We are supposed to continue, business as usual. Have you thought about what that all means?" Jonathan ventured as they rode at a steady pace toward home.

Rosalind shook her head. "Not until this very moment. I assumed we would do what we have been doing these last few months."

"We could do more," he stated. "I'm not quite sure how yet, at least not in detail. I just think perhaps we ought to run the estate as we want to run it."

"So we already do. I'm not sure what you mean. What are you getting at?"

"We have started that process to be sure, but I'd

like to begin it in earnest. I mean we should begin to think long-term."

"I can agree with that. The first thing I want is to learn the best ways to run the estate then implement them. Will you teach me?"

Touched by the request, it was a moment before he could speak. Taking a deep breath, he replied, "I would be honored. You've proven to have a natural instinct for tending an estate. Added to that, I've enjoyed working with you these last weeks. Among other things," he added. He just couldn't resist.

The smile she threw him over her shoulder was as dazzling as it was brief. "Good. As soon as we arrive we'll begin. Why wait?"

Jonathan flashed her a grin of his own. "Why indeed?"

That night after they made camp and he held her, Jonathan thought of all they had accomplished together and all the joy she brought to him and basked in a contentment like none he'd ever experienced.

Chapter Thirteen

"It's good to be back home even if things are still so uncertain and even if it's only for awhile," Jonathan commented late that next evening.

"Mmmm," Rosalind agreed. "It's just about perfect actually."

"Just about perfect? And what more could you possibly want?"

The look she gave him then was nothing short of cheeky. "There is just one thing more I want, or three things to be precise."

In a very formal tone, he stated, "If by my life or my death, I can serve you, I will."

Her breath caught at hearing such words from him. She couldn't help it. Oh, to be defended. To know those words were not mere wind, not to him, made her feel strong and loved in a way she never had before. Still, she tried to match his proper tone. "I want this manor, all the Dubois lands and you."

The teasing smile which transformed his face made her heart skip a beat. "Me? You already have me. In fact, you've had me more times now than I can count," he reminded her.

Heat rushed to her cheeks and she stammered, "That's not exactly—I mean I wish to have you with me on a permanent basis. Stay with me. Be with me as we have been these last weeks." She took his hand then murmured, "There's nothing I want more."

"Stay with you as your steward and your lover? No."

The shock which paralyzed her was nothing compared to the pain that filled her a moment later over his refusal. She released his hand, her own had gone limp in any case, and had to clear her throat before she could go on. "Very well, remain as my steward then."

Jonathan shook his head. "Sometimes you want so much, yet other times you are willing to settle for so very little. I marvel at it. I would only agree to remain as your husband."

For twenty full seconds, Rosalind was speechless. In fact she could not utter a sound, a personal first. "You wish to marry me?" she blurted out once the power of speech returned to her.

Without so much as blinking, he replied, "Yes, I do."

"Have you lost your mind?"

A chuckle burst from him. "No."

"Are you sure? I'm not at all confident I can be the woman you want me to be. If I'm not sure, how can you be? I'm not beautiful like Celina or good like Juliette. You know what I am. I've done terrible things, not just to survive, but because I wanted to."

"You are beautiful," he contradicted. "As for goodness, I see it in you. You prove to me every day it's there. In spite of everything you've done and all you've been through, you are willing to let go of the hate and choose a different way of living. That takes courage. So yes, you are a fighter. You fought to survive and now I hope you'll fight for this. For what could be between us."

A swift denial rose to her lips, but he placed a gentle finger on her mouth to quiet her. "Let us both think on it. There's no need to give me an answer to a question I have yet to officially ask. For now, why don't we just be?"

And why not? A peace unlike any she'd ever known settled over her as she did as her lover advised.

****

Something compelled Rosalind to the old chapel several evenings later. A desire for introspection perhaps? This seemed likely, as she'd never been the religious sort. Not, in any case, since her father had died half a lifetime ago. Lord Andrew Dubois had been a pious man and it was he, not the well-to-do shopkeeper and stepfather who died when she was a toddler and whom she couldn't remember, that she would always consider her father.

Whatever the reason for her sudden desire to be close to the one true parent she had ever known, and in that particular place, she didn't question it. Instead, she took the path to the sanctuary.

When she reached the small clearing, she found the building and the land surrounding it far more overgrown than she'd imagined. It looked as though the place had been abandoned for the better part of a century rather than more than a decade. She navigated the dead leaves and ivy vines as she made her careful way to the entrance. The heavy old doors creaked but wouldn't budge when she tried to open them. Shrugging, she called on her magic, forced them apart then stepped inside.

And knew with absolute certainty she was not alone.

Hoping to find the spirit of her father, instead she found something or someone entirely different. Her mother alone bore that particular scent, like rotting flowers, pungent yet sickly sweet. Turning in a slow circle, she sent out all of her senses, expecting at every moment her mother would jump out and try to do her a serious injury. What Rosalind found instead was the mere image of her, rippling in the frigid, still air. "My lady," she said by way of greeting. She would not call this woman mother, not ever again.

Beatrice shook her head and regarded her for some time before she observed, "You think you've changed, but you haven't, daughter. You are still the same ruthless, self-indulgent girl you've always been. Why are you trying to be something you aren't, Rosalind?"

"You are wrong. I have changed. It took seeing my own death at your hand, by the way, but I did. It wasn't easy and I won't deny I've stumbled along the way, but I am not the same person you left in charge of the Dubois estate months ago," Rosalind told her mother. "There is one thing that hasn't altered, however," she continued after a moment. "I am as stubborn as ever I was. Once I decide on a course, it is set and it takes an act of the gods themselves to sway me. I've decided you will not win."

"Really?" Beatrice's disbelieving amusement was all but palpable.

"Really," Rosalind confirmed.

"You might want to reconsider that. When I am on the throne, you and your sister could rule beside me."

Rosalind let out a very rude snort. "This kingdom isn't yours to give. You will never sit on the throne. Even if, despite our best efforts, you manage to seize power, I would never sit beside you!"

Her mother continued speaking as if she had not heard. "When I am queen, you and your sister can rule at my side, or you can die with the rest in the flames I will use to create this new world. Turn away from these others, fools that they are, and I'll let you live. Join me and I will offer you the world."

"You can offer me nothing. Nothing worth having anyway."

Staring down her mother was easier than she expected. In fact, it felt downright good, so good that she didn't stop there. "Right now, in this holy place, I haven't the means to kill you nor would I want to do it here. In that, you are very lucky because if I did have a mind to end you here and now, you would already be dead. Let me give you one last piece of advice, Beatrice. Run. Run and keep running because if you hurt anyone else that I love, there won't be a hole deep enough for you to hide in where I won't find you."

Without another word or so much as a second glance, Rosalind turned her back on her mother and started toward the warmth and light of the house. Back to those who truly loved her.

****

"Have I changed?" In Jonathan's chambers later that evening, she asked him the question in all seriousness.

"What?" Jonathan turned from the letters he perused.

"You know me better than anyone. At times you know me better than I know myself. Have I changed?"

He regarded her while he gave his full and serious attention to the question. "Yes and no."

Rosalind wrinkled her nose and narrowed her eyes. "What does that mean?"

Jonathan laughed a little, took her hand and pulled her onto his lap. "It means that every day I see more of the woman I have always known you to be. So yes, you have changed. Now the world is beginning to see you as I always have."

He kissed her nose then drew her back against his chest. "What makes you ask, dear heart? Where is this coming from?"

"Beatrice paid me a visit, or at least her apparition did," she admitted.

Jonathan's every muscle tensed. "When?" he asked.

"Earlier tonight at the shrine after we arrived."

"And what, pray tell, did she want?"

His voice was cold with fury now but she did not flinch.

"She wanted me to betray all of you. She offered me the throne."

"And what did you say?"

"What do you think I said? I told her that the throne was not hers to give, then I told her to run. I believe my exact words were that if she hurt anyone else there wouldn't be a hole deep enough for her to hide in where I wouldn't find her."

"She tempted you and you refused her."

"There is nothing she could tempt me with," Rosalind corrected. "Not anymore. I already have everything I want."

"Well, thank the gods for that. I'm glad you have all your heart desires and feel honored to be a small part of those things you wish for."

"A small part?" She shook her head. "You have given me everything I could ever long for."

"That's good because the feeling is entirely mutual. Now come to bed and let me show you what I wish."

She smiled at him and did.

****

Days passed, each much like the next aside from the building tension. Even days filled with the exhausting work of the harvest and the pleasurable, but equally exhausting nights with Rosalind, were not enough to let his body rest. Often when Jonathan finally drifted off, it was into an uneasy sleep filled with vague images of indeterminate origin and purpose.

This dream, when it came, was different. Right from the start, it was not like a dream at all. After a time the images resolved themselves into a forest, beautiful and deep, mysterious and terrible. The place shimmered yet it was clearer than anything he'd ever seen in a dream. His other senses were sharper as well. Taste, hearing, smell, all were more acute.

Soon enough he came upon an abandoned hovel, an eyesore out of its element in such a charming forest. It was downright unnatural to find a refuge of such darkness and ugliness in a place of such goodness and beauty. Despite the lack of any sign of human habitation, he knew to his very bones that the place was not empty. What was more, he was certain evil lurked there. The location was unfamiliar to him, but not the woman sitting near the fire when he entered.

"How wonderful to see you again, Jonathan." Beatrice said without turning to look at him, keeping her face to the flames. "I do wonder at your presence here, however. I thought you didn't have magic." She shrugged. "No matter."

"What are you doing here? Although perhaps I should ask where here is first."

"Here is the realm of dreams and my purpose is none of your concern." Her cold green eyes sharpened. "It seems I should ask not only how you came to be here but why."

"My reasons are my own just as yours are. But since I am here—"

Lightning fast, he reached for the dagger at his side, held it to her throat. "Maybe I should share a little with you after all. How I managed to end up in the dream realm at all, but particularly in the dream realm with you, I know not, but I am not one to waste an opportunity." He pressed the knife just under the skin, enough to draw one tiny drop of blood. "If you die in this strange place will you also die in our own I wonder? Shall we find out?" He pushed the blade in just a little farther and had the pleasure of making her wince.

"You've gone mad," she stated.

To his surprise, she sounded a bit bored. "You think so? Care to test me?"

Beatrice raised a hand, palm first, placed it directly in front of his face but none of the sickly green, fiery sparks of magic appeared. The gasp she couldn't contain made him smile, all teeth. An elemental ferocity rushed through him. "You can't use magic in this realm," he observed. "That's handy. Levels the playing field more than a little I'd say."

"Perhaps, but I can choose when I leave, you can't. Tell my daughter I said hello."

And he was clutching air, grasping at nothing. A

moment later he woke in his own bed, tangled in the sheets.

****

Rosalind woke gasping for breath. No matter how much air she took in it wasn't enough. When her mother actively sought her in the dream realm, she hid herself in the dark wood just outside the clearing where the cottage lay. She did this not out of cowardice, but because she didn't want Beatrice to know their plans. With only minimal control of one's mind possible within that realm, the last thing she wanted was to give the game away. When Beatrice gave up the search, however, Rosalind decided to move closer and conceal herself in some brush near the south wall of the cottage then position herself near an open window so she could be privy to any schemes her mother might devise.

When Jonathan appeared, her heart nearly stopped. Instinct had her moving forward to warn him. It was then she discovered she had hidden herself too well. She was trapped, unable to move or call out and could do nothing but watch in horror as the situation unfolded. With no power to alter it, she was forced to look on as Jonathan confronted her mother until she woke.

As soon as her senses returned, she rose from bed, not bothering with a robe, and marched to Jonathan's chambers. To find him quite unharmed, sitting at his desk with a candle lit, in the royal blue silk dressing gown she loved, writing.

"What in blazes were you doing?!" Scarcely pausing to slam the door shut before roaring the question, Rosalind proceeded to pace the room like a caged animal with her nightgown swirling around her ankles. "Why would you taunt her? Why risk yourself like that?"

"I might be able to answer that question if I knew to what you were referring."

"Don't be obtuse. You know what I am talking about. Your little stunt in the Dreamscape. Taking on my mother. Does any of this ring a bell? Have you lost your mind?" Seeing his stunned expression added fuel to the fire of her fury. "That's right, I was there. I was there, but somehow I couldn't assist you. I think maybe the gods wouldn't allow me to. I was trapped and could do nothing but watch. So, I repeat, what in blazes were you doing?"

"I was doing my best to help. What do you think?" Jonathan answered with maddening calm.

"That's all well and good, but you could've been killed. My mother is no one to be trifled with. You know that better than most."

A small, amused smile flitted across Jonathan's lips. "I am well aware, but nor am I. To answer your question, I did it because I'll risk anything I have to, everything necessary, until she is done," he stated. "Look, all is well and I did what I set out to do. I didn't plan any of this but I still gave her a big scare as well as a serious insult. Added to that, I took a chance at ending her. That part didn't work out as well as I'd wished, but no lasting harm was done. No need to get worked up, I assure you."

When he finished this ridiculous speech then patted her arm in an absent but affectionate way, she had to grit her teeth to hold back a shriek. "No need to get myself worked up? She might've killed you and for what? Ego? Over who is the strongest? You might have died!" She couldn't quite hold the shriek back after all.

"And saved countless others in the process. In my estimation, it was worth the risk. So no, I did not do it for ego and if you don't understand me enough by now to know that then I'm sure not going to explain it to you." He rose to pour himself a glass of sherry. "Why would you care anyway? My death could mean little to you."

The casual, off-hand way he said this made it all the worse. Even more horrifying was that she was sure he believed it. Never had she been so rocked by one simple statement. "Your death could mean little to me? You couldn't be more wrong. I love you."

His entire being went still. For the space of several seconds, he could neither move nor speak. After a time, he managed, "You once told me love is for fools. I seriously doubt you could ever be so unwise."

"I love you," she repeated, eyes closed, partly to block out the pain and partly out of cowardice. How could she bear it if he refused to believe her?

"Don't play with my emotions just to get my attention,"

The warning in his tone had her opening her eyes wide again. "I am not. I would not. I love you," she repeated a third time.

"Stop this, Rosalind. It is ludicrous, downright absurd to the point of profoundly disturbing, and completely unnecessary."

Rosalind shook her head. "My feelings are not ludicrous or absurd and they are very necessary, at least to me. I thought you died tonight. For a moment when I couldn't sense you, I thought you had shuffled off this bloody mortal coil. I realized then that I could no longer keep my feelings from you. I've felt this way for quite some time, maybe from our first night together. From the day I collapsed after that terrible vision for sure. But how could I tell you when I'd done everything in my power to make you believe I could never love you, that I could never love anyone. I—"

Jonathan held up a hand. "Just to be clear, you've been in love with me since Celina escaped?"

Rosalind nodded.

"Perhaps even back to our first night?"

Again, all she could do was nod.

Silence fell and it weighed more heavily on Rosalind than any before until, she could no longer bear it. "Please, say something," she begged. "I finally pour out my heart;, I realize at last that I have a heart and you have nothing to say? I can't believe th—"

"Speak those words once more."

Of the countless ways she had expected he might respond this was not on the list. For a moment she was floored, with no idea whether this was good or bad, but at last she blurted, "What?"

"Say it once more. Please, I'd like to hear it one more time," he repeated.

This time there was a flash of something in his eyes, an intensity that opened a small fissure of hope within her. "I love you, Jonathan Matthew Stot. Let me show you the truth."

****

She opened her mind to him. To know her so thoroughly was both a confirmation and a revelation for Jonathan. Emotions not his own coursed through him and a light filled his soul, rich and deep.

Too soon, all too soon, she withdrew from him.

When he registered her extracting herself, it was almost like physical pain. An instinctive denial rose to his lips which he did not even try to fight.

He gasped. "Don't. Don't leave me, please."

Then it was Rosalind's turn to gasp. "I can feel you reaching for me. How? You are inside my head. How is this possible?"

Jonathan just shook his head. "I'm not sure. Perhaps I have a bit of magic in my blood after all." With a shrug, he dismissed the idea to focus on the reality right in front of him. "It doesn't matter how, it just is. Please don't leave me, not now."

*****

There was no way to describe his tone, it was some cross between beseeching and commanding and it was more enticing, more beguiling than anything she had ever heard before. She did as he entreated and there were no more words between them for a long time. His lips met hers in a caress of unimaginable passion. For the first time, he didn't simply bed her, he made love to her, slowly, achingly. She stayed with him every step of the way. Never in her wildest imaginings had she thought she could be this open with anyone even Jonathan, yet here she was, laid bare in every possible way.

Added to that, the sensual responses of his body and her own that were bombarding her were intense to the point of overpowering. They had made love countless times but never like this, with no shields on any level and she found herself begging for more. To know his very heart, to share in his pleasure, to know he shared hers in the same way was like a drug, one she couldn't stop indulging in. When he pulled her over him, into him, she parted her legs and welcomed him. As he entered her, inch by inch, then slid out just enough to rock back into her, she gasped. Her gasps turned to moans as he set up a rhythm of thrust and retreat which she picked up in an instant.

She could feel his desire building, in mind and body, which in turn heightened her own until it reached flashpoint. In one breathless instant they reached the pinnacle together. Wave after wave of pleasure filled her, physical as well as mental, and the two forces were so entwined she could not separate them. Nor could she separate from him. Their simultaneous release went on and on, had her every muscle trembling, her heart pounding and her eyes clouding over.

Then in the midst of all of this, above and beyond their physical and mental link, she sensed something else. Something more beautiful than anything she had ever encountered even with him. Love, his and hers rose up, mingled, and heightened their connection on every level. Her heart, not to mention her body, exploded like a supernova and they lit up the heavens together.

****

Their mental link was outside the realm of his experience. The force of it hit him like a freight train as he first entered her, yet he welcomed it. So, with no possibility of regaining his mental or emotional footing, he let the tide of sensation wash over him. Although it was overwhelming, it was also the most exciting thing that had ever happened to him.

The link, present now even when they were not touching, increased tenfold with even the slightest physical contact. He couldn't stop touching her, longing for the flashes of pleasure his every stroke brought to her mind and his. With every passing second, he wanted more. Hotter, more intimate caresses, longer and warmer kisses, the feel of every inch of his skin on hers. And by all the gods, he craved to be inside of her. If he had been captivated before, he was well and truly addicted now.

And it wasn't only her body he craved; he longed to know her beautiful mind, in all its glorious complexity. He yearned to hold not just her body, but her heart. As he opened to her he realized, to his great elation, the heart he longed for was already his.

When he was inside her, body, heart, and soul, he gave her own words back to her. "I love you."

****

Much later, deep in the night, she whispered, "Never risk yourself like that again. Promise me."

"I'm sorry, love, I can't promise that. You know I can't, any more than you could. That woman wants the whole world to burn and I will do all I can to stop her. Besides, my risking myself brought us here, didn't it? No matter what happens next, no matter what your mother does, she can't take this away from us. I wouldn't change an instant of our time together, not one word, not one moment because I now know I hold your heart. Rest assured you hold mine."

Although his words moved her more than she could ever say, she turned her dry and cold gaze on him. "What about our future? I won't lose you."

Jonathan shook his head. "We're going into danger and you want me to turn my face away and pretend it isn't happening? No."

"I want you safe," she corrected. "I can't lose you.

I won't," she insisted. "When I return to the palace, you will stay here."

Jonathan sat up, taking her as well. He positioned them face-to-face then took her hands.

Those calm, steady eyes of his, eyes she could get lost in, focused on her. "I'll be damned if I will. My place is at your side as always, now more than ever. I will be here to protect you." He punctuated the statement by kissing her shoulder. "I will be here to argue with you." Bending, he placed another kiss on her forearm. "To laugh with you; to cry with you, definitely to sleep with you." Lips curved in a wicked smile pressed to hers. "But most of all..." In gentle stages, he lowered her back to the bed. His gaze never left hers as he slid into her. "Most of all, I will be here to love you."

Chapter Fourteen

Rosalind went over her ingredients and her plans once more. Getting this right was imperative because she would only get one shot. If Jonathan could challenge her mother, then by all the gods, so could she. Neither of them would rest until her mother was neutralized. Finding the shoe was the first step to accomplishing that goal, so that's what she would do.

She took the pewter bowl she used for such things and dispensed the purified water into it. Then she pricked her finger with her dagger and held it over the bowl, adding the hot, welling blood to the clear, cold liquid. A sprinkle of soil went in as well while the scented candles she made herself, placed and lit on either side of the table, symbolized both fire and air. All of the elements were represented. It was as much as she could do. It was as powerful a spell as she could muster and she hoped it would be enough. All that remained was to cast it.

She took a deep breath and brought to mind the words she had prepared.

Come wind, come rain that I may find what I seek again.

Come earth, come fire that I may touch my heart's desire.

Magic to magic, blood to blood, let visions flood.

Lead me, send me on the right path to save all from

my mother's wrath.

Let every power come to me, one times three.
As I will, so mote it be.

Heat seared along her every vein, but she ignored it and continued to chant.

****

As he sat working in the study, Jonathan's hand spasmed in the middle of writing a string of numbers in a ledger. Pain not his own surged through him and he knew beyond doubt that what he was feeling, Rosalind was also. Staggering to his feet, he hurried to find her.

The sound of the wind reached him when he was still in the hallway. He discovered her in her private chamber standing at her work table, face paler than he'd ever seen it, hair flying wild and blood pouring freely from her nose. As he watched in awe, gaping at the spectacle she made, blood seeped from her eyes as well. When her hands gripped the edge of the table, he found his voice. "Rosalind, stop!"

Her green eyes, even brighter now because of her power, met his gaze but otherwise she did not acknowledge him. She continued to chant.

"Why are you doing this?" Still he got no response from her, other than one fierce determined look.

Just as resolute as she, he strode around the table to her, grasped her by the upper arms, and shook her none too gently in hopes of breaking through to her. "Whatever you are doing, don't. It's killing you. Please."

For just one instant she saw his panic, understood what it meant, but then her jaw firmed and she chanted all the louder.

Speaking past the ferocious ache in his throat was

not easy, but he managed to gasp out one final command. "Stop!" he roared.

The wind whipped up even higher, all but knocking him to the ground and the light in the room became blinding. For one instant he was nothing more than sensation: unpleasant, sharp, cutting and crystal clear. The spell reached some fever pitch then at the exact moment he knew he could bear it no longer, it died away so swiftly that he almost fainted with relief.

The ringing silence left in the wake of her storm gave him a moment to pull himself out of the semi-conscious state her magic had left him. When he could, he got to his feet and although he was still unsteady, lurched to her. "Rosalind?" he called between coughs. Gingerly, he stepped through the rubble to where she had been and when he found her in a crumpled heap on the floor, his heart all but stopped. Clumsy attempts to revive her accomplished nothing. Growing more panicked by the second, he was beyond grateful when her eyes fluttered open and she took a deep, rasping gasp of air.

"Did it work?" she croaked a moment later.

He blinked then answered dryly, "No idea since I haven't a clue what you were trying to accomplish."

"The slipper. I was trying to find the damn slipper. Is it here?" she demanded.

He looked around then nodded. Taking her hand, he closed it about the unmarred shoe lying beside her, mere inches out of her reach.

Laughing a little, she brought it into her field of vision, gazed at her prize a moment then sighed. "Thank the gods."

"Let me help you up," he offered. Not so much as

glancing at the object she risked so much to acquire, he got them both to their feet.

****

He refrained from further inquiry until they were both cleaned up and supplied with cups of hot, strong tea. She knew he'd have questions, probably a lot of them, to which she would have to provide answers sooner rather than later. "I'm sorry I frightened you," she began, "but I needed the shoe."

He appeared calmer than she expected him to be. Instead of yelling or berating her, he sat next to her on the davenport. "Why?"

"It is proof, don't you see? Now we have verification that my mother spelled the slipper after it left Celina's possession."

"I'm sorry, but how is that possible? It's just a shoe, isn't it?"

"No, it's so much more. This is a powerful magical object and when ordered to by any conjurer you care to name, it will give up its secrets."

"That is wonderful. Did you know how difficult it would be?" With an abrupt motion, he rose to refill his cup, though it was only half-empty.

As he did, she noticed that his hands shook though he was trying to hide the fact.

Rosalind shrugged. "I had some idea. It dawned on me that if Beatrice didn't have the shoe with her, she must have left it here. You see, at first I figured she would want it as near to her as possible, for safe keeping you understand. But once I became certain she did not have it with her, I knew she would have wanted it here, protected and as far away from Juliette as she could manage. She didn't count on me, though."

Rosalind couldn't hold back the fierce triumph which rolled through her. "She believed I would be so pleased with my new position as mistress of this estate that I would never look for it or even question where it might be. Well, she was wrong, wasn't she? So very wrong."

"Yes, she was," he murmured.

"Instead, I used a locator spell and found it."

"And almost killed yourself while you were about it!"

His raised voice, so unexpected, nearly made her jump, but she steeled herself and merely raised an eyebrow. "And saved countless others in the process." She had no compunction about throwing his own words back at him.

"Touché," he admitted. "Gods, I need to sit down." He did so then let out a deep breath. "So you've got the shoe. Now what?"

"We keep it safe until the prince summons us, which will be soon. A matter of days, no more. When we return to the castle, the shoe comes with us."

"A matter of days? How do you know that?"

"I can communicate with my sister, mind to mind, across great distances. Juliette has been keeping me informed."

"I see."

"Is it safe here until then? Are we safe? Will your mother know you have it?"

Rosalind smiled. "Don't worry. I've taken care of that little detail. She'll never know I've had my hands on it. Trust me."

"I do. May the gods help me, but I do. It's her I don't trust," he muttered. "So, we wait."

"We wait and prepare. Is there someone we can

rely on to run things in our absence?"

Jonathan nodded. "I'll see to it."

****

Days had passed at the palace without incident. Life for Juliette continued much as it had before, which gave her a lot of time to think. To work up her nerve more like. After much deliberation, she concluded she had to at least try to take her sister's advice. The worst that could happen is that she would make a fool of herself and leave with a broken heart. Either way, she had to know since she couldn't get him out of her head. Besides, she couldn't live without finding out what Robert's feelings were. If she risked nothing, she would gain nothing.

Mind made up, she wasted no more time. While her mother was out for a walk and they were blessedly alone in her sitting room, she rolled the dice and took her chances.

"Robert, there's something I must ask you."

"About?" he asked, giving her hand an absent pat.

Gathering her courage, Juliette took a deep breath. "We need to talk about the kiss."

Every muscle in his body tensed; it was clear she had his full attention. "No we don't."

That curt reply was far from satisfactory. "We do," she contradicted him. "I need to know if gratitude was all you felt or…something more. It seemed like more to me."

She knew she was babbling now, but she couldn't help it. Before she could continue and embarrass herself any further, he kissed her with even more passion than he had the first time. It was fierce, but all too brief. Still, one thing she was sure of, whatever else their previous encounter had been about, it had not been about gratitude alone.

"Does that answer your question?"

She could only nod, mesmerized as she was by him. This response satisfied him, however.

"Good," he murmured, and took her mouth again.

This time he was in no hurry to let her go. He took the smattering of knowledge that he had gained during their previous encounter and put it to good use. Their first kiss had been seduction, utter and compelling. This was one was pure demand. She knew he sought to frighten her off but, curiously, she felt not one bit of trepidation. Fearing him never even crossed her mind.

Even the best of things must end, however, even that kiss. His mouth parted from hers and left her wanting more. As soon as she could speak in coherent sentences, she asked, "Now what?"

"I ask the prince for permission to court you properly once this mess is over. We get to know each other and decide if we are compatible, if we want to share a life just like any other courting couple."

Joy welled up in Juliette and she smiled. "I would like that very much."

"Good. Now go while I still have the strength to let you."

Despite her utmost disinclination to do so, she obeyed.

****

Getting out of the wind and rain was paramount so when he entered the hall Jonathan did not at first hear the voices in the nearest parlor. Once he did register them, it was Rosalind's deep tones that he first caught, mingled a moment later with Celina's lighter ones.

About to pass by and leave them to it, when he comprehended the tenor of their discussion, he couldn't resist the temptation to look and listen unobserved despite the violation of their privacy.

"So have you and the prince...anticipated the wedding vows?" Rosalind had no compunction when it came to asking such personal questions.

Celina flushed. "No, we've decided to wait. Not that it's any of your business."

"Ooo, cheeky." Rosalind chuckled.

"Be that as it may, since we are on the subject, I am rather nervous. Can you offer me any advice?"

Rosalind sipped her tea a moment. "I'll tell you what I wish someone had told me. What I told Juliette when she asked. Just relax. You're both inexperienced, so it may be awkward at first, in fact chances are good it will be, but you'll soon get the hang of it. For the rest, all you need do is be yourself. I've no better advice than that to offer, only a question. Do you love him? So much that you want to express what you feel in your heart and your mind and your soul using your body?"

Celina flushed an even brighter crimson, but met her stepsister's eyes and nodded.

"Well that's a good enough start then."

"But will it hurt?"

"Yes," Rosalind said. "Only a bit at first, especially if he knows what he's doing," she added.

Celina grimaced. "Well, that's something then I suppose."

"Trust me, it's worth it," Rosalind assured her.

"Do you mind that Jonathan isn't of noble blood? I ask because I am marrying a royal when I am of mere noble birth. I wonder, does it matter?"

Jonathan stilled. He had wondered this himself but with all the other concerns on his mind, the question had drifted to the backburner of his thoughts.

Rosalind considered a moment. "It doesn't. What matters more is whether he has a clever mind, a practical bent and a strong, creative body. Jonathan has all of these. His clever mind can keep me engaged of an evening with discussions about literature, religion, philosophy or any other subject you care to name. His practical bent helps me run the estate. His strong arms have defended me and the creative uses to which he has put his body for our mutual benefit, well...I will confine myself to remarking that he is amazing in that arena. To be honest, it's rare that I think of his blood or station. He's simply Jonathan, my partner in every sense."

Celina nodded. "That is good to hear."

The talk veered off into other more mundane subjects. Not wishing to push his luck, Jonathan withdrew.

****

"Marry me."

From her prone position on the bed, Rosalind raised herself up onto an elbow to look Jonathan full in the face.

"Marry me. It's long past time I officially asked the question, don't you think? I love you. You love me. Soon enough we'll be going back into danger and I don't want to die without asking. No matter your answer. I won't say it will be easy, far from it in fact, but I would have you by my side. We could make a good life together."

"Why? You don't have to marry me to sleep with

me." In spite of her racing heart and knotted stomach, she called up a sultry smile from somewhere inside of her.

"You mean more to me than that. Don't you know that by now? I swear sometimes I don't understand you. This is not the moment for you to be willing to settle for so little. This is a moment when you should demand everything. I am offering you a life together. Please consider taking me up on it."

She could've put him off, Rosalind knew. Distracting him with an argument, or their work, or lovemaking would have been easy and she would have if it hadn't been for the concern in his eyes mingled with the sincere desire to have her reply. "Maybe I am willing to settle for less because less is all I've ever been given. You know how it's been for me. What's more, you know what my mother is. Because of that I react in one of two ways, I either demand everything or I expect nothing. When we started working so closely together, I wanted you more each day until I was determined to have you. I thought once we dallied together, the feeling would go away but I just wanted more. Yet that more, it scares me to death. How can I marry you when the very idea of love terrifies me?"

"Believe me, you are not alone in feeling that way. What I feel for you, sometimes it's so strong it petrifies me, but do you know what frightens me most? Losing you. Please make me the happiest of men. Say yes."

"I do want to marry you more than anything, you deserve to know that much. But before I can consider the question in all seriousness, I need you to do something for me," Rosalind said.

"Anything," he vowed.

"Convince me."

"I-I'm sorry? I'm not quite following."

"Convince me I can be the woman you believe me to be."

"You are that woman. I've seen you become your best possible self over these last months and it's only made me love you more. I've told you that more than once. I don't know what other words I can say to—"

"Show me. Show me how much you love me."

His breath hitched and he inclined his head. "I am yours to command, my lady."

****

His heart skipped a beat and every inch of his body went rock hard at her request. He couldn't possibly love her more, but he understood something aside from the mere words was required, so he did as she requested.

He did his best to make her feel the depth of his love with every touch, every caress. Each movement, each stroke of his body inside hers was designed to bring her to the height of exquisite sensation. He used his body then his mind to convey all he wished her to know. When he let her share his thoughts again, the pleasure he gave was reflected back to him threefold.

It nearly sent him over the edge. For a moment his pleasure and hers almost undid him, but he took a deep breath, steadied himself and with a firm grip on his sensual reins, he began to make love to her.

****

As he filled her mind and then worshipped her body, he took her very breath away. She still wasn't at all used to it, his love. Only when she could feel it pouring into, lavished on her, so beautiful she could not think, much less speak, could she believe it actually existed. Combine that with the pure carnal awareness of his body inside of hers and rational thought was impossible.

She had wondered if it would be as amazing this time as it had been the night he told her he loved her. All doubt on that score became a distant memory from the moment he kissed her. He brought her to that first peak with his mouth, as lovely as it was skilled, but didn't join her. She found the sensation of him not just awaiting but enjoying her pleasure as much as if it were his own unbearably erotic.

When he brought her to completion again mere moments later, her mind could not take it in. Her heart, so full of so much, beat so hard, it was a wonder it didn't push right out of her chest. But gods, how she wanted him with her. Skin tingled wherever he touched her, desire, like a fiery wine, raced through her veins, muscles tensed in anticipation. As ever, he did not disappoint. In fact, this time, she realized, there was more, so much more. So much that she could only gasp as he finally entered her. Wordlessly, she drew him to her, reached out to him, body and mind, nothing held back, nothing hidden. He was hers and she was his and she wanted him with her in everything.

****

Aware of her every nuance, he shuddered and slowed his pace. the better to savor her and all she offered. In spite of being in her arms, of being inside her, he still longed. He wanted to hear the words, wanted her commitment. 'Be my wife. Be with me like this always.'

Holding him close, both their hearts racing, she granted him all he wished. "Yes, I will be your wife."

Utter joy filled him and at last he let the tidal wave of emotion and physical sensation carry him away. His orgasm, when it came at last, was like nothing he'd ever experienced before, followed so closely and amplified a hundred times as it was by hers.

****

The squeak which escaped Juliette was involuntary and was, in fact, an utterly feminine, natural and spontaneous reaction to being grabbed and pulled into a hidden alcove behind a tapestry. "I thought we were attending the council meeting." The protest was a feeble one even to her own ears.

"We'll go. We'll just be a little late," Robert promised against her lips. "It's been forever since I kissed you."

For long, delicious moments, she let him. Let the smell of him fill her lungs and the taste of him fill her mouth.

"Are you sure we're safe here?" she whispered.

"Quite safe," he promised, lips so close to her ear, they tickled her lobe.

Indeed they were and so she found herself in a very confined space being held by a very attractive man. A different kind of tension filled Juliette and when he bit her earlobe just hard enough, she shivered.

As he kissed his way down her throat, pausing at the spot where neck and shoulder joined, a small moan escaped her. "We really...uh, should get to the council meeting. They'll wonder where we are." Was that her voice so breathless?

"Mmm. In a moment." The other side of her neck received the same treatment and she arched to give him better access without conscious thought.

His hand, which had rested on her hip, clenched a moment, then released. An instant later, that same hand circled her breast, found its peak. The pleasure of that had her biting her lip to keep from making even the slightest noise.

Her cautiousness was well-founded. Footsteps pattered and voices rang through the hallway bringing her crashing back to reality. Juliette jerked away, but when she started to speak, Robert placed a finger to her lips. They waited, keeping still, as a gaggle of servants, the castle's washerwomen she surmised, passed. When, some minutes after their conversation died away, he grinned then removed his hand, Juliette couldn't help but let out a relieved sigh.

Then she got lost in his eyes. Before she could forget herself and let him kiss her again until she no longer cared where she was, she broke contact. "We have to go. I wouldn't want my mother to wonder." Although she sensed little else could have deflected his intent or cooled his ardor so effectively, that did.

"I hate to admit it, but you are right."

He released her then with a wary look in each direction, he stuck his head out from behind the tapestry to ascertain whether the passage was deserted. When no one appeared, he lifted the arras and gestured for her to step out.

****

For Juliette the days passed in a swift, happy daze, in spite of what was still to do. Each day, each hour she and Robert spent together brought them closer in every way. As a consequence, they continued to sneak off as often as possible, heedless of all risk. The moments alone with him became what she lived for. His kiss, his touch, even the look in his eyes, filled her with heat and the excitement of a marvelous secret.

After one such exquisite interlude in the library where they were nearly discovered twice, Robert grimaced. "We must be more careful. Your mother…"

"A pox upon my mother," Juliette stated with a petulant toss of her head. "I'll not allow her to take one thing more from me."

His gentle fingers brushed a stray hair back from her cheek. "I support that course of action wholeheartedly, but I would see no harm come to you. Perhaps we shouldn't meet alone anymore. At least not until this is all well over."

Juliette shook her head. "No, I told you, I won't lose one more moment of happiness because of her. We'll be more discreet."

Abruptly, he rolled so he was half on top of her with her lying beneath him on the comfortable settee. "I don't like the idea any more than you do. Discretion isn't easy when I feel like everyone can see right through me. I want you, that is plain for anyone who cares to look. It surprises me when I get through another day and there is no whisper of it. It surprises me even more that I've managed to stay out of your bed. I'm not sure how much longer I can keep from—" He whispered an ingenious, overtly sensual suggestion in her ear which left her gasping and blushing.

"It won't be forever," she promised once she recovered a modicum of self-possession. "Soon, we'll stop my mother. Until then…" She drew him down to her for an enthusiastic kiss which he returned in kind.

****

"You ought to stay far away from me, especially

since I can't stay away from you, even though I should," Juliette insisted several evenings later when they were alone on the terrace after yet another formal dinner. "I've never been good at doing what I ought, in case you hadn't noticed." She grinned, unrepentant.

"So I've observed," Robert replied.

More serious now, she continued, "In truth, you should stay away from me. I know we've an understanding between us, and there is nothing more I want in this world than to be with you, but regardless of your feelings or mine, you should steer clear. I've been selfish. These last few days have been wonderful and I don't want them to ever end."

He started to speak, but she held up a hand to forestall him. "Despite that, in the last few days we've also had several close calls. We were almost discovered. I would never want to see you harmed. If my mother were to find out about us before we could neutralize her... Well, let's just say I'm a dangerous woman to love."

"Do I look scared to you?"

Mute, she shook her head. He didn't look scared. He looked very strong, a little frustrated and altogether desirable.

"Did you ever think maybe it's you who ought to run from me?"

More than a little taken aback, she asked, "Why?"

"I'll tell you plainly, I want you in my bed and unless you tell me you don't feel the same, then we'll end up there. Soon."

The look in his eyes all but stopped her breath. It was pure passion, on a tight leash. Greatly daring, she whispered, "And if I do want you?" If I tell you I long to share your bed?"

For an instant something flared in his eyes and he reached for her, then control and sense reasserted themselves. "Juliette, one minute you are telling me to stay away from you and the next you say you want me in your bed. You are not making this easy."

She shrugged delicate shoulders. "Excellent. Let's try for impossible." For the first time she kissed him, flagrantly offering herself.

Her lips were warm and firm on his and they opened to him without cajoling. In fact there was little hesitancy about her as she poured herself into the kiss. All eagerness, she pressed her body to his. Yet even that could not quiet the ache. Her every nerve ending was electrified, acutely, almost painfully, sensitized.

While his hand pressed then kneaded her breast, he broke the kiss and waited until her unfocused gaze met his, cleared. "You have no idea what you are asking for." He ran his hand over her nipple, one slow, deliberate motion, and she gasped. "This is a mere fraction of what I could give you. I could take you so easily, so quickly that I could be inside you before you even knew what was happening. But I want you to know what's happening. I want you with me every step of the way. I want you to be very sure."

"I am sure," she insisted.

"Perhaps so. But I don't think you are ready, not for all it, at any rate. Still…"

Quicker than she would have thought possible, one hand firmed about her breast while the other slid down and ended between her legs. Even muted by layers of fabric, his touch seared and radiated throughout her entire body. In response, heat flickered over every inch of her, but its center remained where his hand stroked her. Each movement of his fingers had ripples of pleasure starting deep in her body and an unfamiliar damp warmth coalescing at the apex of her thighs.

"So there's this," he whispered some minutes later. "But there's also this."

When he'd first touched her it had been fast, so very fast, but now he took her hand and brought it to his erection, giving her plenty of time to prevent him or to break his loose hold on her wrist. She didn't stop him, but let him place her palm firmly on his rigid member. When her hand made contact, she moved it over him, taking his measure. Captivated, she wrapped her slim fingers about him in a secure grasp. His groan drew her attention back to his face. The arrested expression covering his features went passion-blank when she stroked up and down his length.

****

"Wait." The word was barely recognizable, but she stopped. He rested his forehead against hers while he got his breath back. "I could show you more. Satisfy us both without taking your maidenhead."

She inhaled shakily then nodded in response.

"Very well. We'll need someplace a bit more private." He led her out into a starlit night and through a garden to a semi-abandoned gazebo which could not be seen from the castle.

"No one uses this place anymore. We'll be safe here," he assured her.

She nodded then without further preamble, kissed him.

Given this overt encouragement, he let his hands roam where they would, down her back, up her thigh, through her hair. Meanwhile, he allowed his mouth similar freedom. He kissed his way down her neck as he dealt with the laces of her gown then divested her of it. That done, he pressed her onto one of the padded benches in the gazebo. He let his lips and teeth and tongue play at her breasts until they were both wild for more. Deciding he had tormented them both for long enough, he raised her chemise. Still he hesitated and let his hand remain motionless, hovering above her soft, hidden hair. "Are you certain?"

"Yes. Robert, please."

Those three words were enough. A kiss followed this answer. It was a kiss of flagrant invitation, one a grateful Robert accepted. He let his hand roam down a fraction until…skin to skin contact at last. As he began to stroke delicately, the moisture built. Nothing in his life had ever felt so good until she touched him. While he had been focused on her to the exclusion of all else, she had managed to loosen his trousers enough to put her hand right where he wanted it most.

From deep inside of him came a moan and for a moment everything blurred. For a time there was only her hands on him and the demands of his body.

To his surprise, her inexperience was no detriment to his rapidly approaching satisfaction. Aware that he was about to go over some bright jagged peak, he tried to slow himself down, to pull himself back from the edge, found he couldn't. Desperate to take her with him, he found her eyes, kept his locked on her face. "Come with me," he entreated.

****

Juliette had been looking at the strong muscles of his chest, when she sensed his gaze on her. If she'd had breath enough to respond to his whispered, 'Come with me' she would have answered 'anywhere', no matter that she didn't have the faintest idea where 'anywhere' might be. She kept her eyes on his as he did something unspeakably erotic with his very capable hands. And in a sudden flash, she realized what he meant, where he wanted to go and where he wanted her to follow; to a brand new plane of existence, one where carnal delight could be indulged in without reserve. As she surrendered to that grand new world, to him, her body erupted in waves of voluptuous sensation. Her climax triggered his and he gave into it with tremendous relief and with absolute abandon, he lost himself in her.

"So, there you have it. Or at least most of it." he informed her when he could speak.

"Well, yes, I should think so," she replied, still a little breathless.

"Are you all right?"

She touched a hand to his cheek. "Oh, yes. I am very much all right."

"Excellent."

Making use of his handkerchief then hers, he made them both presentable. Then he relaxed back against the cushioned seat with her held close in his arms, her head over his heart.

The distant peal of the clock half-registered, but languidly she counted the chimes. By the time she reached eleven, full-blown panic filled her. "We must go. My mother will expect me to be tucked up in bed when she returns as I pleaded a headache in order to leave dinner early and take the air."

With an inward sigh, Robert agreed and escorted her back to her rooms.

Chapter Fifteen

"May I speak with you, sire?"

"Of course. But why so formal, Robert?"

Robert clenched his hand on the hilt of his sword as was his habit when nervous. "I wish to ask for Juliette s hand in marriage."

Will's grin was so wide it seemed like to split his face. "Excellent! And about time too. Of course you have my consent, especially since I have predicted this all along."

Robert shrugged, but couldn't hold back his answering smile. "So you said and did your best to make it happen too. I have your approval then?"

"You have my unequivocal sanction for the match and my promise that I will procure the same from my father as soon as may be. So long as you realize how lucky you are."

"I assure you I do. I thank the fates every day for putting such an exceptional woman in my orbit and I praise the gods that she loves me."

"As well you should."

"As should you, majesty. When will you ask the beautiful Celina to be your queen?"

"Remember, you address your prince. I should whip you for such impertinence," Will told him, but without heat. "The short answer is, I'll ask when the lady is ready. She's been through an ordeal and I wouldn't want to push her. So long as she is by my side, that's enough for the moment."

Serious now, Robert clasped his friend's shoulder. "You once told me life is too short to delay happiness. Don't wait too long."

He found her in the library, where she so often was. "Juliette."

At the sound of her name she looked up from the book she was reading and a happy light filled her eyes. "Robert, I hadn't expected you."

He strode to her, took her hand. "There's a matter I would discuss with you. Will you walk with me in the garden?"

"To be sure."

Although he could sense her bafflement and beneath it her unease, she followed readily enough. As they walked along the little path in the charming garden, she spoke of inconsequential things for a time, but when he made no move to broach the subject, she did. "You wished to speak to me on some matter which appears to be private. What is it?"

Whether he was ready or not his moment had come. He stopped, took her hands. Shaking inside just a little, he took a deep breath. "Juliette Forbes, will you marry me? I am yours to command ever and always. I know I have so very little to offer you, but all I do have belongs to you. I only wish it were more. There's so much more you should have. You could have married the prince. One day you could've been a queen, but I am a selfish man and so, hope you'll marry me."

She shook her head. "My love and loyalty are the prince's but I think of him as my king and as a brother. I was never meant to be his queen. I am deeply honored to be his friend, but his heart never belonged to me, nor mine to him. I hope you know that."

"I do. It's more than that though." He took her hand, urged her to sit on a nearby bench. "You have magic in your blood, in your very soul. I don't. I wish I had something so precious to offer you."

Juliette shook her head in denial "You've already given me so much. More than I ever dreamed. You have granted me your protection, your passion, the promise of pleasure and best of all your love. What more could a woman want? And what can I offer you? My mother will soon be a convicted traitor. Are you certain you want to marry me when there are so many others who are not plagued by scandal?"

"You will be plagued by no such thing. You will play a vital role in saving this kingdom and so I have no reservations."

"So, is that a yes?" Much as he tried, he couldn't steady his voice and it shook.

"Yes."

The kiss that followed was full of life and light and every good thing in this harsh world. Nothing is more moving, more powerful than passion intermingled with affection and they reveled in it, appreciated it to the full. And knew that the most important thing in the world, love, was theirs for the taking.

****

The tears swimming in her eyes rolled down her cheeks. As he slipped a ring onto her finger, she blinked rapidly, wanting unblurred eyes so she might appreciate it. The light caught on a pear shaped diamond in a silvery bright setting.

She gasped as she held up her hand to let the jewel

catch the light. "Oh, it's lovely."

"Then it is a fitting accompaniment to your beauty. I would want nothing less for you. So, it's settled then, we'll be married."

Juliette's smile came from her very core to engulf her entire being in joy. "Yes, we shall. When?"

"So soon as this is over, if that suits you. I don't want to wait any longer than necessary to make you my wife."

"That suits me very well, but mustn't you ask the king's permission? I've no other recognized guardian, no one for you to speak to, but the king must sanction my marriage."

"I have yet to speak to the king, but I have the prince's consent and he assures me he will do what he can to gain the king's support."

"Even after all I've done, he approved." The tiny fear that Will would hold her actions against her, as he would have been justified in doing, was gone, leaving her relieved. Now all she had to worry about was the king, she thought wryly. "Well, that's wonderful."

"It will be if we live that long," he muttered. When she gave him a censorious look, he added. "I've no wish to spoil the mood, but it has to be said. Your mother is a problem."

"One which we will deal with. I've made my decision. I will grasp the happiness offered me. I tried to stay away from you, but I couldn't. That's done and soon she will be."

He took her hand, kissed it. "From your mouth to the ears of all the gods."

"I have no desire to discuss Beatrice right now. There will be plenty of time for that later. I would far rather discuss wedding plans or, better yet, our honeymoon."

****

Deciding she had nothing to lose, Juliette sought him out at his old rooms, which still contained some of his things and was where he often went during the brief times when he was not with her.

She gave a preemptory knock and entered. He sat at a writing desk in the corner of the room immersed in some correspondence. At the sound of her footsteps, his head shot up.

"We've not been alone since you asked me to marry you. Why?" she said by way of greeting. Not waiting for an answer, Juliette pressed on. "If I've done something, if you are having second thoughts, you need only say and—"

Abruptly, she found she could no longer speak as he ravished her mouth with his.

"Don't ever think I don't want you," he breathed against her lips.

Trembling, eyes wide, she said, "Then why?"

Releasing his hold, he took a deep breath. "I know you are a traditional, not to mention virtuous, woman. As such, you would wish to wait until we take our vows. I can and I will honor this wish, but it's not easy, so I've kept my distance."

Juliette blinked once, goggled. "Whatever made you think that?"

She couldn't quite hold back a giggle when his jaw dropped.

"I assumed…" When she merely looked at him, fine eyebrows raised, Robert stammered. "Umm…" was the best he could come up with.

"You assumed because of my virginal state and the inherent risks of our current situation, I would prefer to remain chaste until this is all well over. Until the kingdom is secure and the world is put to rights we should stay apart, yes?" She shook her head, sighed. "Foolish boy," she chided affectionately. "We are to be married, are we not? What's more, we could die tomorrow so shouldn't we find what joy we can, while we can?"

"Perhaps, but we ought to wait…" Whatever else he might have said died on his lips as her fingers touched them.

"I have no wish to wait."

He murmured, "Far be it from me to deny you anything it is in my power to grant."

Her small triumphant smile lingered for a moment as he kissed her. Then there was only heat, only him.

"I haven't ever done this before," Juliette whispered when their lips parted.

Letting out a shaky breath, Robert said, "I've only ever done it twice."

"Only twice? You seem so…"

"Experienced?" he asked, with a hopeful expression which she found adorable.

Pressing her lips together to hold back her grin, she replied, "I would have said confident."

"I'm not, not really. In fact, I can hardly believe this is happening."

As he whispered this, he trailed his lips down her neck then spoke against her throat. She shivered and could not suppress a moan.

"But it is happening," she said.

"It is. It will if you're sure."

"Oh, I'm sure."

"Good." It was the last word either spoke for a while and soon there wasn't any need for more. His mouth took hers and time ceased to have meaning.

Agonizingly slowly, he kissed his way from her neck to her shoulder. Simultaneously, his hand lowered the strap of her gown. Lifting his head, never letting his eyes leave hers, he lowered the other, let it fall.

"You are exquisite. All that I could wish," he murmured.

When he gazed at her with such undisguised admiration and such naked longing, how could she believe otherwise? Just his eyes looking at her made her shiver. It was almost as palpable as if he had touched her. Gods, how she wanted his hands on her.

A wild heat filled her and suddenly she wanted what remained of their clothing gone. Any barrier separating them was too much to bear now. She needed the smell of him, the taste of his mouth, the brush of his lips on her skin, the very beat of his heart. She craved his strong body beneath her hands. Most of all she needed to know that all that strength was hers to command. Needed to know all that strength was channeled for her pleasure.

He must have understood, as when she began unbuttoning his shirt, he did the same to his breeches. At last, he stood bare before her, all golden skin, lean, but with well-defined muscles, and the face of a fallen angel.

"I might be exquisite, but you are flawless," she claimed.

Her gaze kept going back to the part of him that would soon be inside of her. Erect and larger than she had realized, she was suddenly nervous. Would she really be able to take all of that into her untried body?

"It's all right. Don't be anxious. You've had your hands on me before. This will be even better, I promise."

Memories of the last time he put his hands on her rushed through her mind, hot, visceral and extremely explicit, and all at once the last of her doubt was gone. Whatever pain there might be, whatever happened next, she wasn't leaving his bed a virgin.

To know she fulfilled his desires intensified hers. With a sudden flash of insight, she realized that at the core, she trusted him implicitly, with her very life. And so, she let him take her exactly where they both longed to go.

****

When her gaze zeroed in on his rigid member then slid swiftly away again, Robert sensed her sudden tension and tried to reassure her. As he did, the recollection of their earlier moments together flowed over him and he let it show on his face and in his eyes. That, along with his utter conviction that they would fit perfectly together, seemed to steady her. From that moment, she let all her inhibitions go; he could see them drop from her, the same way he'd already watched her dress fall to the floor. She left him stunned and humbled by her utter trust in him. He swore that it would not be misplaced.

He had promised himself he would go gradually when he took her the first time, but he could no longer deny himself, not a moment longer. So when she opened her arms to him, he went to her. Someone was trembling but he had no idea whether it was her or him.

It didn't seem to matter. It felt as though they were melding into one being anyway.

He couldn't breathe but through her. He couldn't know pleasure but at her hands. Her gasps fueled his and his moans liberated her. With each new touch, glorious sensation built until it was everywhere, in every part of their bodies. And she, well she was in every part of his soul. Never to leave him. Never to be forsaken. Blind, all but mindless, he surged into her over and over until he plunged them both into ecstasy.

****

Juliette found herself wrapped in his arms when she returned to earth. She let out a soft hum of contentment that she knew must be close to a purr, but she didn't care.

"Hmm. I agree."

"You're glad we didn't wait then?" she shyly asked.

"Very glad," he assured her. "I thought I'd go mad with waiting, so no, I'm not upset that phase is all over with now."

She giggled, she couldn't help it. "When I told you I'd rather not wait," she shook her head, "you should have seen your face."

He grunted. "Well, I was a bit shocked. You cannot blame me."

"I suppose," she replied in an ambiguous tone. Now, she determined, was not the proper time to discuss the subject of women's equality so she let it pass.

He settled himself more comfortably and had the advantage of her nestling into his shoulder, hand just over his heart. "Shocked or not, it's done. There's no undoing it and I for one am glad. You are my wife now in all but name, thank the gods."

She tapped a gentle finger on his chest. "And you are my husband."

He smiled and placed a kiss on the top of her head. "So I am. Which makes me a very fortunate man."

She lifted her chin, reached up to touch her lips to his and what was between them flared again. "How soon will you be missed?" he wondered aloud after a moment.

"Not until morning presumably. My mother thinks I've gone to bed."

"Instead you've shared mine. Are you too sore to do so again now?"

His hand, which had at first been playing idly with her hair, had, for the last few moments been travelling downward to her breast. The unique sensation of his fingers and her own soft hair lightly stroking her nipple made her shiver. "I-I am not sore, or at least not very," she admitted in a breathless whisper.

"Excellent," Robert murmured.

The caress intensified, a kiss was added and when their bodies joined, Juliette was happy to note that she was indeed not sore at all.

****

Taking advantage of the morning light that streamed into the library, Will put the final touches to a letter. When Robert entered, Will handed him the missive. "It's time I summoned them. Will you see that Rosalind receives this?"

"Of course. How soon will they arrive?"

"Three days before the ball if all goes well. Time enough for us to refine all of our plans. Their arrival has to remain secret. We must have some place to conceal them. Have you any idea of where?"

"I have a few thoughts." Robert's grin radiated confidence.

****

As arranged, Rosalind, Celina and Jonathan entered via the south gate disguised as tradespeople come to sell their wares. The two women wore heavy veils and serviceable, non-descript gowns while Jonathan did the best he could with a hat and high collared cloak. Having arrived at the palace kitchens, they engaged in a light and friendly bit of barter for the benefit of the rest of the kitchen staff with the fully briefed head cook. She then led them down a steep staircase to a private corridor that ended in a barred door.

"It's all right, little ducks," June told them. "The worst is over. You just walk straight down this passage here and his lordship will be a-waitin' for you."

Footsteps from above rapidly descended the staircase so June shooed them onward with a hasty, impatient flutter of her hands then shut the door behind them. They heard an indistinct interrogatory murmur from a clear female voice then June's firm response.

"I was just fetching the wine for luncheon. The prince wants the vintage that was made in his honor and I don't trust any of you to make it up the stairs without smashing the bottle by accident. I'll be right there."

As promised, Robert was waiting for them. With as little fuss as possible he ushered them even deeper into the tunnels beneath the castle proper. One of the ancient kings had been prey to an obsession with escape routes. Upon discovering a network of natural caverns and tunnels beneath the building, he began to add to them. The passages he created ended at odd places throughout the nearby village. Over the many years of his reign, he built several miles of new routes, creating a veritable warren. But the maps of these had been destroyed and the secret ways forgotten, until Will and Robert discovered them as boys. Considering all the exploring he did as a child, making use of them now to aid in this very grown up adventure was, in his opinion, rather fitting.

****

Will opened the door to the chamber he'd had prepared for Celina. "I-I was going to say I hope you'll be comfortable here, but that hardly seems fitting. I can promise you far more suitable chambers in the very near future, if that is any consolation."

Celina looked around the small cellar room. It was ten-by-ten and contained a narrow cot, an ancient washstand with a chipped ewer, a table and a chamber pot tucked away behind a screen. "My room at Dubois manor was no worse, it's only... I've no wish to be confined even for a short time." She rubbed her arms as much to comfort herself as to ward off the cold and damp which pervaded the room.

"I swear it won't be for long. Then you'll have chambers befitting a queen." He continued after a moment, "This is the safest place I could devise for you. It's in the castle proper, but well away from prying eyes. Few even know these rooms exist. You'll have two guards morning and night and Juliette has done all she can to fortify this room using magic. I'll have her bring you a few books to occupy you as well. I know how much you like to read and our library is world

244

renowned. There's no reason why you can't begin to enjoy it."

She offered him the first genuine smile she'd shared with anyone since her escape. "Your majesty is too kind." Eyes fixed on the floor, she asked the question of gravest importance to her "Will you visit me?"

He hesitated. "There is nothing I would like more, but that would be far too dangerous I fear."

"Please. I know the risks, but if I could look forward to seeing you at least once then I think I could bear with all of this far better."

He took her hand, kissed it. "I would do almost anything to make this easier for you. I'll do my best to see you as often as I can. In truth, I've missed you. I'm not sure how that can be when I hardly know you, but there it is."

"I've missed you as well."

His gaze called to her and she couldn't resist. To be back in his orbit was intoxicating and so when he pressed her to him and kissed her, she allowed it. She tried her best to respond and put all of her longing and desire into that meeting of lips. She let her mouth go hot and soft and open on his, and willed him to respond in kind.

****

Shuddering, he accepted the invitation she offered and found his mouth not only on but inside of hers. The tenor of the kiss was unexpected. When he pressed his lips to hers he had anticipated the sweetness, not the passion. But passionate she was and more than ready to fully participate. Nor had his hands been idle. Without conscious direction, he caressed her neck, her bare shoulders, then her arms, stroking up then down again.

When her hands came up to run through his hair, they trembled. This encouragement, innocent as it was, enticed him far more than other more blatant offers. Despite being a second son meant for the church, women had approached him. None had tempted him so. Years of self-restraint now fell away leaving him aching and vulnerable, hot and hard and wanting. Without warning he craved nothing more than to tumble her back onto the thin mattress on the very narrow cot, strip them both bare and show her precisely how much he missed her and desired her.

A will of iron and an incredibly strong moral compass made it possible for him to step away, to call a halt, but the battle was brutal. "Forgive me," he said when he could speak. Pleased his voice was stronger and steadier than he thought it would be, he tried to find the right words to explain. "I had no right to take such advantage. You are in my care."

"If I had wanted you to stop, if I did not want you to kiss me, I would have said," she informed him, her tone acerbic in the extreme. "I'm not a child, Will."

"No. Nor am I, but what I am is a virgin." Did he just say that out loud? He cleared his throat and tried to pull himself together. "I must beg your pardon again, this time for my crude language."

"Hardly that, majesty." Her eyes danced with merriment, but she said nothing more.

Will's lips twitched but he manfully suppressed the laugh that wanted to bubble up. "My abrupt tone then, perhaps. I never expected to marry, you see. Originally I was to join the church. So, I've never been so... I've never wanted to lie with a woman so much, to be frank."

"If I might speak freely?" When he nodded, she continued, "First let me say, I'm immensely flattered. You'll also notice I am not unwilling, far from it. In fact, I feel the same way, but…"

"But?" After a moment of studying her intently, he smiled and it was filled with rueful tenderness. "You wish to wait until we're married?"

Her tense expression relaxed with relief and she inclined her head.

"As do I, although it's a little difficult to remember that just at the moment. I believe in the church's teachings and I believe marriage, the coming together of two people, should be sacred. That is what I want for us."

"I want the same," Celina assured him.

"Still I must admit, sticking to that is a bit challenging right now. I mean, until this very moment I never realized how easy it would be to just… I mean, I'm the future king, who would gainsay me? No one but you. Not that I would ever force you—" He stopped, horrified at the mere thought of such a thing.

"If I believed for one moment that you would, I wouldn't be here. I understand what you mean."

"I know you do and thank the gods for that. It's just, I've never wanted any woman so much and just knowing you want me too… It makes me want to forget all I've ever learned, everything I've ever believed and take you to bed."

"There's a very large part of me that wants to let you but…"

"Yes, but." He took a deep breath and told himself he did the right thing. "So all things considered, perhaps I should take my leave." He bowed then turned to go. Then turned right back around, caught her up and kissed her again. The caress was brief, yet passionate and full of promise. "I will back. Soon," he vowed.

Chapter Sixteen

The chamber prepared for Rosalind was located a little further along the passage. Leaving the prince and Celina their privacy, Robert showed her to it, with Jonathan in tow.

The place was as simple as Celina's if not more so, yet Robert hoped it would suit her needs, at least temporarily.

"This will do very well for a few days," Rosalind commented after taking a turn about the small room.

"Good. Jonathan's room is just a few steps down the corridor."

Before Rosalind could speak, Jonathan said. "If you don't mind, I'd rather share this room with Rosalind. That way, I can guard her."

Robert cleared his throat and tried to ignore the heat he could feel rising up his neck. Jonathan would do far more than guard Rosalind and they all knew it. He himself was more than aware of what temptations arose when in close quarters with and offering his protection to a woman. Still… "If the lady wishes it."

"I do indeed."

"Very well. You will, of course, have two guards at all times. The princess will have the same. Should anything untoward or at all suspicious happen, however, contact your sister telepathically right away. The prince, Juliette and I will return soon and we'll make our plans. For now, rest."

As he turned to go, Rosalind caught his hand. "Robert, what with one thing and another, I never had the chance to thank you for all you've done for my sister as well as my stepsister. I will be forever in your debt, so if there is ever any way I can serve you, you've but to ask."

Robert bowed in acknowledgement. "I did my duty for my prince, for his princess and for the woman I love, as any would have. Your thanks is most welcome, however."

He bowed once more and took his leave.

****

Will had been pacing the room for several fraught minutes when Robert arrived to attend him in his private chambers as he sometimes did.

Robert tilted his head to observe his friend. "Are you all right, majesty? You seem a bit keyed up."

"I'm fine."

"Are you sure, because you don't look quite—"

"I almost lay with Celina. She was beautiful and willing and I backed off."

"Well—"

"I must be insane. There she was, all but offering herself to me, and I end up spouting moral platitudes." Will laid his head down on the table.

"Sorry, moral platitudes?"

"I told her we should wait until we wed," he explained and beat his head on the tabletop none too gently.

"Oh," Robert replied in the tone of one who now sees the light.

"Yes, oh."

Robert clapped his friend on the shoulder. "Do you know the only thing that can make you forget, at least for a little while, about a woman, aside from another woman? A good stiff drink. C'mon."

Robert took Will's arm then guided him to the sideboard where a very good whiskey awaited. What luck.

Will peered dubiously at the suspicious looking brown liquid in the glass Robert handed him. "What's this, then?" he demanded, narrowing his eyes. "You know I don't drink whiskey."

"The situation calls for something stronger than wine. Drink up."

Will grunted then did as he was told. Liquid fire burned its way down his throat, through his veins until it settled in his belly. Coughing, gasping and shuddering, he managed to get it down. A moment later the warmth which had started deep in his gut radiated out to encompass his entire body and relax each muscle it came into contact with. His sigh was deep if not contented.

"Did that take a bit of the edge off?"

"A bit," he admitted.

But then an image of Celina's pretty face, her hair like golden silk, her soft lips and gorgeous, desire-filled eyes, flashed into his mind, and all the strain of the last hour came flooding back. When he realized the tension coiling inside of him was almost as severe as before, he gave up the struggle against one desire at least, cleared his scorched throat and reached for the decanter. "I need another."

After some time, Robert poured another drink for himself. "Do you believe in the moral correctness of the choice you made tonight?"

"Hmm." Will nodded. "I do. I also believe it to be necessary for the good of the realm. My people must have a king and queen who live by their beliefs, not ones who toss them aside whenever it suits them."

"That's good and I agree. I'm honored to serve a king who has the courage of his convictions. Even so, I've been where you are."

"How did you do it? With Juliette I mean?"

Robert scratched his chin. "Well to be honest, at first I tried to avoid her. When that didn't work, or I suppose it would be more accurate to say, when she wouldn't allow it, we did more than kiss." When Will looked blank, obviously not understanding, he elaborated. "I put my hands on her and she put hers on me. We got right to the very brink once or twice but it wasn't until we were officially engaged that we let ourselves go over."

When the prince just groaned again, the sound the very embodiment of frustration, Robert laughed. "Look, it won't be for long. We'll take care of the Dubois bitch in a matter of days then I'm sure your father will want you married as soon as possible. A month, two at the outside, and you'll be wed."

"I've waited for years. Now that I've found her I'm not sure I can wait two more months. I'm not sure I can wait another day."

"I know the feeling, believe me," Robert replied.

"You're so full of advice this evening; what do you suggest? I mean I can't very well spend the next several months in a drunken stupor."

Robert considered for a moment. "You could avoid being alone with her, as I did with Juliette. If you can't or do not wish to endure that particular brand of torture, then…play. Enjoy each other, up to a certain point. There's nothing wrong with that, she is to be your wife after all. Trust me, that sort of interaction can be very satisfying. All it requires is your mouth, your hands and a bit of creativity. Oh, and control of course." Robert sent him a wicked grin as he downed the rest of his drink.

"I'm aware. I'm not entirely inexperienced," Will assured him, tone dripping with acid. "I do have all the right bits and I think I can muster up some creativity. It's my control I'm concerned about."

"Will, you are the most self-disciplined person I know apart from myself. You'll be fine."

"Maybe. For now, another drink."

Robert laughed and poured.

****

Although Jonathan, Rosalind, and Celina arrived in early morning, it was not until evening fell that Will, Robert, and Juliette were able to steal a few precious moments to catch up on all their latest news. Soon enough, however, their thoughts returned to the matter at hand.

Rosalind lifted an inquiring eyebrow. "You sent for us. When do we make our move?"

"And what news of the traitorous bitch?" asked Jonathan.

Will grimaced. "Beatrice is being watched by my people."

"In all fairness, I must admit I came close to giving the game away after what she did to Juliette," Robert added.

"What did she do?" Celina asked, her sweet, clear

voice clouded with apprehension now.

In a few brief sentences, Robert described the attack on his betrothed. As he expected, everyone present was shocked and appalled.

"So you've called us here and we've arrived. I assume we have a plan," Jonathan said when he was able to get a word in amidst all of the negative imprecations.

Will nodded. "As you know, my father has insisted a ball to announce my engagement take place three days from now. That's when we'll do it. She'll think she's won, but instead, the moment of her greatest triumph will be her greatest nightmare, come true. She'll have no idea what hit her."

"What do you have in mind?"

Will looked to Rosalind. "Instead of presenting Juliette, we'll present Celina as we discussed. You, Rosalind, and you, Juliette, will be standing by to contain the honorable Lady Beatrice Dubois with magic. I will also have a full regiment of my personal guards standing by to help." He turned to his friend. "Robert, your primary objective will be to protect the future queen. Make certain no harm comes to her. Secondarily, you will guard Rosalind and Juliette. Finally, you will do your best, as will we all to be certain no innocents are harmed. Each of you will be placed at various points in the room. Here, here and here," he indicated three spots on a crudely drawn map.

Robert could not hold back his instinctive protest. "But what of the king and of you yourself, majesty? My place has always been at your side."

"Even you cannot be in two places at once. I would have you leave that duty to Jonathan here, my friend.

He will protect me just as I will defend the king to the last drop of my blood. Once we have Beatrice subdued, we'll present my father with the proof of her treachery."

Robert's head shot up at the word 'proof'. "You have hard evidence at last?"

Will could not hold back a fierce grin. "We have the shoe."

Although a thrill shot through him at this news, Robert could scarcely believe it. "You have the shoe, with its magic intact?"

Jonathan inclined his head and took up the tale. "Any conjurer can cast an enchantment which will show that Beatrice spelled the shoe. That, along with Celina's testimony, should be more than enough."

"So it should," Robert agreed. "I would have thought the bitch would have destroyed it. How on earth did you get your hands on it?"

Rosalind waved a hand. "That's due to me I'm afraid. When I realized Beatrice did not have the shoe with her, I made it my business to search for it. I performed a simple locator spell and voila."

"It was more complicated than she is letting on. The spell was difficult and dangerous. It took hours of hard effort with a terrible and hazardous spell at the end of it, but she wouldn't stop. She was brilliant," Jonathan put in.

"I'll say she was," Juliette confirmed. "It would have been warded and any attempt to break through would have caused the conjurer serious pain. Are you all right?"

"Of course I am."

"Don't lie to me, sister. I thought we were past all that."

Rosalind shrugged, "Doing the spell was difficult, but I soon recovered. Whatever transitory suffering I went through, I think it's more important to note that it worked. Now we have everything we need to take the esteemed Lady Dubois down."

"So we do. But what do we do with her once we have her? Where, and even more importantly how, do we imprison her?" Will demanded.

"I have been working on that," Juliette said. "Over these last few weeks I've come up with a spell which I believe will contain her. I also have a place in mind that would hold her. Now that you are here, Rosalind, I could use your input."

Rosalind nodded. "I would be most happy to consult, but there is something else I think I should also be tasked with. If we cannot contain her, I will be the one to kill her."

Dead silence fell at this pronouncement, but after a time Jonathan spoke. "Awful as she is, she is your mother. I'm not so sure—"

"I am. I have the most magic and perhaps the most cause. If it has to be anyone, it should be me. Besides, with everything I've done in my life, my innocence will not be tarnished by the act."

Jonathan opened his mouth to argue that last point, but Robert forestalled him. "Jonathan is right. She is your mother. Given that, who says it has to be you? I would be honored to take on this charge," he stated and offered her a small bow.

Rosalind shook her head. "Juliette, Celina and I have already discussed this. If, in the heat of battle, it must be done and it can be done by any of you, feel free, but be very sure you can finish what you start. As for me, this will be my particular mission. We will capture her or she will die. I will not allow her to escape."

"Very well, Rosalind," Will conceded. "Next-"

"What of me? What is my role?" Celina interrupted.

Will looked to her, all seriousness. "You, my dear lady, are bait. Your job is to stay visible and remain calm no matter what happens. Let her come for you, but don't, by all the gods, let her take you. It's a very delicate balance. Do you think you can do that?"

Her jaw firmed. "Absolutely."

"Good." Will offered her a fierce smile, all teeth. "Now I think we'd best position ourselves here, here and...here," he stated as he indicated strategic points on his makeshift map.

****

The passage Juliette walked along was dimly lit and more than a little damp, but already she knew it well. Visits to Celina, Rosalind and Jonathan—while not a regular occurrence—were sometimes necessary and so it had been tonight. Her stepsister was well tended though not entirely content. Confinement of any sort, for any length of time, tended to grate on the younger woman's nerves, but it wouldn't be for much longer. In two days more all their plans would come to fruition and a ball to outshine any other would be held. And perhaps, she mused, a dreamy smile on her lips, she might even find a moment to dance with Robert again.

So lost in these pleasant flights of fancy was she, that the approaching footsteps went unheard until the intruder was all but upon her. Hastening toward a shadowy alcove, she hid, slowed her ragged breathing, and waited.

She had a moment to wonder who on earth might need or want to be in such a deserted part of the castle when green jewels glimmered in the faint torchlight and Beatrice came into view wearing her favorite black dress. The satin garment was one she put on whenever she meant to do serious magic. Her mother was, as usual, up to something and whatever it was, it was nothing good. The only way to find out what mischief she intended would be to follow her. Juliette's heart, already at a solid canter after her near miss, picked up the pace to a full gallop as she walked in Beatrice's wake.

For several minutes, Beatrice walked the same route Juliette had traversed mere moments before. Juliette grew cold at the notion of how close they were to Celina, Rosalind and Jonathan. Could her mother have discovered where her stepdaughter was being kept? Bile rose in her throat at the mere thought.

When her mother took the left junction and not the right, which would lead her straight to Celina, Juliette drew a deep breath and swallowed against her parched, burning throat. She was desperate to sit down, to let her shaky legs rest, but curiosity as much as a healthy desire for self-preservation pushed her forward. If Beatrice was not here for Celina, what was she here for?

The floor sloped down leading them ever deeper beneath the castle and still Beatrice continued. After ten minutes, she halted at a heavy door of oak with a handle of iron. With a gesture, the lock turned and the door swung inward on rusted hinges.

The glimpse she caught of the chamber beyond was enough to make Juliette glad she had happened upon Beatrice. What she found was the lair of a dark witch. A cauldron stood upon the worktop while bottles of various colors, sizes and descriptions filled with viscous, vile-looking liquids were lined up on crude shelves of unfinished wood. Flesh and blood and bone littered the granite floor. For one instant, the stench of black sorcery filled her nostrils then was gone as the door closed.

To her great shame and misfortune, she was all too familiar with this sort of place. Its similarity to one her mother kept at home was eerie. What was surprising was that Beatrice could put something comparable together here so fast and with such secrecy.

Discovering her mother's lair was one thing, what to do about it was something else altogether. She could and would linger but she was well aware Beatrice might work for hours, even days, at a stretch. This meant waiting for her to come out and leave the place unoccupied was not a viable option. Coming back later on the other hand…no, that wouldn't do either she decided. Determined on her course of action, Juliette turned on her heel and marched back in the direction she had come to a place of concealment.

A swift spell of astral projection was required and so she cast one right then and there. The glorious feeling of lifting out of her body distracted her, but only for a moment. With just a thought, she was inside Beatrice's personal house of horrors.

As she watched, her mother gathered various ingredients and dropped them into an already simmering cauldron. After adding what had to be a rat's tail and a drop of her own blood, the potion boiled then released a puff of bright red smoke. Careful not to spill any, Beatrice filled a small crystal flask with the stuff.

A beautiful bird, a tiny thing with bright eyes and gorgeous blue and silver plumage, sat caged a few steps away. She added a single drop to the creature's water, then watched it drink to ease its thirst. Seconds later the bird fell to the bottom of the enclosure, lifeless. A small, unnerving, wholly satisfied smile played over Beatrice's face. That smile was one Juliette had seen many times before and it chilled her. Deciding she'd seen more than enough, she returned to her own body in an unwise, frantic rush.

Mere seconds after Juliette returned to her own body, Beatrice left the way she had come. Once her mother was gone, Juliette entered the vacant lair. She took a moment to get her bearings then searched through the bottles and found the one she wanted. Beatrice had made so much of the mixture, she surely wouldn't miss a small portion. Whispering a short spell, she conjured a tiny crystal vial then poured a small measure of the brew into it. That done, she left without a backward glance.

Chapter Seventeen

Celina's small room would be more than a little crowded with all of them in it, but it was of vital importance that they all be present that evening, Juliette decided. So she got a message to Will and made certain she and Robert had a plausible excuse to be absent. At the appointed time, she made her way to the tunnels.

"What's this about, Juliette? You know it is very dangerous for us all to meet this way," the prince scolded once everyone arrived.

"Thank you all for coming. I do know the risks and I swear I wouldn't ask except...I've discovered something very important. Something which might well help us defeat Beatrice."

The prince made an expansive gesture. "You perceive us all ears. Do tell."

"It's better if I demonstrate."

She took a dagger standing ready on a side table and pricked her finger. As the blood dripped, she let it fall into a small pewter bowl. "It might be best if you stand back a bit," she advised.

As Will, Celina, Jonathan, Rosalind, and Robert all watched, she took the potion from her pocket and allowed two tiny drops to fall into the bowl to join the blood. For a moment nothing happened, then a dreadful whistling, a high-pitched sound far too akin to a human scream for comfort could be heard. An instant later the contents of the bowl exploded leaving a disproportionate amount of acrid smoke behind.

"What the devil was that?" Will demanded in a sharp tone. He stepped closer and saw that only a blackened circle of oily residue remained in the bowl.

"That is what Beatrice intends to dose your father with if she hasn't already," Juliette informed him grimly.

"Oh gods," Celina breathed.

"We must stop her now. One dose of that and—" Already, Will's hand was on the hilt of his sword.

Juliette held up a hand to forestall him. "Please, majesty, I'd ask you to hear the rest first. I don't believe your father is in immediate danger."

"You don't believe? Unless you are absolutely certain, I'm not willing to risk it."

"Listen, please. She intends to dose him gradually. She means to poison him and make it look as though he has some slow wasting sickness. For you, my prince, it will be battle. That is how she proposes to end you. I have no idea what she has in mind for me, whether it will be as Rosalind's vision foretold or if she'll kill me some other way, but I assure you, she has a very specific plan which she will stick with unless we force her hand."

****

Every muscle tightened as Will fought against the instinct which told him to go and assure himself of his father's safety then wrap his hands around Beatrice's throat and throttle her. Once he gained a modicum of control, he asked, "What do you suggest then?"

"I can create an antidote which we can administer to your father. Let Beatrice dose him as much as she likes after that. No harm will come to him then. After we've captured her, we show this potion to your father. If we can, we prove she added it to his food. Once that is done, she's finished."

"We can't be entirely sure she won't speed things along. Aren't we playing a bit fast and loose with the king's life?" Robert wondered.

Rosalind shook her head. "We have no choice. Juliette's right. She has a plan and unless she is cornered, she'll stick to it. We have almost everything in place. Our own plan to reveal Celina is all but done; this will just add more weight to it. I say we wait."

Will's mouth tightened, but seconds later he relented enough to ask the question uppermost in his mind. "How soon can you concoct this antidote?"

"In less than a day. The poison she has here is a simple one."

"Simple," Rosalind agreed, "but effective."

Will's lips firmed into a determined line. "Do it. Until such time as we can administer the antidote, we take great care. I will taste everything my father's given before it passes his lips."

Robert met Will's gaze. "Majesty, that cannot be. You are the heir to the throne. We cannot risk you."

Will rounded on his friend. "Do you think I value my life above the lives of others, above my own father's? Is my life so much more important because my blood is royal? No, it is not. Nor will I put my father's safety in anyone else's hands."

"Think, Will, think. If she poisons you, we've just made her work that much easier," Rosalind pointed out. "None of us wants that."

"Then who will do it? Who will be my father's

taster? Because someone bloody well must."

"Me of course," Robert stated.

When every face turned to him, each blank with shock, he shrugged. "Next to the prince, it would be easiest for me to accomplish this unobtrusively. I have always been responsible for the prince's safety and while I have never been his or the king's taster before I doubt anyone would bat an eye at the extra precaution given the times we live in."

Straight away, the room erupted with sounds of protest from every quarter.

Chaos reigned for a moment then Robert held up a hand. "It's a reasonable solution. It's our most viable option and it won't be for very long. Thirty-six hours at most, right, Juliette?"

Juliette nodded.

"Well then, there you have it. Just have some antidote standing by for me, just in case," he quipped.

"This is not a joke!" The words were little more than a horrified whisper, but were all the more powerful for that. "If you are going to take it as such, then perhaps I should leave you to mix your own bloody antidote." With no further comment, Juliette turned on her heel and went out.

Robert swore then followed.

"Juliette, wait."

She heard him, Robert knew she did, but she continued walking. She didn't even slow down. Because of the considerable lead she had, he was in the position of chasing her, something which did not put him in the best of moods.

"Can we talk about this?"

Her response was a derisive snort.

Once he caught up with her, he took her arm. "I thought we might discuss this like adults."

She scoffed.

This reply was non-verbal but entirely comprehensible, he decided.

Then she yanked her arm from his and kept walking.

His own temper kindled now, he continued after her. "I see I was wrong." When she never slowed her stride, he decided enough was enough and planted his own feet. "It has to be me Juliette, that's the only way it will work. I am doing this and while I am sorry we didn't get a chance to discuss the matter in private, I do not need your permission." He turned on his heel and headed back the way he had come.

"You think this is about asking my permission? You intend to risk your life to keep the kingdom safe from my mother. My mother. My responsibility. It should be me." She whirled, and struck the rough stone wall of the passageway with her fist. "I know you are right. It can't be me. But does it have to be you?" Breathing heavily, she lowered her forehead to the wall in a posture of utter dejection.

Slowly, he went to her, placed his hand over her still fisted one, fitted his body to hers. "It does. You know it does. I will come out of this alive, I promise, and so shall you."

"Swear it. Swear that when this is all over, you will return, whole and safe. I can't lose you. You are my life."

With gentle hands, he turned her to face him so that she could look into his eyes and see the truth. "By heaven, I swear it."

To seal his vow he gathered her in an embrace to comfort them both and brushed a tender kiss to her lips. For a while they clung to each other, for just another moment they drew strength from each other, then went back to their companions.

****

"Celina, I wanted to talk to you." When all the rest left, the prince stayed behind. He was as serious as she'd ever seen him, so much so that she began to be more than a little concerned herself.

"Of course."

"Are you sure you are all right with the plan? You will be the one most at risk."

For a moment, she studied his face. "It's a risk I am, I won't say eager, but, willing to take. As to being the one most in peril, with respect, I disagree. She might just as easily come after you or Juliette or any one of us."

"Perhaps, but consider, you will be up there, exposed. If there is any part of this plan that you are uncomfortable with, say the word and we will come up with something else."

She smiled at him, her tenderness for him overflowing. She shook her head. "I won't say I'm not afraid. I'd be a fool if I weren't scared, but this is what needs to be done. Oh, and by the way, I'm through letting fear control my life."

"Very well then."

He started to go, but as he did, he heard her voice. "Will I see you tomorrow?"

Without turning, he knew he was lost if he did, he answered, "Perhaps. I will do my best. The risk of discovery is so great. I will try though."

Before he could promise her anything definite, before he could promise her the world, he left her.

****

An hour later, Robert paid a visit to the kitchens. "June, please forgive the intrusion,"

The head cook rose with alacrity and a brisk nod. "It's no intrusion, my lord. How can I help?"

"If we could go somewhere less public? What I have to say, others should not be privy to."

"Of course. This way." June lead him to a small room with a table and two chairs.

"Please sit, my lord, make yourself comfortable. So what can I do for you?"

"What I require most is your sharp eyes, that and your discretion."

Dropping all formality, she replied, "Lord Robert, I've known you since you were in nappies. I even changed yours a time or two. You have both for as long you need. Now what is wrong?"

"I have reason to believe the king's life is in danger. We believe someone will attempt to poison his majesty sometime within the next few days."

June gasped in outrage, but Robert held up a hand to forestall any further comment. "Now we have things in hand, all I need you to do, is to let me know if you see anything strange. Do not approach, do not try to stop it."

"What?"

"I swear on my life that we will make sure the king remains safe. We know where the threat is coming from. Our goal here is to gather proof and we don't want to tip this person off before we can obtain it."

"'This person'? Who? And don't tell me you don't

know."

"June, it would be better for you if you didn't know."

June shook her head and her stern face became downright stubborn and implacable. "You cannot expect me to allow someone to poison my table without at the very least, knowing who."

"June, it's too dangerous."

She waved his concern away. "Dangerous. Humph. There's no need to be a hero. I can take care of myself. Spit it out or I'll have no choice but to go straight to the king."

Robert sighed even as he admitted to a secret admiration for the woman. "Very well. Beatrice Dubois."

June's eyes widened then narrowed in speculation. "Can't say I'm altogether surprised. There's just something about that one. You think she's prepared to go that far?"

"I do."

"Well, that's enough for me then. I'll keep my eyes open."

He sipped the tea June offered him then fell to studying the tiny, neat office. Ledgers for recording household expenses sat in tidy stacks on the second-hand desk; the small window high up the wall let in much needed sunlight, and cheerful white daisies sat in a squat blue vase on a little shelf behind her. As he set the cup aside, he turned his attention back to his companion. "One final thing, when I need you to back me with the king, will you back me?"

"You can be certain I will."

"Good." He rose then she did as well. "June, you

are a treasure." He grasped both of her hands and kissed her cheek.

Her color rose, but all she said was, "Oh, get along with you."

Robert chuckled and headed for the door.

"My lord?"

"Hmm?"

"Watch your back."

Robert nodded. "You do the same."

****

Beatrice decided to implement her plan to poison the king that next night. Just a drop or two to start with, added to a bottle of his favorite vintage, which he shared with others only on rare occasions, and she would be well on her way to having everything she could possibly want.

It had been ridiculously simple to arrange. She approached a young scullery maid, spelled her to poison the king's wine at dinner and waited. All went well enough until Robert acted as taster. Could he suspect? She shrugged. Even if he did, there would be no proof. The toxin was undetectable unless you knew what to look for.

After one moment, fraught with tension that Beatrice couldn't honestly say she was averse to, Robert handed the wine on to the king. Content, Beatrice sipped from her own goblet and enjoyed her meal.

****

"How do you feel?" Juliette murmured, as Robert returned to his place beside her.

"I am fine so far. Your antidote worked."

This statement did nothing to ease her tension, but

when he took her hand and tried to find the right words, the right actions to reassure her, her frightened heart eased a fraction.

"Relax, the toxin works fast. If it were going to affect me it would have by now. I'm clear. Which means so is the king."

He would be all right. For the first time since June had reported the strange actions of the scullery maid, she truly believed it. Hiding the all-encompassing, bone deep relief she experienced then was perhaps the most difficult thing she had ever done in her life.

"Thank the gods for that." Those few words were all she could manage.

Beneath the table, he grasped her hand. "Yes, now just try to act like everything is normal. We don't want to make her suspicious."

"Right."

"Are we quite sure she isn't already?" Juliette followed Will's glance, studied her mother. Beatrice chatted with those near her at table and showed no apparent signs of distress.

"She has no idea. If she did, she'd never be able to behave in any way close to normal believe me," Juliette said.

"Good. Then we're a go for tomorrow night. I want this over. I want her over, once and for all," Will stated coldly.

****

Celina hadn't expected to see Will again that evening, but there he was all the same. She couldn't say she was sorry. "Should you be here? What if you were followed? We're so close I wouldn't want anything to mess up-" Without warning, she found herself unable to speak. With his lips firmly pressed to hers, forming a coherent thought, much less words, was difficult.

After a long while, he lifted his head. "Last night I could scarcely bear to leave you. We have no idea what might happen tomorrow. I had to see you. There are things I need to say to you."

She regarded him for a moment then sighed. "Because you might not get another chance."

It was a statement, not a question, but he nodded all the same then took a deep breath. "From the moment, I saw you, I loved you, but it was not until you were in jeopardy that I understood I would do anything to protect you. You are as much a part of me as my own limbs or my own heart. You are the only woman I would have for my queen." He dropped to one knee beside her. "Celina Dubois, will you do me the honor of becoming my wife?"

When she did not respond immediately, he continued, "I realize we do not know each other well, but we could have as long an engagement as you wish. I swear I will cherish you as my beautiful spouse and queen. Say yes. Be my wife and rule at my side."

Celina had to take a deep breath; she shook so badly, but at last she found her voice. "Yes, I will marry you. I will try…I will endeavor to deserve you."

"And I you, my queen."

He slipped the most beautiful jewel she had ever seen onto her finger. The large marquis-cut emerald in its simple setting was not traditional, but it was elegant, lovely, and suited her very well.

"It fits," he grinned and kissed her long, slim fingers. "I had it specially made for you."

"It's wonderful. I can't tell you; I don't have the

words. None except these: you are my prince, my life, and I love you with my whole heart. Always."

He took her into his arms and kissed her and she knew that kiss would live in her memory forever.

****

The passage was damp and dark as well as one of the most foreboding she had ever encountered. Beatrice loved it as much as she loved the space she had created for herself. What she treasured most, however, was the isolation of the entire area. She could practice her magic in complete privacy. The value of such a place of safety could not be overestimated in her opinion. So when she heard voices, she wasn't alarmed, she was furious. How dare anyone encroach on her chosen domain? Fury, always her first response, was instinctive and potent.

She was a hairsbreadth away from rushing the intruders and damaging them, perhaps permanently, when the cooler aspect of her personality prevailed. Who were they? What were they doing here? Did their presence have anything to do with her or did it have to do with something or someone else entirely? Perhaps she ought to get some answers before she killed them.

To that end, she followed the voices to their source. What she found was two men conversing in low tones with two others on guard duty.

"She all right today?" The dark-haired, middle-aged man asked with mild interest.

One with blond curly hair nodded. "Hmm, if a bit restless. Who could blame her, locked up in here?"

"Well, better locked up than in the hands of that viper Lady Dubois and it won't be for much longer. The ball starts in a few hours," a third commented as he pushed bright red hair from his brow.

"Thank the gods," the older man put in. "Waiting around like this isn't safe and it isn't smart. I told his majesty I disliked the whole plan from the beginning." He cast one sour look at the door in front of him then turned back to his companion, a young man of perhaps twenty, with hair black as a raven's wing.

"Oh stop belly aching, Corm. You 'dislike' anything that requires the least bit of balls," the blond one complained.

Corm just grunted.

"Are you two here to relieve us or what?" Red head demanded.

The blond, eager as a young puppy, stood to attention. "Glass and Cormarthen here to begin guard duty, sir."

"Brandywine and Lewis standing down."

Interesting. It was obvious to her that Will's men were guarding someone. A woman, but who? Even more importantly, why? The answer took only a moment to dawn on her. Celina. The prince had her. How he performed this remarkable feat was a mystery, but she had far more pressing questions on her mind. Why wait to reveal her? Why lock her away for safekeeping? The answer to that she would discover soon, and she would have it from the prince's own lips, she vowed. For now, however, she would take back what belonged to her. Celina would not ruin everything, not when she was so close to having all she desired.

Beatrice waited until the two called Brandywine and Lewis vacated the area. Then, calling on her magic, she sent it toward Glass and Cormarthen. The effect was instantaneous and the two men froze where they stood. Time stopped for them. She studied them a moment, glad to have the chance to practice her new skill.

Striding past them both, she tried the door, but found it locked and barred. Hissing, she lifted a hand already filled with icy green flame and directed it at the lock, then fell back a full step when the flame hit the door. A bright blue force field burst into view upon contact, blazed for several seconds, repelled the flame then faded.

By the looks of it Juliette was responsible for this. Magic always left traces and whenever any conjurer practiced magic a unique imprint remained. This was her daughter's signature and no one else's. One small spurt of pride was all she allowed herself as she considered her daughter's skill. That emotion was soon eclipsed by rage that said skill was turned against her now.

So the girl Celina was protected, not only by human guards, but by magic as well. Pity. Beatrice shrugged. Not for long. Nothing could hold out against her for long. In the meantime she would discover what exactly was going on. It was plain to her that a plan was in the works and she would find it out. Done for the moment, she concealed herself then released the guards so they were none the wiser.

Because her senses were heightened, because she was looking for it or perhaps because her instinct for self-preservation was terrifyingly acute, Beatrice spotted him. He kept a discreet distance of course and if she had not been expecting something of the kind she might never have known he was there but as things were…

Decision made, she turned on her heel and started down the deserted hallway toward the young fellow. She would have certain questions answered and she would do whatever it took to make that happen. Stepping back into an alcove, she waited for him to approach.

As the man tailing her walked right past her, she came out into the open. "Well, hello. Avery, isn't it?"

Startled but adept at hiding it, he whirled to face her then bowed after the merest hesitation. "My lady, I am at your service."

"Oh, how lovely," Beatrice declared. "Could you answer a question for me then, Lord Avery?"

"I will do so to the best of my ability. How might I assist you?"

She stepped closer, rubbed the fabric of his open-necked shirt between finger and thumb before brushing her slim digits over his skin. "I wonder what on earth you might be doing in this part of the castle?"

"I was sent to fetch the prince's favorite brandy, but I've gotten a bit turned around."

He tried for a charming, befuddled demeanor, but Beatrice wasn't buying it at all. She rolled her bright green eyes and made a tsking sound. "I don't think so. Try again." To emphasize her point, she stepped closer.

"In truth, you, Lady Dubois, are the most beautiful woman I've ever set eyes on. When you left the great hall, I followed hoping for a chance to…engage you in conversation as a precursor to perhaps someday winning your affections."

"Insolent boy, I might have believed that if you weren't one of Will's men." In a move almost invisible to the naked eye, she closed the remaining distance between them then simultaneously raised her hand, palm filled with green flame. "Last chance."

One tiny bead of sweat slid down his temple now, the one sign of how panicked he was. "I-I am attracted to you, but it's more than that. I believe you would make an excellent ruler, a far better monarch than King Henry."

Beatrice laughed. "You really are a monumentally bad liar. The prince keeps men about him whose loyalty to the royal family is unquestioned. Every child in Camston knows that."

Avery shrugged. "The prince is very trusting. I was able to slip past his guard. I assure you I'm a better liar than you think. I'm better at a lot of things than you might suppose."

She caught the hand that was running up her arm, all but flung it aside. "Not likely. You're very pretty, but don't you know that when you are lying it's best to stick, as close to the truth as possible? I suppose you won't get the chance to learn now." She tilted her head, considered him. "You've also ceased to amuse me."

With her hand before his face, she engulfed it in foggy green mist and subdued his will to hers. When she was sure it was done, she put him to the question.

"Why are you following me?"

The struggle within was plain to see on his face. But, magic won over his own will and when he spoke his voice was dull and lifeless, not his own. "Dangerous woman, Prince Will said. Possible treason. Mustn't let her out of our sight. Mustn't let harpy see us."

"Since when and for how long?" When he paused and struggled again, she amped up her power. "How long?" she repeated.

"Followed for the last few days. Must continue until after the ball tonight," he intoned.

"What happens then?"

"Don't know. Prince didn't say. Just wants us ready to do our duty whatever it might be."

"The girl you and your compatriots are guarding, who else knows she's here?"

The words came easy now. "Only six of us know aside from the prince himself. We take guard duty in shifts of two. We were sworn to silence on pain of death."

"Who brought her? How did she come to be here?"

"The prince and Lord Robert smuggled her in real secret-like. We deemed it suspicious in the extreme, but only Glass had the audacity to question him. When he did, the prince said it would be for a short time and that it was for the lady's protection. When the lady confirmed this we agreed. We knew at least that while she was under our care no harm would come to her. Still, we did wonder."

"I'm sure you did. One last question, what does the prince intend to do with her?"

"No idea. He joked about taking her to the ball. An unknown woman he's keeping locked away and he's taking her to the biggest fete of the season, possibly ever? Weird."

"Indeed." She stared into his blank eyes then stroked a gentle hand down his cheek. "You've served me well, Lord Avery. A quick death shall be your reward."

As she was about to dispatch him, she heard footsteps.

"Avery, where are you?"

As the man drew nearer, Beatrice tensed. She couldn't afford to kill Avery now, not and have his body immediately discovered. The prince must not know she was on to him, but if an unexplained dead body was found panic would ensue before she could exact her revenge. She also couldn't knock him unconscious and not expect the same result. Grabbing his head firmly in both hands, she stared unblinking into his eyes, said the words of an ancient spell which would wipe away the memory of the last few moments. For good measure, she added, "You will forget you saw me here. Forget we spoke. You were detained, but you are ready to stand guard now. That is all anyone ever need know. You understand?"

"Yes," he mumbled.

"Good. Now go join your friend."

"You were supposed to meet me in the guardroom. You'd better be here and not skipping out somewhere," Glass called out.

"I'm not skipping out anywhere, Richard. I was just detained. It was unavoidable," Avery explained as he joined the other man.

"Detained. Who was she this time?"

Avery just grinned. "Wouldn't you like to know?" He clapped the other man on the back as they headed down the corridor and out of earshot.

Chapter Eighteen

As soon as it was safe, Beatrice headed in the opposite direction, toward what she thought of as her private sanctum. For a space of time, rational thought was beyond her. They were trying to thwart her! A thing no one had even attempted in years. The unutterable audacity! The gall! Fools, to think they would ever manage it. She would be their queen and they would regret ever endeavoring to stop her, of that she would make quite certain. They would discover that the consequences of crossing her would be quite severe.

When the red haze in front of her eyes cleared, she discovered smashed objects strewn everywhere. Books, ripped and tattered, in piles on the floor, shattered glass mixed with unidentifiable liquids and powders and her work table on its side was just the beginning. She looked about, bemused, unable to remember doing any of it, but knowing full well she must have. It had been a long time since she had lost control of her temper so completely.

Breathing heavily, she tried to calm herself. Her head still reeled, she had to admit, but her next move was critical. It was vital she think past the rage to figure out what her next step should be. Celina was here and protected by magic. She'd bet her life, the prince, Juliette and Robert, were involved. Rosalind at the very least had been incompetent if not downright complicit, about Celina's escape. The girl was theirs and they could do whatever they liked with her. So, why hadn't she, Beatrice, been arrested for treason? The lot of them knew what she had done. They knew Juliette was not who she purported to be. Her daughter would have told the prince and the gods alone knew who else, that she had been coerced. Yet here she was, still at large. It made no sense at all and raised many questions.

Slowly, her wild, unmitigated raged coalesced into one single sphere of energy bright as a lightning bolt and the core of an idea formed. All their plans centered on the ball. Well, she had a few of her own and she could make more, starting with ones involving Robert. Since she couldn't get to Celina or Juliette, the delectable Lord Robert would be the key to Juliette's undoing.

In the normal course of things, her younger daughter was little more than a drab mouse, easily cowed, unless she took it into her head to be stubborn. On those rare occasions she morphed into a quietly determined force of nature. Juliette was determined to hold on to Robert, but at what cost? How far would she go to protect him? To the ends of the earth, Beatrice was beginning to suspect. With Robert under her control, she could force her daughter to do anything and wouldn't that be a nice change.

She would use Robert to lure Juliette, the others would follow and she would deal with each of them one by one. First Celina, then the prince. Robert would be next. If Juliette still refused to yield, they would die slowly and painfully right before her daughter's very eyes. Of course, then her task would be far harder, marrying Juliette to the king rather than his son would be difficult, but Juliette would be made to do it, if it came to that. Then she, Beatrice Forbes Dubois, last of her name, would destroy her youngest child.

Things would not happen precisely as she'd originally planned, but she would make do. She would have to move fast, far faster than she would have liked, if she was to manage it all, but she wasn't averse to keeping several balls in the air at once so long as she got what she wanted.

For good measure, she would also punish her eldest for allowing Celina to escape in the first place. If not for Rosalind's lack of vigilance, none of this would have happened. Once she was ensconced on the throne and safe, she would summon the girl and learn from her how the escape had occurred. The foolish chit's incompetence would ruin all of her plans if she weren't careful. Lesson learned, she supposed. Never leave important matters to underlings.

****

Hours later, Beatrice entered the audience chamber with Juliette. The place had been turned into a ballroom for the evening, just as it had been some weeks ago, when the prince and that brat Celina had met. Torches in sconces on the walls and strategically placed candelabra had the chamber bathed in a soft glow. Musicians stationed at the back of the hall near the dais played a waltz. A host of ladies clad in elegant gowns of bright colors mingled among gentlemen more soberly dressed in their formal evening attire. Diamonds and other jewels sparkled on throats exposed by the low cut necklines that were fashionable. This would all be hers, she vowed. She would not let it go. With that thought uppermost in her mind, she made some excuse and slipped away to an unoccupied parlor.

Jaw firming, she passed a hand over her face. Her features changed from aristocratic to more commonplace. Her hair, a rich ebony she had passed on to her eldest daughter, faded to a dull mouse brown. With her height lessened by several inches and her weight increased by two stone, she deemed herself quite unrecognizable. No one would suspect she wasn't what she appeared to be: a matron of a certain age somewhere in the rank of middle gentry. The look in her eyes might give her away if someone studied her too closely but who would spend a thought on one so plain as herself? Pleased, she spent the time left to her considering the rest of her arrangements.

Once dressed in an obtrusive gown she had commandeered from an unsuspecting servant and a hooded cloak which she had earlier secreted in a small private parlor near the audience chamber to avoid detection, she started back. Coupling this disguise with the simple expedient of the glamour, Beatrice hoped to remain unrecognizable and unobserved. She eluded her daughter easily enough, at any rate. She got into position in the south corner of the chamber and awaited her moment. The last few hours had been torture, but that was all but over now. Very soon Robert would appear and she could put her well-honed, contingency plan into action.

As she peered about trying to see everything and everyone from all possible vantage points, she was shocked to find Rosalind stationed in the southwest corner of the room. On full alert now, she searched each face and found another familiar one. Her bloody steward, Jack or Jason or something, was at the southeast end. With Robert in the northwest area at last, and the prince at true north, that accounted for them all. By the gods, they were all here and waiting for her. Well they would get far more than they bargained for, she would make certain of that.

After some swift revision of her plans, she headed in Robert's direction with unerring purpose. Let the games begin.

****

The door to the withdrawing room where he waited to make his entrance opened then at the sound of approaching footsteps, Henry turned then stiffened. Through teeth clenched in a ghastly smile, he demanded, "Who might I ask is this and where is Lady Forbes?"

Will took a deep breath. This was the moment, now or never. Either his father would support him or he would not. Either he would force him to wed a woman he did not love or he would not. Either his father would imprison him for disobedience and treason, or he would not. "She is in the crowd. There's a lot I need to tell you, Father, but for now, will you accept that this is the woman I danced with and this is indeed the woman I wish to wed?"

Henry studied his son's face for a long moment. Then he transferred his scrutiny to Celina. "Do you love him?" His manner was brusque, his tone more so, but there was deep affection for his only son behind it.

"I do indeed. So very much."

"He loves you for sure and certain otherwise he would not have gone to all this trouble to find you."

"Would you do any less for the woman you love?"

This surprised a short bark of a laugh from him.

"Touché, my dear. Touché. You and I might just get on." Turning back to face his son, he continued, "And what does Juliette Forbes say about all of this? The loss of her prince must, of course, have left her desolate."

"By no means, Father. She loves Lord Robert, never me. She never wished... She was under duress and—"

Henry's already thunderous expression darkened still further. "Beatrice," he spat. "Of course. Where is she, Will?"

"She's also in the crowd and won't be going anywhere. Will you trust me to deal with her for now? I have a plan, one that will ensnare her, but I need just a little more time."

"For what it's worth, I've always trusted you, son. Very well. Bring me her head at the earliest opportunity then."

Clearing his throat, Henry turned back to Celina, reached for her hand then his son's, joined the two. "Well, Will, I can't say I approve of the way you went about it, but if you are satisfied at last in your choice of bride then so am I."

Will beamed. "I am most satisfied, majesty, and would beg your leave to announce the happy news as planned."

Henry agreed. "By all means."

****

"What do you mean, she's gone?" Will asked Robert.

"What I said, she's gone. She told Juliette she needed to speak to some minor lord, but she slipped away using magic. Juliette's beside herself. If Beatrice used magic, she wouldn't have felt a thing until it was too late. She will blame herself now."

Will closed his eyes in supplication to any gods who might listen. "As well she might. The success of this plan depends in large part on us being able to contain Beatrice."

"I know. She is well and truly cloaked. I have my people looking for her, but this castle is the largest building in Camston. Not to mention all of the outbuildings, the land itself. It'll take time."

"Quite. Just do it. When you find her, let me know."

"Of course, majesty. What about the rest of the plan?"

Will considered for a moment. "We go ahead with it just as arranged. We no longer have the element of surprise and that's a real problem, but if we are lucky, what we intend to do will still draw her out."

"Very well, sire," Robert replied and rushed to do his prince's bidding.

****

Robert stationed himself at his assigned post again and waited. The audience chamber was large and so he was able to edge away from the crowd and stand in a semi-private alcove near an adjoining corridor. He wondered whether the night would be an entire waste and had to admit this was a very real possibility. Since he couldn't be sure of that, however, he continued to watch for anything or anyone remotely suspicious.

"Stay still or I will gut you before you can make a sound," Beatrice whispered right into Robert's ear.

He froze as instructed, encouraged to do so by the knife in his back.

"What do you want?"

"Well, you, obviously. I need leverage with my daughter. You're it."

"Leverage?"

Beatrice nodded. "Don't be dense. My fool of a daughter thinks she's in love with you. Ergo, as long as I have you, she'll do everything I say."

"You're wrong. She doesn't *think* she's in love with me—she is—which is why the last thing she wants to do is marry the prince. Even so, if that were all, if it were only her own heart and mine at stake, then she might consent to wed him. But such a sacrifice won't save the kingdom from you, it'll destroy it. She won't throw away everything just to watch you obliterate all the royal family has built here. Still less will she let innocent people die. She will never agree."

"Oh? I can be very persuasive as you have cause to know. Now, be quiet," she whispered.

Robert ignored her and kept right on talking. "What's more, none of us—and by us I mean Prince Will, Juliette, Rosalind, Celina, Jonathan and myself—will let it happen."

"You think it's your choice to make? I assure you, it isn't."

"Beatrice, I hate to be the one to tell you this but… it's over." After a moment, he laughed. "Actually, I lied. I'm glad I'm the one who gets the honor. The king will soon be informed of your treachery, as will the entire kingdom. Because you see, we have all the proof we need: Proof of you spelling the shoe, of you forcing your daughter to play out this charade and take Celina's place, of your plans to murder the royal family, of your plans to take the throne for yourself, all of it. Your daughter will never be queen. Nor will you. You are beaten. Just accept it."

She scoffed. "Accept it? No, I think not. You and your merry band don't hold all the cards. Now, unless you want all these innocent people hurt, you'll move, keeping it slow and quiet, toward that hallway there." She tilted her head to indicate a passage some fifty feet to their right.

When he refused to budge, she pushed the knife into skin then showed him her other hand, green-flamed and stinking of the dark magic she held in her palm. "You see this? I could kill you with it. In an instant or with agonizing slowness, the choice is yours. Co-operate and perhaps I'll let you die quickly."

His utter lack of reaction to that statement had her letting out a hiss of frustration. "Perhaps other methods of persuasion might be more effective. I could lock everyone in the great hall and set it aflame in moments for example. Is that what you want?"

What he wanted was to break her neck right then and there. It would be so easy and so very satisfying. He could hear the snap of it echo in his head, but he couldn't be sure she wouldn't do damage on her way down. He couldn't take the risk, so he forced his feet to move. She led him to a small private parlor just off the main hall. Once inside, she used magic to close and bolt the door behind them without ever taking the knife away from his back.

"Now what?" He couldn't help but ask the question, although he regretted the impulse almost as soon as the words were out of his mouth.

Now we wait. Turn around," she ordered. He obeyed then gazed at her. "Once she realizes you are nowhere to be found, she'll come looking, not to worry." She glanced over, gauging his height and weight. "In the meantime, I had best secure you."

Before he could even think to resist, she magically locked his hands. A heartbeat later, he was in the air and looking down on his captor.

"Is she tuned to you, I wonder?" She eyed him, head tilted like a curious bird. "If you were to be injured, let's say, would she come running?"

Robert swallowed hard. The eager, almost hungry look on her face made his blood run cold as much as it sickened him, but he'd be damned if he'd let her see how much. "She can't sense me if I block her. She taught me how to do that you see, just in case of an occasion like this. If you think I'll let you use me as bait any more than you already have, you are sadly mistaken. I'll die before I'll call her to me," he vowed.

Beatrice's eyes hardened and her chin took on a determined set. "How very noble. Do you have any notion of what I can do to you, Robert? I swear by all the gods, before I'm through, you'll plead to do whatever I ask of you. Then you'll beg for death. Once I'm done with you, I might, if I'm feeling generous, oblige."

She lifted a hand and sent green fire to engulf him. She used her power to lift him higher into the air and lock all his limbs spread-eagle. His scream filled the room and his last conscious thought was he was grateful Juliette was not there to hear.

****

As she mingled with the crowd, Juliette waited for her mother to wreak havoc. When nothing at all untoward happened, the sick feeling of dread in her gut increased tenfold. She looked to the northwest side of the hall, seeking Robert's reassuring presence as if by instinct. The position designated for him was empty. Their meticulous plan called for Robert to be in the crowd awaiting Beatrice yet he was nowhere to be seen. Just as alarming, if not infinitely more so, her mother had disappeared while her attention was elsewhere.

"She's gone! She must've used magic. I never realized. I thought she would always be within sight of one of us and if I attempted to stop her from going across the room she might get suspicious so I let her go, but now she's nowhere to be seen. Robert's isn't in position and I can't reach him telepathically anymore. I just spoke with him, told him Beatrice would be out of my eye-line for a moment and now she's gone; he's shielded, blocked. Can you spot him?" she mentally said to her sister on the other side of the room.

"Sorry, I can't. I don't see either of them," Rosalind replied, also by telepathy.

Alarm streaked through Juliette faster than lightning. "We need to call a halt. Something's wrong."

"No. We don't know that. Until we are sure, we do the best we can without him. She may still show."

"Rosalind—"

"Listen, Juliette, she might have him stashed somewhere, in fact, I'd say it's a good bet she does, but we won't know where unless we capture her. This, here and now, is our best chance to do that."

"He could be hurt. He could be dying. I—" Her every instinct was screaming at her to go after him, but she fought the impulse back and tried to think things through rationally. "He's not dead. I'd know." Of that she was unshakably certain. "So maybe she wants him for leverage. She wants me. Oh, gods, Rosalind, she took him to get to me." Bone-deep terror coupled with rising hysteria threatened to overwhelm her.

"Probably," Rosalind agreed. The calm in her sister's tone could not reach Juliette. "If she does show, I will need your help. If she doesn't, I swear I'll help you look for him and I won't stop until we find him. But right now, I need you to stick to the plan. Okay?"

Juliette shook her head. "If he dies, I can't live with that."

"And if countless other innocents die? You can live with that? I can't." Her sister's mental voice was cold and sharp as a knife's edge.

"I'll worry about everyone else in this bloody world later. Right this moment, I have to get to him. I have to get to him now!"

"No! You have to stick to the plan. It's almost over; just hold on a few moments longer. Please." She took her sister's silence as assent and turned her attention to the top of the room.

****

The prince stepped forward to address the lords and ladies. "My people, I have called you here to share glorious news. I have, at long last, chosen a bride. I present to you, Lady Celina Dubois, your future queen."

The entire crowd sent up a joyous roar, but Juliette could do little to conceal her tension. This was the moment they feared because it was the most likely moment for Beatrice to make her move. With her nowhere to be found, it was all but certain.

When the presentation continued without incident, Juliette was positive her mother had abducted her lover.

The people had their future queen and they were

beyond ecstatic. Behind her, the noise of celebration escalated yet she did not register it as she barreled through the crowd. Celina was, at long last, with her prince, but Juliette had to find her own. Her beautiful Lord Robert, her protector, what had her mother done to him? As her bodyguard, he was always near unless she and the prince were alone. In the past several days, he had not let her out of his sight for more than a minute or two at a time and had said he would not leave her until the plan was a success. Yet now he was nowhere to be found. Only her mother could be responsible.

The fates were with her and she noticed the distinctive green of her sister's dress disappear around a corner. Rosalind would find their mother, as promised.

****

Rosalind had not expected to discover her mother, at least not so soon. Still less had she expected Robert to be held imprisoned ten feet in the air. The distinctive sound of a dagger being unsheathed brought her back to an awareness of her own predicament. She looked to her left to see her sister at her side, knife at the ready and in the very act of running in. Rosalind grabbed Juliette's arm. "Sister, wait!"

Juliette rounded on her. "Wait?! Robert is in there. She has him and I'll not stay my hand another moment. Get the prince, get Jonathan, mobilize the castle guards, bring whoever you must, but I'll not stand by and watch this happen."

With that she was gone, leaving Rosalind to do as she was commanded.

"Jonathan, I need you." As she ran back down the passageway toward the ballroom, the message she sent was simple and to the point. Thankfully, telepathy could convey all the emotional nuances one could desire. So every bit of her frustration and alarm must have gotten through as he was with her in seconds.

"What's happened? Where's Robert?" The demand was short and curt.

"Beatrice has him."

"What? You're sure? Do you know which way they went?"

"As sure as I can be, having seen them both with my own eyes in the first room you come to down that corridor there."

When she indicated a passage some little distance away, Jonathan turned to go, no further explanation needed, but Rosalind caught his arm.

"No, I need you to remain here. Bring the prince as soon as may be, but make certain Celina stays well away no matter what."

"No, I'm with you."

Much as that statement and even more the look in his eyes thrilled her to her toes, Rosalind shook her head. "The prince needs to be warned."

"So we'll warn him." His face set into the stubborn lines with which she was growing all too familiar.

"No, Juliette has already gone after our mother. We will need all the sorcery we can muster to defeat her. Now we can continue to argue about this, but every second we waste is one second closer to people dying and one of them could be my sister."

"Rosalind—"

Out of patience and out of time, she said the one thing she knew would trump his every objection. "I need you to do this for me. Please."

He still looked desperate to argue, but finally had to give it up. "All right ," he agreed. "But I want you to promise you won't do anything crazy, at least not without me there to catch you."

Her every muscle stiffened. "Do I seem at all incapable to you?"

"No. You know very well that's not at all what I meant," he protested.

"Wasn't it?" She shook her head and turned to leave. "You're wasting time. Go."

When he whirled her back to him, she had one moment of startled clarity then lost herself in his kiss. Hot and bright, it was over almost as soon as it had begun.

"Stay alive until I come for you."

"You do the same."

He let her go and she rushed to meet her fate.

Chapter Nineteen

The scene that met Juliette's gaze when she entered the private parlor was one straight from a nightmare. Robert, her lover, was entrapped.

"Mother, release him. Now," she ordered in a deadly calm voice.

"Juliette, get out of here. I won't have her hurt you." Robert begged.

"Be quiet, Robert, this is between my mother and me."

"Juliette," he pleaded again.

She spared him one glance, just one, but that was enough to break her heart. He was battered and beaten, and blood trickled from a split lower lip, but his fierce spirit remained unbroken. Yet for the first time, there was true fear in his eyes, not for himself she knew, but for her. That she would not countenance. Her mother would pay for every moment of pain she had caused, to Celina, Rosalind, Jonathan, the prince, herself, but most especially to Robert.

"You will release him," she repeated.

Her mother threw back her head and laughed. "You think so? Why on earth would I release the delectable Robert when I at last have the means of controlling you?" Beatrice circled her captive then glanced back at Juliette. "Just look at the two of you, so foolish, so vulnerable. From the moment I saw you with him I knew he was your Achilles heel and vice-versa. Your love has made you weak, daughter." Without warning, she sent a bolt of energy toward Robert.

As it struck him, he howled with pain.

Juliette shrieked, "No! Stop!" It was herself she found stopped, however. When she rushed forward, she discovered her mother's magic prevented her from going any closer. "What are you doing?" she demanded once she could speak.

"I'm helping you. Your love has made you weak," Beatrice reiterated, as if explaining that one and one equals two. She stepped close enough to her daughter to whisper in her ear, "Be strong and we can rule together. Finish him. Use what's in you. I know you want to."

For one awful moment, Juliette did want that, so much. She wanted to use her magic, not on her betrothed but on her own mother. Her desire to use her gift to harm became almost overwhelming, so much so that she began to shake with it. It was her love alone which allowed her to master that urge. Love for Robert and her sisters, even for Beatrice herself. In spite of everything, Beatrice was her mother after all. Trembling, she stepped back from all the older woman offered. "No," she stated in a firm, decisive tone. "I won't use what I am to harm. Not even to harm you. If you think I would ever use it to harm the man I love, then you don't know me."

"You would throw it all away? Crown, kingdom, prince? You would toss all of it out? Over him?" her mother asked in wonder.

"All that and more," she said, voice rock-steady now.

"Then die with him, for you are no daughter of

mine." Her mother turned from Robert to her.

"Mother, let him go right now," she ordered.

"Juliette, get out of here," he begged again. "I won't have her kill you."

Looking away from him, she shook her head. "I won't let her harm you."

He closed his eyes then opened them again as pain scorched him and he screamed. "Go! I can face my own death but I'll be damned if I'll accept yours. Leave me!"

Juliette shook her head. "Never. Not while I am alive."

****

Will and Celina were enjoying their first dance as a betrothed couple when Jonathan approached them. The music was just ending and under cover of the ensuing applause, Jonathan drew the prince aside. "Forgive the interruption, majesty, but you'd best come."

Will studied Jonathan's face for a long moment. "I have not known you for long, but I'll take you at your word. Give me a moment."

The prince stepped once again to the top of the room and raised a hand to gain everyone's attention. "Forgive me, but there is a matter of great importance my queen and I must attend to. Everyone please, continue to enjoy your evening."

Ignoring the gasps and murmurs from the crowd, not to mention the shocked exclamations of his father, he took Celina's arm and headed for the nearest exit. Belatedly, Jonathan followed.

"What happened?" Will demanded as soon as they were out of earshot.

"Robert never showed. Beatrice has him. Juliette

and Rosalind both went after them."

Will didn't even bother to curse; there wasn't enough time. "Which way did they go?"

"Toward the south passage."

He kissed Celina's hand, intending to leave her behind, but she clung.

"Wait. What are you planning to do?"

"I plan to find her and stop her. I need you to stay with Jonathan where you'll be safe."

"With all due respect, sire, no. I have cowered before that woman for half my life, but I won't anymore. Not ever again. I won't say I'm not terrified to face her now, but where you go, I go."

"Celina, I understand and believe me I appreciate the sentiment, but—"

"I am to be your queen, am I not?"

In that moment, with her eyebrows raised and her bearing regal as any woman's he'd ever seen, he'd never been prouder of her. And he'd never wanted her more. The need to protect her was all at once in direct opposition with the desire to have this amazing woman at his side in everything. As was often the case when it came to Celina, his desire won. He inclined his head in supplication. "As you command, my queen." He turned his attention back to Jonathan, who was straining with impatience.

"This way, majesty," he said, indicating a corridor to their left.

****

The scene which met Rosalind's eyes was worse than any she had feared. Robert was ten feet in the air, bleeding and semi-conscious. Her sister sprawled out on the floor, receiving the full brunt of Beatrice's power. Juliette's every muscle tensed in a rictus of pain and her sister's echoing screams would haunt Rosalind for the rest of her life.

"Free them both. Now. In fact, if you cause even one more person one more second of pain, I swear by all the gods, I will end you. Personally, I hope you make a try for it. Give me a reason to kill you. Please."

Without bothering to speak, Beatrice raised a magic-filled hand. But Rosalind was faster. She raised her own and sent a silvery blue wave of energy straight to her mother. It never reached its target. Beatrice raised her shields; barely withstanding her daughter's onslaught.

"While Juliette would never use her gift to harm you, believe me when I say I have no such compunction."

When Beatrice made an instinctive movement back toward her prey, Rosalind cautioned, "Don't move another inch. You're dead if you try."

Beatrice hissed, but she stilled.

****

When Juliette returned to her senses, she fervently wished she had not. Like an old woman with aches in every bone, Juliette got to her feet and despite the blinding pain in her head she could see Rosalind and Beatrice were at each other's throats, almost literally. Rosalind was barely holding her own. Juliette called up her own magic, more than she ever had before, more than she even knew she possessed then sent it all toward her mother. She added her power to her sister's and strengthened the barrage against their mother's shield. A storm of energy, a whirlwind of enchantment shot in Beatrice's direction.

Her mother's shield rippled and they redoubled their efforts. Rosalind sent all she had, holding nothing back for her own defense and finally the shield cracked. It fractured, in one small spot at first then the miniscule fissures spread and, like a pretty piece of glass, it shattered. Rosalind sent a wave of magic at her mother while Juliette conjured a whip of power which pierced her mother's already splintered shield. The whip wrapped snakelike around Beatrice's hand, raised to deliver what might well have been a killing blow.

A shocked stare at her restrained hand held Beatrice transfixed for a moment. Then she turned to her younger daughter and blasted Juliette with magic.

Undaunted, Juliette put up her own shield and shifted her position. Circling ever closer to Robert, she kept her guard up as she made her way around. Beatrice tried to block her but it was too late. With a spell and a burst of sorcery, Juliette freed her lover then shielded him with an enchantment of her own as best she could. With Robert severely injured but alive and as protected as she could make him, she shifted her focus back to her mother.

****

Will entered with Celina and Jonathan close behind. Without taking her attention from her mother for even a second, Rosalind registered their presence.

Jonathan began to head toward Rosalind but the prince restrained him. "Trust me."

Will had to resist his own similar protective impulses. The desire to sweep Celina from the room along with Juliette and Rosalind while he and Jonathan dealt with Beatrice was strong, but he fought it back. Aside from all else, their right to see justice done, perhaps even mete out a bit of it themselves being one serious consideration, the ladies were essential if they were to accomplish Beatrice's confinement. There was no getting around that simple fact. No mere participants, Beatrice's daughters and stepdaughter were to be the instruments of her capture. So they had to remain in the very thick of danger, despite his wishes. "Lady Rosalind, Lady Juliette before you take any further action, you will explain."

A long moment passed then calm and collected, Juliette inquired, "What would you have us do with this traitor, your majesty?"

Beatrice adopted her usual confident manner and began, "Sire, you cannot believe this. My daughters are both deranged. Surely—"

"Silence! Lady Beatrice Dubois, you will answer the questions of your prince truthfully on pain of death. Otherwise you will be silent. Why was Lord Robert restrained?"

When she did not answer, Will's fury grew. "You are a traitor. There is clear and undeniable proof."

Royal authority rang in Will's tone, but Lady Dubois's expression remained impassive. "What is more, as such you are one whom I wish to execute. Much as I personally desire that this should be your fate, a prince must think of his people first, and foremost among them, is his queen. So, I will defer to you, my future wife, since it is you who arguably has been most directly harmed by the actions of this woman. What say you?"

"Imprison her. Strip her of all: magic, lands, title, money, dignity. Isolate her from others for the rest of her miserable life. I hope it is long. Until now, I did not know what I would say when this moment came. I am relieved I cannot order anyone's death, not even Beatrice's, Do this and justice will be satisfied."

****

Rosalind's eyes became sparks of pure green flame upon hearing this. "You are far too kind, Celina. She came close to destroying us all. She treated you like a slave for half your life. Do you not wish her death?" When Celina said nothing and instead arched a brow as if to say 'Should I wish it so?' Rosalind turned to Juliette. "And you, Juliette? She involved you in treason against your will. Would you not be revenged? If things hadn't worked out so well as they have, if you'd been discovered by a less merciful prince, she would have sent you to your execution without a second thought."

"True," Juliette agreed, "and she should be punished, but if she had not done what she did, I might never have met Robert. Perhaps she ought to die, but I don't believe either you or I should be the one to do it."

"It has to be done," Rosalind insisted. "She won't stop. She'll never stop. She won't quit until she makes me as much of a monster as she is. She won't call a halt until the entire kingdom is under her complete control. I can't, I won't allow that." Rosalind's whole body shook with fury.

"We will make her stop. We will make sure that she can do no harm ever again," Juliette insisted.

A laugh came from behind the temporary barrier. "She's right, you know. I want the throne. I won't live caged. No matter the prison you place me in, no matter how strong, no matter how deep, I will crawl out and I will get what I want."

Rosalind made an incoherent, animal sound of rage and turned her power up a notch.

Pain contorted Beatrice's face but she did not cry out. "Enjoy it while you can, daughter. Just know that the one thing I want most now is for you and all you love to die screaming."

Rosalind moved then. Wanting the sweet taste of violence more than she ever wanted anything, she enveloped her mother's mind with her own and upbraided every synapse, every neuron until Beatrice's brain was on fire.

"Rosalind, don't." Jonathan's voice filled her head. "Please."

"Why not? Why shouldn't I? Why shouldn't I show her what pain really is and then and only then give her death?"

"Because you have to make a choice. Life or death. Good or evil. You don't make that choice just once; you have to make it every day, sometimes every minute. You have to choose but know this, whatever you decide I am with you."

"Can we truly imprison her?" This question she directed to Juliette.

"We can. I swear it. With your help, with our joined powers, we can create a prison for her that she will never be able to get out of. We've already started."

"She will be guarded day and night by my most trusted men. This I vow to you," Will said.

"Swear it. All of you swear that you will never allow Beatrice to escape."

One by one they did as she bid them, even Robert semi-conscious as he was.

Violent shudders shook Rosalind, but Jonathan was

right and she knew it. Each day, each moment in this life was full of choices. This time, by all the gods, she would make the right one. Leaving the barrier in place, she deliberately withdrew from her mother's mind. She lowered her hand inch by inch until it lay open at her side. With a sharp sound somewhere between a gasp and a sob, she reached for Jonathan and found herself enfolded in his strong, loving arms.

"I choose you. I want a life with my sister, my stepsister and their men, with all those who might love me. Most of all I want to make a life with you. I love you. Stay with me, please."

"I will never leave you. I'm not going anywhere. I love you."

For a very long time, he just held her and she drew strength from his love. At last however, she turned to Juliette. "What do I have to do?"

"Add your power to mine. Can you do that?" When Rosalind nodded, she commanded, "Then do it and say these words. *Incantorum captua, alpha et omega.*"

As soon as their lips formed the words, Beatrice began to scream. Wind and fire and water raged and the room shook, but the two women repeated the spell over and over, and were joined by the others at the last. Candles flickered out, pictures fell and shattered and still they chanted.

Eventually Lady Dubois's voice faded and her body slowly disappeared until she was gone.

"Did we succeed? Is she contained?" Rosalind demanded.

Rosalind waited while Juliette looked with her third eye and saw their mother. Then her sister smiled.

"She now lies in the deepest darkest pit below this

castle. She is using magic to try to escape, but she can't. Oh, now she's using her fists. Hmm, well, we'll see about that won't we?" Juliette clucked her tongue and murmured, "Temper, temper." Then with a small gesture, Juliette used her power to knock Lady Dubois out cold. "Some people just don't know when they are beaten," Juliette informed Rosalind with a sigh.

"So it's finished?" Celina asked some moments later.

"It is," Rosalind passed a shaking hand over her tired eyes but managed a weary nod.

"Is anyone else hurt?" Will demanded. "Is Robert all right?"

"I'll be just fine. Juliette will heal me. All I need is a bit of rest."

"So, all that remains is to inform my father."

Robert made to rise. "Shall I come with you, majesty?"

Will placed a hand on his friend's shoulder. "No, you rest, my friend. All of you, I cannot express my thanks for the service you have done for the realm, and for my betrothed. For my part, I will never forget it and you will all be well rewarded"

"Justice is its own reward. We all agree; she had to be stopped," Juliette commented.

"And now she is, thanks to all of you."

"And you," Celina reminded him.

"Well, everyone get some rest. Very soon we'll all have a drink together to celebrate."

"You're forgetting something." Celina smiled when Will looked at her, a bit bemused. "The ball. You and I had best clean ourselves up as best we can and make an appearance."

****

"Are you all right?" Robert asked Juliette.

"No but I will be. Will you take me up?"

He bowed and acceded to her request. Yet leaving was not so simple a task as one might expect. Those guests nearest the parlor had heard and felt a bit of the action and come to investigate. Word soon spread; there was nothing any of them could do to stop it. Consequently, it was a quarter of an hour before they were able to wade through all of the well-wishers and gossips who sought them out and head upstairs to their own chambers. When they did, she let out an immense sigh of relief and all of the tension engulfing her disappeared. The effort involved in maintaining the façade of her customary calm had brought her near to tears, but now came blessed release. She let her shoulders droop and her utter exhaustion show.

"It's hard to believe it's over." The dead of night was long past and the morning sun appearing when Robert offered to escort her to her chamber, but Juliette took a seat for a moment in a quiet alcove they passed. All the adrenaline sustaining her was gone now and her body crashed in reaction.

"We stopped her. No death on the gallows. No kingdom under her command. No marriage to the prince. No bedding a man I don't love. After all this time, I'm free. All of us working together were able to end it. Now she won't hurt anyone else ever again."

"You know without you, it wouldn't have been possible. You could have gone along with her plan. If you had given up, given in to her at any point…well, I don't like to contemplate what might have happened. You were so brave. The way you dealt with her was nothing short of amazing. I've never seen such utter calm, such grace in such a fraught situation. Remarkable. That's not even mentioning that you saved my life again."

"I still can't believe you are alive and whole. You'd tell me if anything was wrong?" she asked, and even she could hear how anxious her own voice sounded.

"I would," he assured her. "You healed me thoroughly. Relax."

For just a moment she closed her eyes trying to will the terrible scene away. "When I realized she had you and then I saw you, held captive, I lost it. For an instant, I was blinded by panic. Then all I could see was you. You, your love, gave me strength because I knew if it was the last thing I ever did I would rescue you. I knew I couldn't live with myself if I let you die, not when I could've saved you. I couldn't have done any of those things alone."

He caught her hand and kissed it. "My love." He pressed his lips to hers then took her arm. "Come. Let me take you back to your rooms. You should rest. There's little more to be done tonight."

Grateful, she leaned against him as they left the hall.

****

Silence pervaded as Jonathan led Rosalind to the guest quarters Will had prepared for them. Shock was setting in, she realized and she wondered if anything could break through it.

"Rosalind, please talk to me."

"I almost killed my own mother. What more is there to say?" She sank to the edge of the bed as dull and lifeless as a puppet with its strings cut.

"Damn it—"

She held up a hand to forestall him. "I planned to do it, prepared to do it and came close to succeeding and the worst part is that, by all the gods, I would have enjoyed it. What does that say about me?" Temper flashed and she was relieved that she could feel anything at all.

"It says you are human. That woman did terrible things to you all of your life. She would have destroyed the kingdom. She poisoned everything she touched. I think it's natural that you would want to put a stop to her by any means necessary and enjoy doing it too. Even with all that, you didn't kill her. You did the right thing."

"Did I? What if she somehow gets free? What then?" The thought would keep her awake at night for a long time to come, perhaps for the rest of her life.

"Listen to me. She won't get out. Not ever." He put a finger to her lips when she started to protest. "But if she did, we would deal with it. You are safe. All of us are. Juliette, Celina, Will, Robert, me, the king, the realm. Understand that this would not be the case without you."

"Or you. Thank you."

Tears came then. Hot, cleansing and seemingly endless, they eased just a little of her pain. Pain not over that night's incident alone, but over every occasion of brutality perpetrated by her mother and by her herself over the long years.

When the storm slowed, Jonathan dried her eyes but did not end their embrace. She kissed him and knew that soon enough she would start the long, arduous process of healing but for now, she let him hold her and she drank in the love and safety and comfort of it.

****

As they approached her door, Robert hesitated. "Don't go back to your rooms. Come to mine."

Sweet gods, yes, was all Juliette could think. Then she stopped thinking at all for a moment as her whole being reached out to his.

Seeing Juliette's arrested expression and perhaps misinterpreting it, Robert hastened to add, "Those rooms are full of bad memories for us both. I don't want you thinking of Beatrice anymore tonight. If you don't wish to share my bed, I can sleep on the settee in the sitting room. There isn't a moment that I don't long to be with you, of course, but only at the right time and place and only if you wish it."

She opened her mouth to speak, but Robert had more to say. "I suppose what I am trying to say is that you've been through so much today and if you need time to process, if you need to rest, I understand."

For a moment she was so overwhelmed by every kind of feeling that she could not speak. He was always thinking of her, putting her first. That was what it meant to be loved by him. She was a fortunate woman.

Just as she was finding her voice to tell him so, he drew breath to speak again. "Whatever you need, I will do."

At last she found her tongue and at last he allowed her to use it. "I do need you, in my life, in my arms, in my bed, especially tonight."

"The feeling is mutual."

Deciding that nothing more need be said, he held out his hand and she placed her slim fingers in his as they made their way to his bedchamber.

****

"Will it hold?" Henry asked his son as he circled Beatrice's prison.

With the majority of the guests gone and Beatrice caught, his son judged it safe enough to tell him the whole of the tale from the spelling of the shoe, to Beatrice's plans to poison her king and murder her prince on the battlefield.

Shocked astonishment had soon given way to fury and Henry demanded to see the traitor with his own eyes. With alacrity, Will led him to Lady Dubois's cell and now they stood before it.

"We believe so."

"You mean Lady Forbes and Lady Juliette believe so. What do you believe?"

Will gathered his thoughts then replied, "I believe that Lady Forbes and Lady Juliette have done all they can. But I also believe that while there's life, there's hope. What is hope for her is dangerous for us. No one must be allowed to communicate with her. Also, she must never be allowed certain objects lest she use them to perform a spell. Juliette and Rosalind can help with that. In short, she must be watched until the day of her death."

Henry's jaw firmed as it always did when he had to make a harsh decision. "It confirms what I have long suspected; while she lives the kingdom will never be safe. I ought to execute her now, this very moment."

"If that is your will, but I would advise against it."

"Why? For the good of the realm, she should be struck down. How else will the people know the strength of their king? What she did...it cannot be allowed to stand. Such treason must be answered."

"And so it will be, but the chance that she will escape is miniscule; we will make certain it is nonexistent," Will argued.

A moment or two passed in charged silence then Will decided to speak. "In addition, I'll tell you plainly, I want her to suffer for a long time before she dies alone and unmourned."

"I take it this is also the wish of your betrothed?"

"Yes, it is her most fervent wish."

"And the others? They agree as well."

It was a statement, not a question, but Will answered it nevertheless. "With some debate, yes."

"Very well, I will take time to consider the question. In twenty-four hours you will have my answer. Unless my mind changes within that time, I will let it be known that this is how we deal with traitors. She will be imprisoned, denied all access to power, to companionship, and left to rot. Once she is a shell of the woman she once was, then and only then will she be executed."

"Thank you, Father."

Henry made a derisive noise. "No need. In fact, it is I who should be thanking you. I am the one that owes you a debt. You and yours captured that viper, brought her to me and kept my kingdom—our kingdom—safe. I'm proud of you. Now, I'm sure your betrothed requires your attention. Go to her."

Grateful, Will bowed and did just that.

****

Cleaning up such a mess—magical and social as well as political—took longer than Will expected and far longer than he liked. It was vital that he tell the nobles as little as possible. Yet, he had to tell them enough to satisfy their relentless curiosity or they would ask even more questions. The more questions they asked, the more likely someone might stumble on the complete truth, and if that happened, panic would ensue. Worse, if anyone ever found out how close the royal family had come to being assassinated, every enemy they had would see them as fair game and chaos would reign.

By the time he finished with the nobles, he was ready to drop. All he wanted was a tub of hot water and a bed to sleep in for twelve hours straight, not necessarily in that order, until he saw her. She sat in a corner of the hall waiting for him to finish the rest of his duties. Most of the guests had long since left and the musicians were playing one final song, so Will took his future bride to the floor.

"We never finished our dance," he explained when she lifted an eyebrow in question.

She smiled up at him as he led her in the first steps of a waltz. "When can we be wed?"

"Other than as quickly as possible? I'm not sure exactly, but soon."

"Hmm. Soon. Good."

Celina put her head on his shoulder and in that moment he knew there was no place he'd rather be.

Epilogue

Four months later

The day of Will's wedding dawned as bright and beautiful and clear as could be wished. It had all taken what felt like an eternity to arrange. Both Robert and Jonathan had already married, with Rosalind and Jonathan taking their vows a mere month after dealing with Beatrice. Juliette and Robert had married just a little over a fortnight ago and were already well ensconced at Windbourne, their beautiful new estate, less than a day's ride from the castle. The two were still often at court to assist the running of the kingdom and were, in fact, second only to the royal couple in influence.

Jonathan and Rosalind had been living happily at Dubois Manor since their marriage. The harvest had been exceptional and they as well as their people were happier than ever. Each time they visited Will and Celina, which was often, one or the other had a new, exciting idea for improving farming and the general running of an estate. Will suspected reform would always be close to their hearts. Such things would take second place at least for a time since they were already expecting their first child.

Although they were all living apart and beginning their own lives, today they were once again all gathered together. In token of how much their relationship had changed, Celina named her stepsisters as matrons of honor, just as she had been maid of honor for both women. The stepsisters were dressed in shimmering royal blue satin with yards of lace trimming and the bride, he was assured, had the most exquisite dress ever produced. Despite his incessant pestering for details, all he could get out of Juliette was that it was a low cut garment of white silk trimmed with lots of lace.

With Jonathan and Robert named as groomsmen, and dressed in black satin coats and tails, with white shirts with blue cravats to match, well, the most important aspects of the wedding were covered. Who cared about the rest of the innumerable details involved in holding a royal wedding with five hundred guests and twenty times as many onlookers?

And so it was that he stood waiting at the front of the great cathedral to greet his bride. The church was a masterpiece of architecture with its high ceilings, arches and vast, stained glass windows all made by the most talented artisans. The rows of carved oak pews would hold the requisite five hundred people, five hundred and fifty at a stretch, if the attached tiny chapel were opened for use. Draped over the head of each pew all the way down the aisle were bunches of white roses and violets. Larger, more intricate arrangements were also placed at the front of the sanctuary. The entire effect was one of romantic elegance.

You look a bit pale," Robert said.

Will waved his friend's concern away. "I'm fine. I just didn't sleep well last night. Can you blame me?"

"Not at all," Jonathan put in.

Will could not keep from pacing. "How much

longer?"

Robert chuckled. "Not long."

Minutes later the enormous doors creaked open allowing a shaft of warm sunshine to fall upon the aisle and Celina stepped in. The beautiful vision that was the woman he loved floated in his direction. When she was close enough, he offered her his hand. His bride-to-be smiled and placed her palm in his.

A word about the author...

Shirley grew up in Baton Rouge, LA and started writing at an early age. Always talkative, when she was eleven she began to put her thoughts on paper, writing stories inspired by some of her favorite writers, Laura Ingalls Wilder and Madeline L'Engle. As she grew older, she developed a love of romance and in 2009 she decided to try her hand at paranormal romance. She has written two novels since then and several unpublished screenplays.

Shirley graduated from Nicholls State University where she majored in History and minored in English. Since graduating (she doesn't like to think about how long ago that was) she has worked at some of the best libraries in the Baton Rouge area. She makes her home there and enjoys spending time with family members. She also loves seeing movies, reading, and going to the park with her niece in her free time.

Currently, Shirley is hard at work on her newest venture, tentatively titled *Fire and Ice*. It is a re-imagining of the Hans Christian Anderson fairy tale, *The Snow Queen*.

Visit her at http://www.shirleypmccoy.com

Thank you for purchasing
this publication of The Wild Rose Press, Inc.

If you enjoyed the story, we would appreciate your
letting others know by leaving a review.

For other wonderful stories,
please visit our on-line bookstore at
www.thewildrosepress.com.

For questions or more information
contact us at
info@thewildrosepress.com.

The Wild Rose Press, Inc.
www.thewildrosepress.com

Stay current with The Wild Rose Press, Inc.

Like us on Facebook

https://www.facebook.com/TheWildRosePress

And Follow us on Twitter
https://twitter.com/WildRosePress